a pound of flesh

SYDNEY HUNTER

Squabbling Sparrows Press

A Pound of Flesh

Published 2024 by Squabbling Sparrows Press: Copyright © 2024 Sydney Hunter / Andrene Low. Originally published as DietVale 2021 & 2023 using ISBNs: 978-0-9951235-7-1 and 978-1-99-116153-6

This edition paperback ISBN: 978-1-99-116159-8

Squabbling Sparrows Press

"When you say
you'd do anything
to lose the weight,
do you really
mean it?"

1

Dammit, I could already see my epitaph. The slab of marble above my head wouldn't have 'Quietly in her sleep' chiseled into it, rather stating 'Death by shape wear' as the cause. Honestly, I'd worn wetsuits that were less depilatory in their treatment of my lady bits.

As I lay back on the luxurious super-king that dominated the bedroom, the opulent décor soured my mood. Like everything to do with my old life, it no longer gave me joy. The ivory silk curtains I had spent weeks dithering over no longer glowed. The same was true of the crystal chandelier that David, my soon to be ex, had hated with a passion.

I was soon back in the present. The iron grip of my foundation garment had me breathing like a newbie at a Lamaze Class. This only added to the anxiety that had been building all morning thanks to the impending visit to David's lawyer.

The thought of facing my husband, of having to discuss the divorce, filled me with a dread I couldn't shake. But I had to calm down if I was to make a modicum of sense and stand up for myself. David had always talked rings around me, to the point I'd stumble over my words. I was just as sure he would have employed a lawyer with a similar gift of the gab.

I closed my eyes, fighting to rein in my racing thoughts. A whiff of the lavender-scented candle burning on the bedside table didn't cut it. My frazzled nerves were way past that, the lovely aroma not enough to ease the tension in my body.

I was hyperventilating to the point I was in danger of blacking out.

Come on, you stupid tart, get a grip.

This pep talk, along with a few measured breaths, and the black spots faded back to wherever they'd come from. As calm as I was likely to be, I attempted to stand so I could search for another outfit. One in which I resembled a slimmish over-stuffed sausage was my best hope.

I couldn't do it.

Stuck amid my earlier fashion malfunctions, I was like a cast sheep.

Flailing my arms and legs, I tried to roll onto my side, but my torso was a solid block of Lycra-constricted fat and bone, mammary glands, and useless ovaries.

The tears that had been my constant companion in recent months spilled over and rolled down my cheeks and I gave in to the temptation to wallow. Had my ovaries shown themselves to be more than decorative, things might have been different.

Smacking my stomach hard in frustration did nothing to remedy my situation. Instead, a boom echoed around the bedroom.

Damn it. Bloated again.

I hated my body with a passion, with 'disgusting' being the best way to describe it. Hell, if I found myself too gross to masturbate with success, was it any wonder David no longer wanted a bar of me?

I snaked my hand down between my legs and ripped open the poppers that were hanging on for grim death, moaning in pleasure. I felt a momentary relief, but it quickly vanished when the front crotch panel shot up and over my tummy, returning to its original size from the pack. This was small enough that a ten-year-old would have been hard-pressed to shoehorn themselves into it.

With nothing holding it in, my stomach wobbled out of control, leaving me looking as though I was pregnant. At least, from the spare tire of the rolled-up undergarment, and down, it did.

"Oh, for goodness' sake."

After slamming my hands down on the bed in frustration, I lifted my hips and the back part of the crotch disappeared under me at a rate of knots. If I'd opted for the G-string version, I would now have been the proud owner of shredded hemorrhoids. On the bright side, I could now get into a sitting position and, after a short breather, I clambered to my feet.

From a morbid sense of self-hatred, I looked in the full-length mirror sitting at the end of the walk-in wardrobe. Even from that distance, it wasn't pretty. I would have been okay with my old glasses, but having had laser surgery to correct my dodgy eyesight, there was nothing to protect my fragile ego.

I had given up thinking back to how attractive I was when I first caught David's eye. There wasn't a diet I hadn't tried to regain my glory days. The merest lip curl from my husband of twenty years and there wasn't a chocolate bar without my name on it.

Each fall from the diet wagon took an ever-greater toll on my psyche, requiring more chocolate, carbs, or fat to heal it. More often than not, it took all three to restore any sense of equilibrium.

Turning side-on to the mirror, I succumbed to my absolute self-loathing and, giving in to gravity, let my gut hang out. If it hadn't been so sad, it would have been funny, but it gave me an idea of what would fit.

I entered the wardrobe, dread filling me. What I wanted was in David's corner, down the back. There I rummaged through the few things of his remaining since he moved into the guest suite over the garage.

He'd been furious about this, but I wasn't moving out. The divorce was his idea, although he hadn't been in a hurry to follow through. No, he had taken his own sweet time until the call yesterday. He'd then had the nerve to tell me I needed to be at his lawyer's office at one-thirty today, sharp. I'd longed to tell him the time wasn't convenient, but lacked the nerve.

I'd sifted through most of the hodgepodge of garments before I found what I was looking for. I held the dark blue dress up in front of me and turned to face the mirror.

"Perfect." If I looked pregnant, I may as well wear maternity, even if it was musty and full of memories of my phantom pregnancy. David's joke that the missing fetus was last seen wearing a purple jumpsuit like The Phantom of comic book fame still hurt. Even after all this time.

Sure, the smock was out of fashion, but at least my tummy wouldn't need to be squished flat. To free myself from the torturous shapewear wasn't as easy, with the muscles in my arms not up to the challenges set by the boa constrictor-like bodysuit.

I had to resort to hacking at it with the kitchen scissors to escape its death grip. My relief at being free was short-lived when I saw my boobs were back to their sagging, unperky selves. Talk about a let-down.

My hands shoved under them, I then lifted, twisted, and rotated until I liked their shape. Pity there wasn't a bra capable of replicating the look. I had tried a Wonder Bra once, but by the end of the evening, I—and even my boobs—had been exhausted.

My girls looking twenty years younger and a couple of inches higher than they were naturally were what did us in. The disappointment voiced by David when I had removed the confection of lace and industrial-strength boning left me unsure who was the biggest idiot.

Me for thinking I would get away with it, or him for expecting a miracle.

The drive into the city was stressful. It didn't matter that I had left myself plenty of time for the trip. All it took to grid-lock the city was a single fender-bender or someone to think about having one. Livable city, my sizeable butt. If it hadn't been for all my friends living here, I would have given consideration to moving away.

Leaving the car in a parking lot that would require me to sell a kidney to cover the fee, I hurried to the café where I was to meet Sue-Ng. She was the pocket-rocket divorce lawyer recommended by Lorraine.

Progress was slow: my heels, while slimming, were precarious enough that if I hurried, I would twist an ankle. I'd be late over limping into this meeting with David. How late I was running became obvious when I spotted Sue-Ng waiting outside the café.

Dwarfed by an enormous briefcase, double-gripped in front of her slight frame, the New Zealand-born Chinese coped with its weight without issue. "You're late, Marilyn! I wanted to brief you before the meeting. We'll have to wing it."

She took off, and I did my best to keep up. Our destination was the tower that housed Screw, Shaft & Swindle, or whatever name David's firm of lawyers went by. Not a simple task, with Sue-Ng pulling ahead with each step. "Hold up. We aren't all wearing sensible shoes," I gasped out.

Sensible was an understatement. She was wearing running shoes that looked to have covered a lot of miles. They were at odds with the tailor-made burgundy skirt suit that fit her like a glove. By comparison, I was a lumbering beast. Hippo in high heels was the description that sprung to mind each time I caught my reflection as I strode by yet another honest-to-a-fault plate-glass window.

After a couple of close calls, I concentrated on putting one foot in front of the other, rather than torturing myself with a multitude of side glances. Sue-Ng didn't slow when she hit the marble floor of the large foyer at our destination. I did likewise and came close to taking a tumble. Windmilling my arms kept me upright, but put a real strain on my ankles.

Sue-Ng's repeated pushing of the 'up' button did nothing to hasten the lift. By the time it dinged its presence, there were half-a-dozen be-suited gents with us, all eyes glued to the illuminated display above the doors.

Blast it.

I'd wanted a mini briefing from Sue-Ng on our game plan and, despite our destination being the penultimate floor, we were still the first to get off. When we exited straight into the law firm's reception area, it blew any chance of a final catch up.

It didn't take a brain surgeon to know David was furious I was late. The overt checking of his watch and sneering in my direction were impossible to miss. His actions were melodramatic enough that I was expecting to hear a chorus of "She's by the lifts," like I was at an English pantomime.

Well, he could screw himself if he was expecting me to apologize. As usual, I wasn't game to voice this.

Sue-Ng hadn't even given our names to the receptionist when a shark in a suit popped out of nowhere. A brief look in our direction, and he glided to David's side. The gray sheen of the predator's suit was a perfect match to the dull metallic luster of his eyes. There was nothing gray about his smile. His teeth were toilet-bowl white and gleamed against his tan. He reminded me of someone, although I couldn't think who. Or was it I'd met him before? Not if his introducing himself was genuine and not some weird legal mind game.

He ushered us into a humongous boardroom with sweeping views of the harbor. His movements were just as slick when he made for the far side of the large table.

Not to be outmaneuvered, Sue-Ng skipped around the other end, beating him to it. She then hurried to sit with her back to the windows, before motioning for me to take the seat next to her.

On David and his lawyer sitting opposite, I grasped why she had made a mad dash for these seats. The light streaming in the floor-to-ceiling glass had them squinting. That was until The Shark took a remote out of his pocket and dropped the shades.

Giving no one a chance to speak, David's lawyer then started on what was a prepared and well-rehearsed piece. It was akin to something from a soap opera. The upshot was that David was as poor as a church mouse and in no state to support me after the divorce. Also, he wanted to get the whole mess over with. What a jerk. My mouth opened, but soon closed again. It was a struggle what shocked me most. That David had frittered away a fortune. Or that he blamed me for holding things up.

Sue-Ng had no trouble finding the right words. After thanking The Shark for a masterful summing up, she hefted her large briefcase up onto the pristine surface of the boardroom table. She then shimmied it around until the locks faced us, the table now as battered as The Shark's serene countenance. Doubtless, the gigantic domes on its bottom gouging the French polish were the reason for his horror.

Oblivious to this, she opened the case briefly and grabbed a bound document off the top of the financial fire hazard inside. I was having flashbacks about how long it took to print that lot when she dropped the document on the table in front of David and his lawyer. "Perhaps the next time your client tries to conceal his true financial worth, he should change his one and only password."

This must have been the report from the forensic accountant Sue-Ng had convinced me was money well spent. It was excellent value if David's pallor was anything to go by. His face now matched his lawyer's teeth. The Shark didn't appear affected unless you counted the tic flickering in the corner of his right eye. After turning to the next page, he put his hand up to cover this 'tell'. When he then put his elbow on the table and leaned into his hand, it didn't fool me.

Good luck with that mate, you're busted.

"There's nothing concrete here that isn't part of the public record. A good accountant will show a loss." The Shark's smile was once again in place.

"Our forensic accountant would not agree with you about that." Sue-Ng stood and lifted the block of paper out of her briefcase before slamming it on the table. "This is what we've uncovered so far, but I'm sure there's more where this came from."

The Shark made quick work of scanning the contents page before speaking in a controlled manner. "Will you excuse us?" He was already standing.

David staggered to his feet and trailed the lawyer from the room.

No sooner had the door shut than I bombarded Sue-Ng with questions, but she didn't answer. Her head bowed, she scribbled on a yellow legal pad she'd grabbed from the top pocket of her briefcase. After she held it up for me to read, I couldn't bring myself to ask any further questions.

It was as if she'd hit me with a gag order.

2

I scribbled yet another question on the crowded legal pad, and Sue-Ng replied in kind. It required squinting at her abysmal handwriting, and saying the individual letters in my head, to decipher each word. With handwriting this atrocious, she could have had a promising career in medicine.

On getting a nod that I had read her last reply, Sue-Ng ripped the top sheet off the pad and screwed it into a tight ball. She tossed this into the briefcase, followed by the pad and pen, closing the lid with a hollow boom. The lock was engaged before David, and his paid shark returned.

They didn't look happy. The Shark's killer smile had swum away, and his eyes were darker than when he'd been playing his friendly 'let's get along' cards.

The men had only just regained their seats when Sue-Ng went on the attack, proving everything Lorraine had said.

"Of course, we realize the report doesn't include the entirety of David's holdings, but we can go to court and get an Order of Discovery. Or ..."

The two men leaned forward, squinting against the full glare of the sun. The remote The Shark had left on the table was now sitting in my lap, and I wasn't handing it over. The better illuminated David's squirming, the happier I was.

"Or we could settle this now," continued Sue-Ng. She then showed a deft sleight of hand when she retrieved a couple of sheets of paper from under the briefcase. She spun these across the table toward The Shark, with his reactions fast enough to have him stopping them from aquaplaning off the gleaming tabletop.

The men scanned the contents, with David paling even more than earlier. The lawyer's teeth, visible in a scowl, were gray by comparison.

"This is preposterous. I can't afford this!" David's face once again showed a surplus of broken capillaries.

"You have three options, gentlemen." Sue-Ng splayed her hands flat on the table on either side of the briefcase.

"Three?" said The Shark and David in unison.

I fought to stop myself from asking the same question.

"One." Sue-Ng held up her left hand and tapped the forefinger with her right. "You settle as we've outlined here. Two." She counted off another digit, giving the men the fingers while she was about it. "We go to court and secure the Order of Discovery. Or three, we send the report to the tax department and let them sort it out."

It took a moment to register that the gurgling sounds were coming from David and not dodgy plumbing in the cavity above the floating ceiling panels. There was no avoiding his ashen face as he slid off his chair and into a heap under the boardroom table.

The lack of reaction from The Shark made me think he was as used to David's community theater episodes as I was. I had to give it to David. This was his best performance to date. Maybe the idea of handing over half his money had spurred him onto this more Shakespearian offering.

On realizing there was no breathing coming from under the table, all hell broke loose. The way The Shark got on with CPR suggested he had had to revive clients before. Meanwhile, Sue-Ng screamed at the receptionist to call for an ambulance.

I was the only one not taking part in the melodrama, unable to believe David wasn't faking it again. The paramedics arrived and took over from The Shark. However, despite all this attention, David wasn't up to an encore. It was a shame because he would have loved to receive the critical acclaim that he would have thought was due.

They recorded his time of death at 2:37 p.m.

He left the building in a black zippered bag, well on his way to being stiffer than he had been in my presence for well over two years, if ever.

Back in the boardroom, I voiced the question hovering on the faces of The Shark and Sue-Ng. "What happens now?"

"It depends." Sue-Ng's statement hung low and ominous over the boardroom table.

The Shark lifted a brow, telling me he wasn't biting.

My lawyer huffed in annoyance, forced to take the lead. "Did your client update his will?"

"I instructed him to do so with one of my associates." The Shark's teeth were again on show.

"This could take years to sort out." It disturbed me to see Sue-Ng was also smiling. Money-hungry so-and-sos, the lot of them.

I waited until The Shark looked in my direction. "Did your associate confirm David got around to changing his will?"

It was all I could do not to laugh at his confusion. No doubt he expected people to do what he told them. It would appear he was unaware of David's inability to complete anything without continual, around-the-clock nagging.

It was a role I had relinquished the second the waste-of-space had moved into the apartment over the garage. Reminding David to take his heart medication had been the thing I had missed the least.

Oops.

"One moment." The Shark got to his feet and disappeared through the door he and David had used earlier.

He wasn't gone for long.

He did not look happy on his return.

Meanwhile, I was ecstatic.

3

Despite the modest size of my hotel room, it was bleak, even though I had all my worldly possessions with me. On looking around the tastefully decorated room, it was hard to shake off the feeling that something was missing.

Months had passed since I told Sue-Ng to liquidate everything, in a spur-of-the-moment decision. I still got a surge of power in my solar plexus when I thought about it. Funny, but my words had had quite the opposite effect on David's lawyer. Perhaps down to the fact David was still in transit to the morgue.

Not that the seasoned legal professional appeared put off by the death of my hairy-backed, doughy late husband. No, it was more a case of being done out of a hefty fee because David hadn't updated his will. As it was, my being sole beneficiary, there had been no need to contest it.

With no kids or long-lost relatives waiting in the wings, it had been straightforward gaining access to the estate. The extent of this hadn't come to light until after I gave the forensic accountant full access to all the records. It was then the true extent of how much David had planned on screwing me on a financial front became apparent.

The other thing that came to light was David's mistress. Or the Mini Me, as I had coined her. It also explained why people kept saying it was such a shame I'd put the weight back on. They'd seen David gadding around town with a younger, slimmer version of me.

The one thing I hadn't sold was the apartment David had set Mary-Lynn up in. Yes, even the woman's name was similar, no doubt to avoid him getting confused in the sack when calling out her name. I had taken great delight in joining her when she was sniffling over the open casket and whispering that I was doubling the rent. Even though dead for a couple of weeks, and in receipt of a mortician's makeover, I was positive David flinched. His cheeks were for sure rosier than those of his mistress.

A knock at the door of my hotel room brought me back to the present. While the instruction to Sue-Ng to sell everything had been down to the shock of the quickie divorce that David's death gifted me, I had no regrets. Shrugging off my old life along with all its excess baggage was liberating. Especially when all that baggage was chock-full of clothes that no longer fit my body or my life.

My closet was now full of loose-fitting outfits that could

cope with my weight fluctuations. If I needed to dress up, I threw on the blue maternity frock and accessorized the hell out of it. This was a far cry from the clothes David had insisted I wear. The same style favored by Lorraine and my other friends. All the years next to him at events, nodding when I should, and smiling when inside I was screaming. I had been the perfect corporate wife until he fired me.

"Marilyn? Are you in there?" Sue-Ng's voice was faint through a door designed to stop fires and the racket of inebriated guests staggering back to their rooms in the small hours.

With the memories dislodged, I struggled off the bed and rushed to open the door before standing to the side. Rather than take advantage of my unspoken invitation, she handed me a fat envelope, explained that she was on her way to court, and raced off. I hadn't even closed the door when I heard her stabbing the 'down' button. Sue-Ng's "Don't spend it all at once" snuck between the metal doors as they hissed closed.

Holding the envelope against my chest, I leaned back against the door, managing to both close it and open the letter at the same time. On seeing the number of zeros on the law firm's escrow account check, my legs failed me and I slid in a heap to the plush carpet.

Unaware I was crying until a second tear splattered onto the trembling check, I had to swipe at my eyes to stop any further damage. It didn't matter how hard I concentrated, my math skills weren't up to the challenge of calculating my hourly rate over the course of the marriage.

I straightened the sheath of papers that held the check in their bosom and made quick work of skimming the contents. It took a while to understand how they had calculated the crazy estate total. "That's ridiculous!" I had known house prices were through the roof, but three-point-two million was more than the house was worth.

It had tons of land for being so close to the city, but was old and riddled with problems. Enough that even the most dedicated house flipper would back away. If whoever bought it had any sense, they would bowl it, or get the fire brigade to burn the place to the ground for practice.

I would even throw the first match in a reverse ribbon-cutting ceremony, if it weren't for me never wanting to see my old home again. Any memories it held I had abandoned to the fates, pleased to be shot of the whole thing. I had even moved out before the funeral, because it wasn't as if David could change the locks on me as I had done to him. At least not without a seance.

I spent a pleasant afternoon pretending to spend my windfall. Scratch that, it wasn't a windfall. I'd worked hard for every damned dollar. Years spent performing CPR on a marriage that suffered an irregular heartbeat from the day of the over-blown ceremony.

It hadn't been my fault David had drunk so much at the reception that he had had trouble getting it up. Also, not my fault he had poured so much alcohol down my throat that I had laughed it off as being no big deal. Unfortunately, all of that happened before they dished out the little blue pills like candy.

David's only way to move on from what he claimed was his complete and utter humiliation had been counseling.

I wondered if this hadn't been the real nail in the coffin of our marriage, rather than my inability to conceive. Either way, David soon looked to bolster his manhood in places other than our marital bed.

On taking another look at the check propped up in front of the television, I realized the major expense I faced in establishing a new life was a house. No, make that a home. One without memories stuffed between the loose floorboards. And, much as I had loved the large rooms of my old house, I was thinking of something smaller for the next stage in my life. Perhaps I should kick the Mini Me out and take over the love nest?

I'd already scoped out the neighborhood from a mix of research and morbid curiosity. The main reason was to get my head around who would screw my late husband by choice. Of course, before moving in, I'd have to have the place fumigated. Something involving women dressed in purple velvet and armed with burning bunches of sage. Did the Catholic Church undertake exorcisms these days?

However, with the sort of money I had at my disposal, I didn't need to bother. Hell, I could even head overseas if I wanted to, although I was unsure of where I would go. There was a lot to be said for keeping a few familiar things around after purging myself of everything else. I hadn't even seen that much of my girlfriends since David popped his clogs.

Whenever we got together, all we did was rip apart our other halves, never mind that they paid for the lunches. With

David gone, I had little to talk to them about and they weren't interested in the challenges I was facing. It was as if they preferred me when I was miserable.

No, apart from an abundance of cash, my life was empty.

I tapped away at the calculator app on my phone, adding up ball-parks on things I would need. I even included a few that were more want than need. Despite this, I didn't come close to spending it. Who would have thought David would be worth as much dead?

The way he had told it, we were scraping by. Technically, that would have been the case if I hadn't sold everything, sometimes at below-market prices. Asset rich, cash poor, although not anymore.

I'd already talked with Sue-Ng's accountant friend about how to invest the money. The bulk had gone to an off-shore trust, in Central America of all places. Somewhere the government couldn't get its sticky fingers on it and where I could pay little or no tax. Tax avoidance, rather than evasion, was how the accountant put it, so legal if not ethical.

This wasn't the only asset protection I was investing in. If I couldn't find a bra to contort my boobs into something worthy of Instagram, I knew of a surgeon who could help. Just as Lorraine recommended Sue-Ng as the perfect lawyer for the job at hand, she recommended Mr. Ian Stamford as the best boob man in town.

My friend's perky D-cups, with the gravity-defying properties of something out of NASA, were a testament to this. Heaven knew she got them out at every opportunity. She hadn't even waited for the stitches to be removed to show them off for the first time. In a restaurant! The Mexican wave of dropped cutlery had been deafening.

The irony of implants adding weight to my body didn't escape me. Now that I was single again, I was desperate to lose the poundage. There was also not wanting to settle for someone as average as David, or even me. Sadly, in my current state, it was all I was likely to attract. Ugh, even thinking about getting naked with a guy in my league was gag-worthy.

Yes, double standards, I know.

Of real annoyance was that even though I was carrying a ton of extra weight, none of it had found its way north of my waist. If you were into the fruit and veg morphology, pear-shaped didn't cut it, with my body tending to the malformed butternut squash end of things.

Well, no more.

4

Balanced on the plush couch at the plastic surgeon's, I was nervous. Fertility treatment had seen me poked, prodded, and explored more than enough for one lifetime. However, if that was all that stood between me and boobs capable of uplifting my soul and launching the next phase of my life, then I would cope. Not that I was after a pair of those fridge-magnet puppies. Perky, yes, but still natural-looking was the goal.

After reading the same advertisement for the third time, I closed the Italian Vogue on my lap and placed it back on the dark mahogany coffee table. I straightened it until it was in perfect alignment with all its glossy neighbors. A reading selection that was this high end and up-to-date guaranteed each breast would cost me a fortune. And it wasn't as if you could get them done in instalments.

There was a muted ding, followed by the receptionist

standing and peering at me over the top of the tall counter. "Mr. Stamford will see you now, Mrs. Channing."

The woman was in good shape for her age, even if it was hard to determine what that might be, other than over forty, or maybe even fifty. Maybe she worked for contra instead of wages? Not a wrinkle marred her serene countenance. And if she'd ever had jowls, they were long ago incinerated in line with industry standards.

Struggling free from the depths of the couch, I was glad of my loose-fitting new clothes. The couch was squishy, with getting out of it akin to something you would do during an advanced yoga class.

When I sat in the visitor's chair across from the surgeon, his youthful appearance didn't surprise me. I'd researched the heck out of him, rather than taking Lorraine's word for it. Anyone going near my girls with a scalpel needed to be legitimate. However, he didn't look quite as he did in the photos online.

Still, if you were a plastic surgeon and you played golf with other plastic surgeons, it stood to reason you were getting a little work done now and then. Perhaps a little work wasn't the best description. From the looks of things, the surgeon had had everything but a boob job, unless it was a reduction. It was difficult to gauge with any man-boobs well hidden under the three-piece suit he was wearing, like a badge to his hourly rate.

"And what can we do for you today, Mrs. Channing?" That he said this while looking at me with a critical eye was unnerving. He hadn't even looked at my chest yet, having found more than enough to focus on above my neck. Despite being rich, I refused to fund his next golf trip to Hawaii.

"Ah, I'd like to talk about a breast augmentation." Sure, I was okay calling it a boob job in my head and amongst friends. No way was I using the term when speaking to the man who would wield the scalpel.

"Really?" He punctuated this single word by lifting an eyebrow, something I hadn't thought possible considering the help they'd already had. His tone did nothing for my confidence.

Perhaps there was another surgeon available with a better bedside manner? Mind you, would I want to entrust my new tits to someone else? Knowing my luck, I'd end up with the surgeon responsible for the brow lift opposite.

"Yes, really!" I put as much force as I could into my reply, although I was still struggling to find my voice after all the years of being muted.

Even faking it had the desired effect, with the air of up-sell dropping a notch. The surgeon then went into his spiel about the pros and cons of breast augmentation. So precise was his recitation, that it was as if he was skimming through a handbook in his head. As though he was reading me the Miranda rights, but for tits and not assholes.

I couldn't fault Stamford's examination. Not since my first school ball had someone groped me like that. And just as then, my efforts to distance myself from the action were so successful that it was as if my girls belonged to someone else. Much easier than dealing with any unwanted and embarrassing reactions, with him the first man to touch them in over a year.

Only after I'd dressed, and my breasts were my own again, did we discuss cup size, shape, and options like over or under the muscle. Under the muscle, if I was to avoid them looking like a couple of poached eggs. He'd then buzzed the receptionist and arranged for me to undergo a few tests.

A nurse carried these out in a side room that was clinical in the extreme. There were no squishy couches in here. It was all hard, sterile surfaces and no-nonsense equipment. The first thing the nurse did was weigh me. The last thing she did was take my blood pressure. And that's where things went tits-up.

My blood pressure wasn't so much high, as stoned out of its freaking gourd. My best chance of getting new boobs was to grab the implants off Mr. Stamford's desk and leg it.

"Now, we can put you on beta-blockers for six months to help drop the blood pressure to a level where we can operate without risk, or..."

The surgeon left the alternative just out of reach. It didn't matter. I already knew what he would say. I didn't need him to voice it. I didn't give him a chance, stuttering out, "But I've tried every diet under the sun, and none of them worked."

Instead of leaving with a date for surgery, I left with a prescription for beta-blockers, promising Mr. Stamford I would get it filled. And I did, because if nothing else, I was obedient, a rule follower.

Not that I planned on just sitting around popping pills. If

there was a way that I could speed up my weight loss, then I would be all in.

At least, that was my plan. Until checking online, I hadn't realized there were so many spas on offer in New Zealand. Places that would dispatch the thatch, trim the brows and IPL you to within an inch of your life, but all without losing an ounce.

Residential fat loss centers, however, were thin on the ground. You would think the TV show Weight Loss Warriors would have people clamoring to be locked up, starved and forced to labor for hours, but no.

Personally, I had always found the show too much akin to a documentary about Third-World-prison systems to find it entertaining. Not that this stopped me from watching it.

I then undertook a cursory search of overseas centers, starting in Australia, before working my way on to the more accessible parts of the USA and Europe. Sure, I could afford them, but the idea of being on my own on the other side of the world filled me with trepidation.

I'd never been much of a traveler, preferring the comforts of home to ritzy five-star resorts. I was also aware of the irony that I was living in such an establishment for the foreseeable future.

There was also the brand-new Lexus sitting in the hotel's basement parking garage to consider. It had been my only significant purchase since receiving the mega pay out, and I was keen on putting a few miles on the clock. That wouldn't happen if it was rusting away in long-stay parking at the airport.

A sense of pride in my purchase of the vehicle swathed me. It was the first time I had bought a car on my own. Originally, it was my parents who dictated the choice of vehicle, and then David.

His propensity to harp on about the resale value had meant non-stop Hondas, to the point I hated them with a passion. The Lexus was the most ostentatious, impractical thing I could find without going over-the-top. Even though I could afford one, I couldn't negotiate the supermarket speed bumps in a Lamborghini.

The girls said I was mad and should have bought a Tesla. And if it hadn't been for David saying no to a Lexus in the past, I would have.

Leaving my laptop to hibernate, I swiped through the contacts on my phone until I found the one that I was after. My frenemy answered on the third ring, as though she had been expecting my call.

"Lorraine, do you have a second?" It never paid to assume she was free to talk. Shame she didn't extend this courtesy in return. I would often be halfway through my greeting when she bombarded me with whatever crisis was befalling her. The problem was that if anyone knew of a suitable 'fat farm'—spa to you and me, darling—it was Lorraine.

"I do!" Lorraine sounded as surprised about this as I was. It was more common to be left waiting for her to call back at a time that suited her.

Unprepared for this immediate audience, I stuttered for a second or two, unsure how to proceed, deciding that just stating what was happening was the best approach.

"I, ah, went to see Mr. Stamford about the boob job and it can't go ahead."

"And ..." said Lorraine, this single word encapsulating that the woman was full of expectation of learning something juicy she could spread around our group.

I had given up asking her to keep anything in confidence, as it seemed to be a pathological impossibility. Tell Lorraine and you told everyone. It had saved me a lot of phone minutes over the years.

"It's my blood pressure." I stopped in hopes she would catch on.

My hopes were in vain. Either she didn't know about the link between hypertension and excess weight or, more likely, she was being obtuse to force me to say it aloud.

"It's my weight."

"Oh, yes!"

Her glee in this brief acknowledgement was obvious, with it being followed by the rustle of wicker. This was a sure sign Lorraine had settled into a chair in their conservatory, ready for me to spill my guts.

Damn, I should never have phoned, but to back out now would be pointless.

"I was told I need to lose at least fifty pounds."

I didn't bother going into the course of beta-blockers because I had discarded that as time-consuming. I wanted new boobs ready for next summer and that wasn't happening if I was mucking about taking drugs. After having the prescription filled, I had stuffed the bottle in my purse without a second thought.

"What about Weight Watchers?"

Her suggestion had me grinding my teeth in small circles. She knew more than most how that had worked out in the past. Was she that thick, or was she winding me up?

"I was thinking of somewhere residential. I don't want to be tempted."

That Lorraine and my other friends were the ones who tempted me went unsaid. There was no need, with us both well aware of it.

"There is this one place," Lorraine started but didn't finish, and I hoped to hell she wouldn't leave me hanging. To be strung along over several days like the mouse to Lorraine's cat. Lord knew it had happened before, with whatever interaction taking days, not minutes, and proving frustrating as hell.

Dammit, I didn't want to lay myself bare like this. But if that was what it would take to get her to divulge the information, so be it.

After opening my jaw to ease the tension, I pressed on. "I need this. My life is as good as on hold until they operate."

Her answer came faster than I could have hoped for, or even expected.

"The Vale. Down on the Coromandel Peninsula. It's full-on, though, and only for the elite, so you might not get in."

In summary, I wasn't elite. Thanks for the vote of confidence, Lorraine.

There was a sudden intake of breath from the other end

before Lorraine pressed on. "But I was told about the place in confidence, so you didn't hear about it from me."

"My lips are sealed." In a lifelong habit, I followed this up by zipping them shut, even though she wasn't privy to the motion. "Do they have a website?"

I preferred any establishment I was dealing with to have a website I could visit. That way, I could get a sense of the place before committing to anything.

"Just a mo."

The change in Lorraine's voice confirmed we were en route to another part of the large, rambling Remuera mansion. There was then a lot of scrabbling at the other end before she spoke. "Got a pen?"

A rummage in the top drawer of the small bedside table and I found one sporting the hotel's logo, along with a notepad similarly monogrammed. After scribbling the website address down, I read it back twice to confirm I had it right.

Rather than comprising words that translated to the actual name of the establishment, Lorraine dictated a random collection of letters and numbers. A Mensa chapter Christmas party would have been stuck recalling this lot. Then followed the usual ritual of agreeing to lunch and 'we must chat more often', before I tapped the call shut and fired up my laptop. I had to type in the URL one letter at a time, all while checking everything was correct, that my zeros weren't Os or vice versa. Convoluted in the extreme, it even included symbols, giving the address a Cyrillic look.

The website, however, was clean and professional. Even

better was that the spa offered what I was after. Fast-track weight loss under professional supervision at a location so remote that escaping would burn more calories than you could snag during a blow-out at McDonald's.

The name was the one off-putting thing about the place. The Vale at Shady Meadows made it sound less like an exclusive spa and weight-loss center and more like an upmarket lawn cemetery. So long as it was the place where fat went to die, I could live with that.

5

For once in my life, I didn't hesitate. I filled in the online application form, hoping The Vale would take me. The way Lorraine told it, there was no guarantee the spa would accept me as an inmate, although the website referred to guests.

Hah, it didn't matter how luxurious it looked, with all those professional photos and beautiful typesetting. Once I checked in, it would be like a prison.

Although, this was the only thing it had in common with those facilities overseen by the Department of Corrections. As well as weight loss, the retreat offered yoga classes, dietary advice, a cinema, and a pool.

Perhaps one of the most comforting things about the place was that they had a money-back guarantee, with my credit card not being hit until I checked out.

It was also women-only, which was a relief, because I'd had

enough of sweaty men grinding away next to me to last a lifetime. Lovemaking with David had always been a damp affair, with the soggy memories having me shuddering as he never could.

With the form completed and submitted, I snapped my computer shut, leaving the rest to fate. However, the wait was shorter than I had been expecting, with an approval email arriving the next morning. This both confirmed acceptance of my booking and let me know what my assigned alias would be.

Maisie Smith? Were they serious?

On scrolling down, I saw the reason for this was to maintain their clients' anonymity. Apparently, they'd had problems with paparazzi in the past. A bubble of excitement gurgled away in my tummy. Or it could have been gas. Either way, I quite liked the idea of mixing with celebrities over breakfast, even if I eschewed the limelight myself.

I also received a link to their online registration, including a page and a half of terms and conditions. These related to keeping quiet about the spa's location and my booking with them. There was enough legalese that I knew if I breached any of them, it would cost me big time. The last section related to my next of kin in case there was an emergency.

My elderly mother couldn't cope with anything drastic from the cushioned comfort of her La-Z-Boy recliner at the rest home down south. Nor did I want to assign this task to any of my girlfriends. Instead, I typed in the contact details of Sue-Ng's law firm. She, more than anyone, would know what to do in case of anything dire occurring.

They also wanted to know my hair and eye color, height, weight, blood type, blood pressure, and if I had any distinguishing marks. Most of this I knew from a lifelong association with my body. The answers to all the medical questions were in the report from my consultation with the boob man.

The next question was one I couldn't answer. I knew I had a mole high on my back. But marking it on the line drawing of a human body on the website? That wasn't happening without clever camera work in the bathroom.

I marked it as best I could by dragging and dropping the mole symbol from the menu on the sidebar. I also added a few piercings and a couple of tattoos to check out what they'd look like before deleting them and clicking the NEXT button. The request on the following page made me second-guess the advisability of completing the booking.

A nude selfie?

Were they serious?

I was in danger of the registration timing out before I could bring myself to strip. The process of taking the photo via the full-length mirror on the back of the bathroom door had me breaking out in a cold sweat. I did, however, use my phone to obscure my face in the photo.

Not long after I hit SUBMIT, I received another email. This one confirmed all my details, along with listing an anchor tattoo on my forearm and pierced nipples.

No, no, no!

I absolutely deleted those before hitting the NEXT button. I know I did.

I wasted no time hitting REPLY, desperate to put things right. However, an automated message stated that if I wanted to contact management at The Vale, I needed to do so via the online contact form.

This didn't work.

Neither did the link to the original registration page.

Damn.

As upsetting as them thinking I was a redneck, was reading the menu and finding out I was going vegan for the duration. Kale and I did not get along.

With my visit to the fat farm a mere two weeks away, I saw no point not to indulge a little in the interim. A back-to-back binge of lunches, dinners, decadent desserts, and a LOT of chocolate ensued. The highlight of this feasting was a going-away dinner with my girlfriends at Flossie's, the most talked about restaurant in town. Despite it not living up to the hype, I still made the most of it, tucking into a large steak with all the trimmings.

If I was subsisting on tofu and kale for the next six weeks, I wanted to boost my levels of whatever it was a large slab of meat provided. The creamy potatoes that accompanied the steak were the perfect thing to top up my potassium and calcium.

Unfortunately, these 'supplements' didn't sit well when I did up my seatbelt the following morning, ready for the drive to The Vale. What had been succulent the night before had coalesced into something that did me no favors. And with the waistband of my snug-fitting yoga pants close to chopping me in two, I was anything but comfortable.

I was zooming down the freeway when my overindulgence sped its way through my gastrointestinal tract, demanding a mercy dash into a service plaza. It was this or risk besmirching my gorgeous new leather upholstery.

While unpleasant in the extreme, the relief was immense. On climbing back into my car, which I hadn't so much parked as abandoned, my stretch pants were no longer in danger of leaving permanent marks.

And it would also help with that all-important first weigh-in.

A snap decision—one of many, after years of researching everything to death to satisfy David—had me taking the back roads. This would avoid traffic and speed traps. The joy of a new car was seeing what it could do. That couldn't happen if I was in bumper-to-bumper traffic and in fear of being done for speeding. The GPS soon had me out in the country and away from the city's gravitational pull.

Despite a dry summer in the city, the fields were lush, rolling in gentle waves before lapping against the native bush that topped the surrounding hills. The road, too, was in good shape. It was time to let my new baby show me what it was capable of.

It didn't take long to realize it could handle a lot more than I could, and I eased off the accelerator for fear of putting myself in a ditch. The first thing I'd do when I was back in town was sign up for advanced driving lessons.

Images of myself dressed head-to-toe in black leathers, tailor-made to fit my new boobs, flashed in a delightful slide show inside my head. That was until lights flashing in the rear-view mirror broke my concentration. I was tootling along at 40mph and had a dozen cars queued up behind me. Rather than speeding up and dealing with the pressure of keeping ahead of them all, I pulled into the next farm driveway. I couldn't believe my eyes when the little old lady in the Nissan Micra at the end of the queue flipped me off when she sped by. In a move out of character, I returned the gesture, although chances were the myopic biddy will have missed it.

Before pulling back onto the road, I opened the sunroof and turned up the volume on my favorite station. Singing like no one was listening, and hoping they weren't, I got back on the road.

The rest of the drive was uneventful but pleasant all the same. The highlight was the drive through the bush at the back of Kawakawa Bay. There I turned the radio down and listened instead to the local birds and cicadas, with their voices filling the air. The smell of the damp undergrowth had memories of trips out this way when I was a teenager, flooding back.

That was before I met David, when I was full of confidence, thin and happy. Well, happy with life. I hadn't liked my body back then either, being skinny as the proverbial rake and built more for speed than comfort.

This boob job of mine was long overdue.

The journey slowed after I left Thames township, where I'd stopped for a light lunch at McDonald's. The road was narrower and the corners more frequent. While the car could handle these at speed, the drop-offs had me driving with care. I'd given myself ample time for the trip. There was no need to risk life and limb.

As noted in The Vale's instructions, and confirmed by Google Earth, my final destination was a small paved area at the side of the road. It was also halfway to the middle of nowhere. However, it was there I was supposed to park and wait for them to collect me. I was to complete the rest of the trip in a vehicle better suited to the roads.

Roads that I couldn't even check out on Street View, with the Google vehicle preferring to stick to the main road north to Shelly Beach. There wasn't a chance I was parking my gorgeous baby out there for six weeks. I was as likely to return to find the car, or at the very least, the wheels, missing.

As well as checking out the parking spot as best I could, I'd also searched Google Earth long and hard for anything looking like The Vale. At least based on the photos on their website. Despite zooming in on any open areas on the hills above Coromandel Township, I had come up empty-handed.

Soon enough, houses popped up more frequently, announcing I was once again approaching civilization, with me soon spotting what I was after. The bright green signage on the gas station was eye-catching, with my turn into the forecourt slow and measured.

I didn't ease in next to the pumps, instead pulling in hard on the left-hand side and parking the Lexus well out of the way. I couldn't have parked next to the pumps if I'd wanted to, with a filthy 4WD hogging the space closest to the buildings. The side closest to the road was home to a ridiculous gold Hummer, like something out of a porno.

I was about to enter the small shop that formed the basis of the gas station when I had to jump back. A rangy man with greasy shoulder-length hair stormed out, his entire focus on the smartphone gripped in his grimy hand.

I bit down on the pointed "excuse me" that hovered on my lips. It was best not to antagonize his sort. Any further words failed me when, instead of getting into the beat-up 4WD, he threw himself into the porn-mobile.

He must have stolen it.

The automatic doors then closed behind me, prompting me to wave my hand above my head. I wasn't looking where I was going when I entered the shop, my eyes still glued to the Hummer.

"Can I help you, love?" said the chap standing behind the counter.

"Oh, ah, yes." I didn't turn to give him my full attention until the ugly gold vehicle had roared out of the station and off down the road. It was as though the hounds of hell, or the cops, were in pursuit.

"I wonder if I can park my vehicle here for the next six

weeks? I'm happy to pay. Somewhere secure and under cover, if possible." As if to reinforce my reason for this, I pointed at my car gleaming in the sunlight.

One look at the Lexus and his mien flipped from professional enquiry to small-town gossip in the blink of an eye. "And where will you be, love?"

Tempted to say it was none of his business, he was all that stood between my beloved car being safe or it being parked in the middle of nowhere. In the end, I went with the excuse I had thought of only last night.

"I'm joining friends. They've rented a beach cottage up the, ah, coast. The road is, um, rough. I don't want to take my new, my car." Despite having run through it several times on the drive down, I still stumbled through the lie, my words disjointed and staccato.

Still, it was better than telling a stranger I'd booked in for six weeks of borderline starvation and enemas. And all so I could get a new pair of boobs. Even thinking about it had my cheeks warm. "I'm meeting up with them at a nearby café."

"Is that so?" Gary, if he was the manager on duty as the sign above the register implied, appeared surprised, although I wasn't sure why. The tilt of his head questioned my plans, although he soon changed his mind. "I guess I wouldn't want to take that fancy car of yours off paved roads, either."

Along with preserving my dignity, the small lie also meant I'd stuck to the Vale's rules that I'd agreed to online. I guess I could understand their desire for privacy given their celebrity clientele.

"That's right. I'd hate to cause any damage."

As annoyed as I was by this delay, I kept my feelings in check. Maybe if Gary answered his phone, we could have sorted this up front. To steer him back to securing lodging for the car, I asked, "So, could you help with parking?"

"I can. There's plenty of space out back in the big shed. I'm sure Bill wouldn't mind."

"Bill?"

"The bloke who's shed it is. Not part of the station, you see."

"Is he around so I can ask him?"

"No, love, he's dead."

6

Unsure of how I was to negotiate a price to store the Lexus with someone who had passed on, I stood in front of the counter, dithering. "Roxanne!" Gary had shouted this at the top of his voice, causing me to jump. We waited. "Roxanne!! His volume had doubled, but this time it didn't take me off guard.

There was shuffling before a girl flung aside the multi-colored, plastic fly screen that separated the shop from the private spaces out back. She had her music turned up so loud that I recognized the song, even though she'd shoved the buds deep inside her ears. Her expression of teenage angst was also loud, with every decibel directed at me.

Rather than waste breath speaking to her, Gary pointed first at her and then at the stool behind the counter. He repeated this when she didn't move as fast as he would have liked. It wasn't until she was in place, her belligerence on full show, that he led me out the front doors.

He then swung to the right, and we walked down the side of the garage to a hodgepodge of tin sheds that cluttered the back of the lot. After stopping next to the sliding doors on the biggest, he pulled an enormous bunch of keys from his back pocket, his pants lifting in relief. A quick flick through the multitude on offer and Gary selected a large key. He slid this into a padlock that appeared older than the patchwork of corrugated iron skinning the building.

The lock opened with surprising ease given the rust that coated it, but the squealing when he slid the door to one side set my teeth on edge. Inside, the shed was much lighter than I had expected, with most of the roof given over to plastic sheeting rather than long-run iron.

The smell of oil, sawdust, and long-forgotten projects was one that took me back to my dad tinkering away in the shed at my childhood home. A true workman's shed.

"Now that's odd." Gary stopped without warning, and I ran into the back of him, forcing him to step forward.

With nothing other than a pristine Morris Minor parked in one corner, I asked, "What is?"

"Bill's car being here. It's been missing since before the pig hunters found him at the bottom of that cliff." He strolled over to inspect the vehicle, with me trailing along. "Everyone's been on the lookout for it." He ran his hand over the hood. "Collector's item, you see. But I can tell you one thing, it wasn't in here earlier. The cops will want to hear about this."

"The police? Should I store my car somewhere else?"

"What? No, she'll be right, love. It was an open-and-shut case. Silly old fool was out hunting by himself and must have slipped. Pigs savaged him something chronic before those hunters found him."

"Pigs?" I said weakly, with the Big Macs from earlier doing their best to be back on the menu. Make that with double fries and a sundae, with a dollop of chocolate sauce to follow.

"Nasty things, wild boar. Did you know they can eat a sheep, bones and all? Couple of hours and they'll be done. And that's a healthy animal, not an injured bloke like old Bill."

I didn't know.

I didn't want to know.

"Excuse me."

I stumbled out into the fresh air, breathing in through my nose, all the while avoiding images of people being eaten alive by pigs. It wasn't a simple task given I had been up-sold bacon on my burgers. Gary continued with a chomp-by-chomp account of how this had happened. I shoved my fingers in my ears and distanced myself to the point I was over by the corrugated iron fence. The property was a shrine to iron.

As if realizing I was no longer behind him, Gary turned and, although his lips moved, I couldn't hear anything. I waited for him to understand his gruesome account was more than I needed to know. However, it was only when his lips had stopped moving that I pulled my fingers out of my ears.

I now understood why Roxanne kept her music at full volume.

"Sorry, love, didn't mean to upset you."

Not trusting myself to open my mouth, I instead waved my hand to acknowledge his apology.

"If the shed's all good with you, we can put your car in there now. No need to charge you anything."

Whether his charity was down to small-town kindness, or his having me close to barfing all over the yard, I wasn't sure. Either way, I couldn't accept it.

"No, I'd prefer to pay. You can give the money to a worthy cause if you like."

We were back at the Lexus before Gary spoke again. "Bill was always a big supporter of the local animal shelter. We can give it to them, if you like?"

I agreed, unlocked the Lexus, and climbed in. It was another ten minutes before I parked next to Bill's car and dragged my bag out of the trunk. Progress had been slow because of Gary walking in front of my car like a signalman from the first days of motoring. Locking the shed door had then taken on a ceremonial air.

Back out front, the forecourt was now free of cars, which was just as well. Roxanne sat with eyes closed and the music cranked up so loud she didn't have a clue we were right next to her. Only when Gary nudged her did she open her eyes. However, the sullen teen didn't show an ounce of surprise, so perhaps she was aware of us, after all.

Soon enough, she jumped off the stool and, after flinging the fly screen to one side, skulked through. She didn't go far, though, instead turning and watching us through the still swaying strips of plastic.

Gary stood at the cash register and scratched his head. Leaning forward, he peered at the plethora of buttons on the state-of-the-art till in pride of place on the counter. "Not sure what I should put parking under."

I didn't have time for this. All this messing about had me in danger of running late, with this something The Vale had warned against. Desperation had me grabbing a packet of chewing gum from the stand next to the register and slamming it down on the counter.

"How about I buy this and get two-hundred-dollars out in cash? I can give that to you for the animal shelter." His relief was clear by how quickly he took my purchase and rang it up. I signed the receipt to show I had received the cash and then handed it straight back.

All of this under Roxanne's watchful—some might say avaricious—gaze. Despite not hearing much, I doubted she missed a thing. I was therefore relieved when Gary folded the money and put it into the pocket of his shirt and patted it, the drop in the teenage girl's demeanor palpable.

Of more concern was her eyes widening when I handed Gary my keyring. While it was doubtful that he'd need to move the Lexus in my absence, I would rather he could, if it was necessary.

At any other time, my keyring would have been bristling with keys, but not any longer. Not wanting to commit to an apartment before leaving town, I had instead hired a storage unit, with this secured by a keypad. It hadn't been easy finding a unit though, with these in short supply thanks to people buying crap they didn't have room for. It was for this reason I'd had to pre-pay three months in advance.

Thanks to running shoes and a wheeled suitcase, I was at the taxi stand around the corner with time to spare. I shared the old-school bench seat with a woman who must have been in her eighties and who had a small child in tow. A grandchild, no doubt. Neither of them looked keen on conversation and I wasn't one to strike it up without encouragement, so we sat.

Shattering our peace was the beat-up 4WD from the gas station pulling up in front of us. This was something that would have led to a turf war at any taxi stand in the city, but that didn't raise an eyebrow here.

I was fretting my taxi would have trouble pulling in with this grubby vehicle in the way, when the curb-side window whirred down. The driver then leaned across the passenger seat, his gaze soon enough catching mine. "Mrs. Rogers?"

It took a second to realize he was talking to me and that this beat-up vehicle must be my taxi. I had forgotten I'd booked it under my maiden name in an act of rebellion at being free of David. "It's Ms. but yes."

With my identity confirmed, he jumped out, marched around the front, and collected my bag. While the vehicle wasn't taxi-standard, his outfit of walk shorts, white shirt, and a potbelly, thanks to hours behind the wheel, was spot-on. He put the buttons on his shirt to the test when he slung my bag in the back. Ditto the expensive French cosmetics I had packed the night before.

I held back on telling him to be careful, with any damage already done. All I could hope was that when I opened my toiletry bag, everything hadn't coalesced into a skin-smoothing-wrinkle-beating goo. Glass bottles could be a curse.

I had already tried the handle of the back door when he marched by me and opened the front. "Sorry, love, my usual ride's out for the count. You'll need to sit up front with me."

This at least explained the state of the vehicle, and while not happy to be sitting next to him, I demurred and climbed in. I hadn't had time to get comfortable when he jumped in and floored it, pressing me back into an immaculate seat.

While the outside of the vehicle was rough as guts, the interior was pristine. There was even a box of tissues in the center console in case of spills. The small cardboard pine tree, swinging from the rear-view mirror, gave off a reassuring smell of taxi.

All that was missing was a meter with this doubtless in his usual vehicle. It did, however, have me glad I'd agreed to a price upfront with the lady at the taxi company.

It didn't take long for me to realize that completing the trip in silence was out of the question. As with all taxi drivers, Colin liked a chat, although the spew of words he kept up for the first five minutes of our trip didn't match the term. Verbal diarrhea would have been a better descriptor.

He touched on the backgrounds of everyone we passed. He went into the history of buildings, roads, and anything else not nailed down. He even proved knowledgeable about the flora and fauna and modern farming methods. None of which interested me.

We turned onto Flays Road and his diatribe changed direction, too. It was one I'd rather have avoided.

"Such a shame about old Bill. It was out this way they found him. He was a character, all right."

He appeared ready to carry on, forcing me to blurt out, "What sort of ferns are these?" My question was one of desperation. Anything to avoid stories of people being eaten by pigs. Personally, I couldn't have cared less about the native plants thrashing themselves against the side of the Land Rover as if to stop us from passing. But if it would shut him up, I'd summon my inner gardener.

"Oh." He seemed put out at my having cut him off. "Oh, these are Dicksonia fibrosa."

In response to my blank look, he added, "Golden tree fern."

I was out of distractions. Unless I wanted to get into the grade of gravel on the road. Soon enough, he was back to talking about Bill.

"The strange thing was he didn't have his pack with him, or his gun. If he'd had his gun, he could have taken potshots at those porkers and kept them at bay. They ripped his throat clean out, they did."

"Stop!"

Colin looked at me as if I was bonkers for interrupting a story he'd doubtless dined out on many times.

"Stop the car! I'm going to be sick!"

The speed with which he applied the brakes had me close to losing my lunch all over the dashboard. However, his emergency stop was academic. Unable to get out of the vehicle in time, I opened the door wide, leaned out as far as I could, and introduced the Golden Arches to Flays Road.

Colin inched forward, allowing me to avoid the remains of my burger. I stumbled from the vehicle and gave up more of my lunch, grateful when he moved the vehicle to a clean spot after each expulsion. After a couple of dry retches, I knew there was nothing left. However, on my clambering back in, a brief nod from Colin stopped me.

"Oh, I'm so sorry." I leaned over the passenger seat and snatched several tissues from the box before wiping the door.

He checked for longer than I'd have liked before he gave me the nod that said I'd cleaned to his exacting standards. This had me balling the tissues and stuffing them in the plastic bag hanging from the knob of the glove compartment. Despite the occasional whiff, the little pine tree was up to the challenge of masking them from my driver.

We hadn't gone more than another twenty feet when Colin said, "He'd scratched 'Cooking P' into the dirt. Cops figure he must have stumbled across a cook lab."

He went quiet, although not for as long as I'd have liked. "Guess writing that was quicker than methamphetamine." He thought about this for a beat before continuing. "Now, isn't that funny? I wouldn't have a clue what P stands for. Do you?"

My headshake was more of a wobble, thanks to that purging and not having the nerve to tell him to shut up. I mean, how on earth was I supposed to know what the initial used to describe the drug of choice stood for?

"Yep, meth labs, the modern-day equivalent of an old-school dope patch. It happens here, too. It's not just in the big smoke, ya know."

I avoided the inevitable argument about Aucklanders being money-grubbing, house-gobbling, road-hogs and leaned back into my seat, turning my head to stare, unseeing, out of the window. Peace was impossible, with Colin and the dueling banjos showing no signs of shutting up.

All I could hope was that we were getting close to the designated pickup spot. However, as I took in the impenetrable bush on both sides of the road, I wasn't optimistic.

7

As we continued to inch forward, Colin peered at the coordinates on his GPS. "You sure about this parking spot? I can't think of anything like that out this way."

"That's where my friends said they'd collect me." I kept my response brief, not wanting to prattle on. I already looked like an idiot asking him to drop me out here. No need to gild the lily.

However, my runaway mouth had other ideas. Continuing with the lie of going further afield with friends, I hurriedly added, "The parking spot showed on Google Earth." I then took another look at the screen of my phone as if to double-check.

With his suspicions allayed, he again inched the vehicle forward. Meanwhile, I kept a wary eye out for the tag on the tree mentioned in the instructions emailed to me a day earlier.

Another email I couldn't reply to in order to rescind my redneck credentials.

Scanning the bushes on my side of the road, I was now as unsure as my driver. Civilization was a long way behind us, with any establishment expecting me to park my car out here seeming less legit all the time. It confirmed my decision to park in town was the right one.

"There, there!" I pointed at a bright pink tag nailed to a tree that overhung the corrugated gravel road. "The parking spot should be around this corner, on my side."

Colin didn't speed up, which was just as well. While the parking spot was visible on Google Earth, it seemed the photo was an old one. Rather than a graveled space as I'd seen, it was now only a scruffy gap between the ferns. If he had been driving any faster, we would have missed it, and given how dense the undergrowth was, my car might have been okay after all.

Still, I'd have hated driving up this road, with the potholes and ridges more challenging than the speed bumps at the local supermarket.

I expected Colin to swing into the space so he could turn, but he didn't. Instead, he cranked on the handbrake, killed the engine, and got out. It was only when he pulled a machete out of the driver's door pocket I grasped what he was up to.

The blade looked lethal, making quick work of the ferns curving in on all sides. By the time he'd finished, there was a discernible space in the bush, and I could even make out tatty patches of gravel. However, Colin didn't stop there, proceeding to stomp all over the space, checking for stability. It wasn't something I would have thought to do. Even creeping forward into the bush as far as possible, turning the Land Rover was no easy feat.

I'd never have managed it in the Lexus. Not without removing paint and scraping the undercarriage. Or worse, sliding off the side of the hill and into the bush. We were back on the road and facing town before he spoke again.

"You sure your friends said they'd pick you up here?"

He was now displaying as much trepidation as I was feeling. This had me pulling up my metaphorical big-girl pants—perhaps not so metaphorical—and convincing him I'd be fine.

"I've got my phone, and it's fully charged. I can call you if they don't turn up."

He opened his mouth but didn't have time to speak before a crackle of static and a woman's voice filled the cab.

"Colin, you copy?"

He retrieved a mic from under his seat, stretched on the cord, and pressed a big button on the side, causing it to beep. "Receiving..."

"I've got a pickup for you in ... Kennedy Bay... Six passengers... American..."

The pauses were for effect and, sure enough, they elicited the desired response. He peered at me, then dropped his gaze before replying. "I'm on my way."

He was now less concerned with leaving me in the middle of nowhere, instead focused on exchanging me for what would be a massive fare, given the distance alone. Add to this the reputation Americans had for being big tippers, and I was as good as on my own.

"If you're sure you'll be okay, love. I'd offer to drop you back in town, but I'll be heading in the other direction when I get to Kennedy Bay Road."

I imagined he was crossing his fingers on the hand I couldn't see, hoping I wouldn't change my mind and insist that he drop me back in town. While tempted, I'd come this far, and with each mile traveled, those perky boobs of mine were inching ever closer.

"I'm due to be picked up in," I glanced at my Rolex, "ten minutes. No harm can come to me in that short a time. It's a beautiful day." I trailed off, unable to come up with any other pluses to standing on the side of a gravel road, deep in the bush.

He took me at my word, hopped out of the cab, and unloaded my bag from the back. After carrying it to the cleared piece of bush, he plopped it down on the edge of the road before striding back and opening my door.

Having paid by bank transfer the day before, I swung my legs around and slid over the side of the bench seat until my feet hit gravel. I retrieved my handbag from the footwell, and once I was clear of the door, Colin slammed it shut with the finality of a job well done.

It was a shame he left at a greater rate of knots than we'd arrived. Coated in a thick cloud of dust, I had to lift my arm to form a mask of sorts. Any sounds of the departing taxi were now down to my imagination, with the stillness of the bush closing in. It was quiet, except for the local birds chattering as though they hadn't seen each other in weeks.

And it would appear they had a lot of catching up to do with no let-up in the squawks, cheeps, and whistles that flitted about in the dense bush.

Then, as if they'd caught up on all their gossip, they fell silent; eerily so.

I turned my back on the road and peered into the bush. There were birds there, sitting on branches, stock-still. There was no preening, no stretching of wings. There wasn't even any shuffling along branches in hopes of a better view. They sat frozen and quiet, as if waiting for something to pass.

I stepped closer to the bush.

What had spooked them?

Could it be there were feral cats up this way? The ones that politician wanted to wipe off the face of the earth. However, when he'd mentioned getting rid of any domesticated pets, he'd lost the vote of every cat lady in the country.

My arms folded across my chest, I rubbed my upper arms, working at the goosebumps that had popped up unbidden. As I backed away from the bush, I scanned its depths from left to right. Something was off. I just didn't know what. But the sensation of being watched didn't go away.

As focused as I was, it was hearing the crunch of gravel underfoot that had me grasp I was back on the road. I stopped where I was, my gaze still trained on the bush, my ears straining to pick up on the smallest sound. And when they did, it wasn't the local birds getting on with their day. No, it was the roar of an approaching vehicle.

What on earth was I thinking, agreeing to a pickup spot as remote as this? David always said I was stupid. Could it be he was right?

I was giving serious consideration to hiding in the bush until I was sure it was my ride when the gold Hummer porn-mobile thundered around the corner.

What was that thing doing out here? And what if it was the same creep driving?

I'd staggered back from the road when the gold Hummer came to an abrupt stop, dead in front of me. The window slid down to reveal the scruffy bloke from the gas station. Rather than look at me, he was peering at a crumpled piece of paper he was holding against the steering wheel. Soon enough, he examined me with as much depth.

He may or may not have washed his hair since I last saw him. But he had pulled it back into a tight ponytail, making him look more clean-cut than he had been earlier. The other thing that looked clean was his shirt, even if all I could see was the sleeve, with his arm propped out of the window. Gone was the grubby black singlet of earlier.

I was edging toward a full-on panic attack over why he had stopped when he shoved the grubby sheet of paper through the window. It was a copy of my Vale registration form, but one without my naked selfie in evidence, thank goodness. "Is this you?"

"Yes, that's me." Now that I knew he worked for The Vale, I

gave him a small wave and my friendliest smile, hoping to soften his demeanor. He was not happy. He looked even more ticked off now than when he came close to bowling me over when he left the gas station shop.

The reason for this soon became apparent.

"Where's your car?"

His accent was feral, concentrating on all the bad points of the New Zealand twang. It was not something one heard often in the city, and there was nothing polite about his inquiry. It was aggressive. This had me glad I'd practiced my response in the bathroom mirror of my hotel room until I could spit it out without stuttering or blushing beet red.

Despite all the rehearsals, I still needed to lubricate my mouth with my tongue before I could speak. "It ... it was playing up on the trip here, so I left it with a mechanic in town. I would have called you, but ..."

But, thanks to all the cloak and dagger, they hadn't given me a phone number.

My response did nothing to placate him. His brow crunched down further. This became even more obvious when he opened the door and slid out of the ridiculous tank of a vehicle. He stood on the edge of the road, legs braced and arms crossed. If he was trying to intimidate me, he was doing a good job.

"How did you get out here?"

Again, I reverted to my prepared script. "Ah, a local was collecting his car from the mechanic, and he offered to give me a ride."

He stomped over and planted himself in front of me. "Did you give the mechanic your real name?"

I craned my neck and squinted up at him, trying not to think about all the other terms and conditions I had ignored. My voice was stuck in my throat, although I soon spluttered out. "Um, I had to. The license plate..."

I couldn't come up with anything else. Even someone as feral as this guy would have to know I couldn't use an alias. Not when the fictitious mechanic could check online to see who owned the car.

We had now arrived at the point where I longed to scream, "I've changed my mind." To grab my suitcase and drag it back into town. Shame my body wasn't up to the task. Come to that, neither was the suitcase.

"What about the person who gave you a ride?"

I shook my head, unable to spout yet another lie.

He shoved his hand in my direction, opening and closing his fingers while barking, "Where's the ID you were told to bring?"

This had me scrambling to get my license and passport out of the zippered pocket deep inside my handbag before passing them to him. Only after he'd scanned them did his body language drop a notch from, I'm going to kill you for breaking the rules, to a simple pissed.

I flinched and even stumbled when he shoved the documents back at me. I knew I wasn't imagining his smirk when he grabbed my suitcase, again getting closer than he needed to.

Bastard.

It therefore astounded me when he placed my bag in the Hummer's trunk with care. I'd been expecting more of the luggage-handling capabilities of Colin, the taxi driver. When he opened the rear door and stood back, waiting for me to enter, he again took me by surprise.

Climbing in was easier said than done, with the step being a good couple of feet off the road, thanks to the vehicle's enormous size.

The other thing that wasn't in its favor was that it shrieked look at me. Thank goodness for tinted windows and being in the middle of nowhere. I wouldn't want to be seen dead in this thing anywhere near civilization.

The term wanker came to mind for anyone willing to be seen in one on purpose, being right up there with stretch limos on the lame scale. Certainly, it smacked too much of a big entrance at the school ball for my liking.

It was an effort to lift my leg and step onto the footplate. I was beyond mortified when this resulted in a fart so toxic my chauffeur staggered back. To further add to my mortification, he then waved his hand back and forth in front of his nose, his gagging exaggerated in the extreme.

My humiliation was complete.

Unfortunately, this wasn't quite true.

There was no way my leg muscles were up to the challenge of stepping into the vehicle. I had to resort to scrambling in on my hands and knees. The driver picked the wrong time to step forward and close the door.

To a background chorus of more coughing and retching, I clambered onto the back seat, slid over as far as I could, and settled in. From force of habit, I pulled the seatbelt over my shoulder and secured it. This, more than anything else, reinforced how big the seats were.

For the first time in a long while, I felt small. I could lay full length across the back seat without messing my hair or bending my legs, and at five-foot-eight, it was not as if I was short.

Nor was I tempted to try it. Not with bubbles of flatulence threatening to convert the Hummer into a mobile gas chamber each time we rattled across another rut in the road. I suspected this was also worrying the driver if the number of times he looked at me in the rear-view mirror was anything to go on.

My relief must have been as clear as his when the road became a soft dust bowl that was easier on the vehicle and my gastric opus. It would be a nightmare if it rained, but being late summer, the road was bone dry, and so he whistled to a song no one else was privy to.

This was odd because the dashboard featured a stereo that appeared flashier than the one David had had in his car. The one he'd loved to crank the volume up on, and that gave me a headache. The one that made conversation impossible.

About twenty minutes later, I noticed grass growing in the middle of the dusty road. The ferns on either side attacked the pristine gold paintwork with a passion rarely seen with foliage. There were even a few worrying crunches.

If it bothered the crazy man in the front, he didn't show it. When I again caught his gaze in the rear-view mirror, the calculating nature of his examination freaked me out. I was so out of my depth that I was close to drowning, and with good reason.

Stuck in a strange vehicle, with an even stranger man, heading for who knew where. Only now did an apprehension I should have felt earlier make itself at home in my gut.

Unless it was gas?

8

What seemed like hours later, but likely wasn't, we drove into the open, with the tinted windows not up to the challenge of keeping the bright sunlight at bay. While the narrow road carried on, disappearing into the trees up ahead, we swung through enormous gates that appeared industrial, even military, in nature. A peek out the back window showed them being shut and locked behind us.

It was then that I noticed the tall chain-link fence, with its razor wire topping. What was odd was that this angled inwards. Could it be my jokes about being an inmate weren't so far from the truth? The only thing that calmed my nerves was Lorraine's assertion that the place was above-board, with many she knew returning year-after-year.

The driveway meandered through gardens that lacked any

flowers. They were more cleared bush than anything featured in magazines. However, when we crested the brow of the hill, the panorama spread out before us, showed me why titivating the gardens would be overkill.

The view was spectacular and of the variety often seen in high-end real estate brochures, the colors so vibrant as to appear retouched. I was doing my best to check it out when the Hummer jerked to an emergency stop, throwing me hard against my seatbelt.

I knew I wasn't imagining the suppressed laughter coming from the front. My driver appeared to have irritating people down to a fine art. So far, it had been annoying, but nothing more. If I complained, I would appear delusional. It was also not my way, preferring to keep my opinions to myself to avoid open confrontation.

The building we had stopped outside was nothing like I had been imagining and nothing like I'd expected to see at a high-end spa. It was relocatable, complete with large skids, making it easy to move around. Closer inspection showed it to be a shipping container, and a big one at that.

"Ah, are you sure you've brought me to the right place? It looks nothing like the images on the web—"

Any further words died on my lips when he wrenched himself around in his seat and shoved that crumpled note right up in my face. Close enough that I got a whiff of cheap aftershave and engine oil.

I pushed back into my seat, distancing myself from his

grubby fist and providing the focal length required to read the blasted thing. However, before I could make out more than a couple of words, he snatched it back. It would appear seeing the Vale logo at the top right-hand corner was all the answer I was getting.

This did nothing to settle my nerves, and I was relieved when he turned back to face the steering wheel. I didn't like the way he looked at me, with it having a calculating quality that creeped me out.

Not waiting for him to get out and do so, I unclipped my seatbelt and opened my door. On lowering myself to the ground, I let go of any cubic feet of gas left in my system, relieved this didn't lead to anything more substantial.

He exploded out of the vehicle in response to my accidental gassing, his filthy look having me glad the ugly thing was between us. He stalked around to the back, wrenched open the rear door, and dragged my bag out with complete disregard for the contents. He then dumped it next to the front steps in the middle of the building.

On looking up, it surprised me to see wide eaves, and a roof covered in native grasses. It was something that would have made it as good as invisible on Google Earth. Other than this nod to an off-grid lifestyle, I was relieved to see three large satellite dishes anchored to the roof. Given the remote location, I'd worried about being cut off from civilization.

A small ADMIN sign sat to the right of large floor-to-ceiling sliding glass doors that allowed a view of the interior.

The setup in there went a long way toward explaining why I'd be paying so much on departure.

Reception was like something out of a design magazine, and while the chairs were plastic, they were Philippe Starck Ghost Chairs. A far cry from the stackable variety seen at barbeques the world over.

They were also not a good idea at a fat farm. If I was to sit in one of those, I'd be stuck wearing the blasted thing like a pair of see-through underpants until they produced the tire irons.

While I'd like to go in and register, the driver was between me and the door, and I intended to keep as much distance as I could. He made my skin crawl. To avoid the confrontation hovering between us, I turned and concentrated on the view. His eyes were daggers in my back, leaving me fighting the urge to turn and apologize. It was something that required me to subjugate years of compliance and doing what I deemed right.

And the vista was one hell of a distraction. The land rolled away from us in a mix of bush and farmland, bordered by the sparkling waters of the upper Firth of Thames. Ponui and Waiheke Islands sat splendidly in the middle of this aquamarine sea.

"That will be all, Lance."

The woman's voice, having come out of nowhere, had startled me, leaving my heart hammering. Her hard New York accent was also unexpected, being more common in sitcoms than in the depths of the New Zealand countryside.

However, the scorn she'd injected into her simple demand was impressive, with the greasy twit moving far quicker than if she'd been polite. He was back in the Hummer in a flash. As quick to follow was a bout of coughing and cussing, and all the windows whirring down at the same time. He gave me one last dirty look before he floored it, coating me in dust.

If the woman standing unmoving on the top step thought anything of this insubordination, she didn't show it. I was unsure whether this was because she was unconcerned or had sufficient Botox on board to paralyze an elephant.

I'd describe her as monochromatic. Hair black. Skin white. With a lot of help in both cases, being my guess. Her lipstick was a red, so dark that at first glance, I'd mistaken it for black. The shapeless smock that hung from her shoulders was crisp enough it could doubtless stay upright on its own. This slap to the face of fashion was snow white, had large patch pockets, and concealed any curves she had.

Despite the prêt-à-porter camouflage, my money was on the woman having fewer curves than an ironing board.

What was it about women who weighed one-hundred-pounds dripping wet that they ended up running places like this? It was inhumane, that's what it was.

"You must be 'Maisie Smith'," said the woman, making her way down the steps, her movements somehow regal.

It took a moment to appreciate the greeting was hers, with her lips not having moved, that I saw. Give her a dummy, and she could succeed in vaudeville.

"Yes, that's right." I was conscious of nodding as woodenly as any ventriloquist's sidekick while agreeing to this stupid alias.

She held out her hand in greeting, leaving me no option but

to step forward and take it. The warmth of her grip was a surprise, and not something shared by the woman herself. Despite having just met her, I knew she was what my late dad would have called a cold fish. Certainly, her eyes were reminiscent of some I'd seen at the fishmonger's I frequented back in the city.

"I'm Candice Hawkie. Welcome to The Vale at Shady Meadows, where dreams become reality."

Damn it, her American accent made it sound more like a lawn cemetery than ever, and I struggled against the smile that threatened. That her eyes narrowed suggested I'd failed in this endeavor. At least, I think they narrowed.

However, if Candice thought she was hiding her true age from me, she was out of luck. I'd been on many an outing with the high-maintenance ladies who lunch, something that had my gaze dropping to her hands.

Sure enough, they were out of whack with her face and neck by around thirty years. While her face belonged to a twenty-something, her wrinkled mitts sure didn't. If there was a procedure to remedy this, Lorraine would have had it by now.

As if able to discern my thoughts, she dropped my hand and made her way back up the steps. There she waited beside the door, signaling for me to enter. "Please, do come in."

Yet again, I wondered at the advisability of interring myself here. I knew next to nothing about this place other than the snippets from Lorraine, with even those second-hand. And who knew how much my frenemy had held back thanks to her love of keeping others in the dark?

However, years of being subservient first to my parents and then David had me bending over to retrieve my suitcase.

"No need to worry about your luggage. We'll take care of it for you."

This was more like it! Upon entering a reception area bereft of personality, my gaze skittered around. My hope was a chair more suited to my Rubenesque figure than those fragile-looking ghost chairs. There was nothing on offer, although there was a door marked PRIVATE off to the left.

Behind me, Candice slid the outside door shut, silencing the cicadas and confirming the glazing was double, or even triple. "Delia's away sick today. We can go through to my office and fill in the paperwork there."

To the right of reception, her office was also a study in minimalism. It didn't even benefit from the view, thanks to skinny windows that hugged the ceiling. I guessed it helped her concentrate on her work, whatever that was.

On seeing the visitors' chairs in Candice's office, I relaxed a little. Here the chairs didn't have arms, although my current weight would still put the crisscross metal frames of the Barcelona chairs to the test. I was on edge until the piece of classic design took my full weight, and any residual bounce subsided.

I noticed Candice's matching chair didn't bounce at all.

I also noticed the clipboard on the glass coffee table between us. Strange that there were so many empty spaces, considering how many questions I'd answered in that online form of theirs.

Unsure of how to broach the subject, I waded right in. "I don't have an anchor tattoo or pierced nipples."

To reinforce the truth, I pushed back the sleeves of my top, revealing my forearms. But I stopped there. She'd have to take me at my word after this. If she needed confirmation, she could check on the naked selfie I'd submitted.

She said nothing, and with no movement in her face, I was in the dark about what she thought of me adding these features. Not my fault there was something screwy going on with the software.

"But I have got a mole on my back."

Again, there was no response other than her sliding the clipboard, with a pen on top, over to my side of the coffee table.

"Even though we got you to fill in all your details online, we have to show you a hard copy of everything." She tried to lift an eyebrow before continuing. "For legal reasons."

Very legal reasons if the wodge of paper jammed under the clip was an indicator. While the first couple of pages repeated everything I'd already completed online, there were a couple of extra questions for me to answer. The rest was dense legalese.

In a six-point font.

The type was gray.

It was as if they didn't want me to read it.

Thanks to this, I was having second, and maybe even third, thoughts. This had me close to handing the agreement back, unsigned until a quick gander at my chest urged me on. If this was what it took to have my body bikini-ready for next summer, then I was in, boots and all.

The years of David harping on about me reading anything I signed had me going full on Pavlov's dog. I was struggling through Clause 4 when Candice sighed. It was the first genuine expression that the woman had given since I met her. The subliminal pressure from her was worse than the internal pressure from my late husband to read the damned thing from start to end.

"Look, I'm sure this is all fine." Abandoning any pretense of being able to see the type, let alone understand it, I flipped straight to the back page and signed with a flourish. Interestingly, here, at least, I had to sign my real name. That I'd done so, skimming nothing in between, should have David spinning in his grave. Good, I hoped the asshole's ass was getting splinters with every rotation.

The bulky contract was still flipping back into place when Candice took the clipboard from me with a speed that hinted at eagerness. She was on her feet in a flash, but I struggled to follow suit. Fearful of putting too much downward force on the Barcelona chair, I was careful when I gained my feet, taking as much pressure on my thighs as I could. No simple task, as I hadn't been near the gym since long before they stopped sending me reminders featuring dinosaurs.

I used the opportunity of Candice putting my signed contract in the top drawer of her designer desk to shake the cramp out of my legs. I was still doing this when she turned in my direction.

"Now, if you'll just give me your handbag, we'll put it in the safe."

"My what?"

"Your handbag. As per the contract you've just signed, we need to hold on to your handbag. For security reasons."

Damn it. I should have read the fine print. Even if that had her huffing and puffing like an asthmatic in springtime.

With nothing for it, I retrieved my eReader, phone, and charger and handed over my beloved Hermès bag, hoping it would be as safe as she assured me. It didn't inspire confidence when, after thumping it down on the credenza behind her, she opened it wide and peered inside.

After a thorough search, she held up the bottle of beta-blockers. "Hmph, you won't need these by the time we've finished with you." After dumping them back in my handbag, she eyeballed me again.

"Your keys, Maisie? Where are your keys?"

It confused me why she didn't know, although I soon realized the greasy twit hadn't told her about my fictitious car troubles. Too busy choking over my gastric shortcomings.

I rattled through my explanation, my eyes never daring to leave her face. There was no way of knowing whether she'd seen through my lie, with her brief nod at the end of my ramblings, rather non-committal. It was only when I'd mentioned the mechanic who was tending to my car that her eyes had flickered.

That dealt with, Candice reached out, beckoning with her

fingers, and leaving me befuddled. But Lorraine had been teasing about that, hadn't she? Not if the hard glint in the spa manager's eyes was any indicator.

"But I like to read at night. And what if I need to get hold of someone? Or they need to get hold of me?"

"We've given your contact details to your lawyer, and if you need to phone anyone, you're welcome to use our landline. Cell coverage is patchy here." She then took my eReader out of my left hand, flipped the cover open, and looked at the device before returning it.

"You may keep hold of this, but you can't download any books while you're here."

Thinking as I was about can't versus not allowed, my question was slow in forming. "But, the dishes on the roof," I jabbed my eReader toward the ceiling. "Don't they mean I can download new books?"

"Those old things? No, they date back to when the New Zealand military was in residence. With them decommissioned, we're at the mercy of the cell tower in town for our communications."

Well, this would make it tricky to stay in touch with my friends on Threads and Facebook. They'd think something dire had happened to me, even if I hadn't planned on telling the truth about why I was out of town.

My plan was to focus on the beauty treatments while not mentioning where I actually was. I wasn't likely to post a selfie of me giving myself a right seeing to with a rubber tube and a bag of saline. I wasn't one of those TMI social media types.

If what she said was true, the cell reception must be chronic. When Candice tried to take my phone and charger, it startled me. Such was my attachment to these devices, that she had to peel my fingers away one at a time to do so.

She then dropped them inside my handbag before turning back to face me. When she again held out her hand, I was in the dark about what she was after. There was nothing left, unless you counted my jewelry, and I doubted she was after that.

How wrong I was. After a bit of fumbling with catches and clasps, I handed over my earrings, necklace, and even my Rolex. Apparently, there was no need to keep track of time while I was here.

"Now, if you'll follow me, I'll show you to your room."

For someone as washed-out as she was, she sure rattled along. Not even those clumpy white ankle boots of hers slowed her down. She would have given Sue-Ng, the pocket-rocket lawyer, a run for her money.

I had fallen back a few feet before the tube of toothpaste in front of me came to a stop, allowing me to catch up.

"That's the yoga studio."

On looking where she'd pointed, I recognized the studio from photos on their website. What the website hadn't shown was the drop-dead gorgeous view beyond. You could take it in while in a Downward Dog, with your ass saluting the sun.

Strange that the building didn't have a sedum roof in the photos on their website. It must have been a recent addition.

It was a second before I understood Candice was no longer at my side. Luckily, she wasn't too far ahead and wasn't walking as quickly as before. I caught up, and she continued pointing out more of the facilities.

"Dining room. Medical center."

She rattled these off in a monotone that matched her persona, pointing to them as if they were emergency exits. It was a relief that we were walking on a wooden boardwalk with the open ground roughly mowed and thus peppered with outcrops of tussock and bracken.

At least scooting along on the walkway, I was less likely to trip as I swung my head from side to side. The one thing all the buildings had in common was their eco-friendly roofs and an array of modern-looking satellite dishes.

"And whereabouts is the pool?" Despite it being ages since I had been out in public in a swimsuit, the pool looked heavenly, from what I saw of it on their website.

"It's at the top of the property. Sadly, the filtration system isn't working. So, the pool is closed for maintenance." She remained close-lipped about when it would be up and running again, and I concluded it wouldn't be while I was staying there.

I was still contemplating the direction she had pointed in and thinking how nice a dip would have been when she announced we had arrived at my room.

Swinging my gaze back, I was gobsmacked.

The building looked to be as utilitarian and relocatable as that housing the admin department. There was nothing designer and expensive about that board and batten cladding. Steps led to a narrow porch, with a large window to the left of the door.

As well as a small satellite dish, and the ubiquitous native grasses, the roof had a couple of solar panels and the spouting finished in a large water butt. Strange, the website said nothing about the place being this green. I had been expecting high-end, not low impact.

This couldn't be right.

There must have been a horrible mistake.

9

I was still working on the courage to voice concerns that my room was nothing like that shown on their website when Candice opened the door. She then entered and waited for me to follow, her toe-tapping signaling I wasn't moving fast enough.

Ever obedient, I hastened to enter, with an appraisal of the crisp, clean interior decor, smoothing my ruffled feathers. They were now as soft as those in the plump duvet that sat on the king-sized bed. Here, at least, the room matched up to the photos on their website.

"There's an information pack in the top drawer of the bedside cabinet."

Without bothering to see if I had noted this, she opened the closet and passed me a sterile pack containing a small bucket, assorted tubing, and spouts.

"This is an enema kit. You'll need to complete your cleanse early in the morning to be ready for your sunrise yoga session."

The words enema and sunrise yoga fought for supremacy over what horrified me most, leaving me speechless. She was on the small deck in front of my room before I realized something.

"Ah, you forgot to give me my room key." I held my hand out in readiness.

"Maisie, there's no need to worry about that." Her use of that stupid alias meant it took a second to register she was speaking to me. "Our security is top-notch. The perimeter fence is there for your protection. It's not just to keep out the wild pigs, you know."

After this bombshell, she left, pulling the door shut and imbuing me with some small sense of safety. Still, it wasn't as though anyone could break in there and expect to make a clean getaway. Besides, anything valuable of mine was sitting in her office or concealed in the false bottom of my suitcase.

Taped alongside my new phone were a couple of blocks of Dark Ghana and a spare credit card. Candice wouldn't realize the phone in my handbag was a dummy unless she worked out the PIN, and, for once, I hadn't opted for 0000. I'd impressed myself with how well I'd faked handing everything over.

After putting the bucket back in the closet where it couldn't taunt me, I took a leisurely look around my room. It was a relief to see the furniture and fittings were top-notch. Less impressive was that there wasn't a TV atop the dresser, just a glass and jug of water with a couple of slices of lemon floating about.

The other thing conspicuous by its absence was color, pinpointing who had been in charge of the interior design. If the woman stood against a wall in here, she'd disappear.

Next to the closet was a door I was hoping was to a bathroom, as promised in the brochure. But with so many other things being different to what the website had led me to expect, I wasn't holding my breath.

After sliding the heavy wooden door to the side, a cave-like bathroom confronted me. I'd stepped into the gloom and was looking for a switch when light flooded the room. On stepping back into the bedroom, the light switched off again.

While this was okay during the day, going for a pee in the middle of the night would be blinding. Closer examination of the door frame showed a discreet electric eye at knee height. With any luck, I could step over it in the dark without doing a Tonya Harding.

There was no gray in the bathroom unless you counted stainless steel. White subway tiles covered every surface other than the ceiling and a deep strip above the double vanity. An enormous mirror consumed this space. It was one that'd have me wanting to wear a blindfold before getting naked. That or running the shower first to fog the damned thing up.

On hearing the whirr of an extractor fan, I looked up, squinting against the brightness of the large bulb. The fan was part of this light fixture and also automatic by the look of things. It was a necessary feature, given there weren't any windows.

While waiting for my bag to appear, I retrieved the

instruction manual Candice had told me about and plonked myself down on the bed. A couple of bounces confirmed it to be in the Goldilocks zone. After slipping off my shoes, I lifted my legs onto the bed and settled in to check what was on offer. Could there be other things they had neglected to put on their website? If nothing else, checking everything out would fill in the time left until dinner.

At least, I hoped I would get dinner because the website had been vague regarding the number of meals each day. I very much hoped it was more than one because I had tried the 5/2 diet and couldn't hack it. The girls all raved about how easy it was, but for me, it hadn't been so.

At ten o'clock on the first day of fasting, my stomach had thought someone had cut my throat. And this hadn't gone away, despite their assertions it would. Instead, it had gotten worse as time went on, leaving me light-headed and nauseated.

From the outside, The Vale manual looked like something you would get at a chain motel. There any other similarities ended, with no rules about pool opening hours, or how much the porn cost. It was about what time you gave yourself your daily enema. The line drawing of a large woman on her hands and knees with tubing disappearing between her butt cheeks had made mine clench of their own volition.

That I would need to carry this out at four-thirty in the morning hadn't rated a mention on their website. Anything before six was the middle of the sodding night in my world. It wasn't the "early in the morning" Candice mentioned before leaving.

To make matters worse, I'd be on my hands and knees on the tiled floor in the bathroom when I undertook the task. All I could hope was that there was underfloor heating.

It took ten minutes to skim through everything on offer. Some of it I was looking forward to, other bits, not so much.

The manual smacking me on the nose alerted me to having nodded off. It had been a long day, with more action than I was used to.

I'll just shut my eyes. Not for long.

When I looked up at the clear blue sky, I was confused. The thunder was getting louder, and yet there wasn't a cloud in sight.

"Maisie, wake up, or you'll miss dinner," someone shook me.

It wasn't easy to pull myself free of the delightful dream that had seen me dancing on David's grave. I had a lot of dancing and even some stomping left in me. It wasn't until I was once again conscious that things righted themselves. The thunder must have been the fifty-something woman next to my bed knocking on the door, and Maisie was my assigned alias.

My response wasn't immediate. I was too busy taking in her snug-fitting outfit. No, make that the ridiculously tight activewear someone had shoehorned her into. It was black as a ninja's, but there any eastern influence stopped. If you were to scale a wall in this get-up, you'd risk a nasty bush fire.

To add to the ugliness of the ensemble, there were Vale

logos embroidered on the front of the top and side of the pants. The stitches on these were being put to the test with breasts and thighs the designer hadn't envisaged when working on the project.

Shaking my head to clear it of images of myself dressed the same way, I stopped to consider her greeting.

"It's Marilyn."

"I'm Belinda, also known as Beverley, but you can call me Bev, so I know you're talking to me. Damned, stupid idea."

The woman was right. The whole alias thing was a tad over the top for a fat farm.

"Perhaps you should call me M?"

Bev laughed and held her hand out. "We're sounding more like Bond characters all the time."

The ease with which she helped me stand said she was in better shape than she looked. However, it wasn't until I stood next to her, I realized how large she was. Sure, she was carrying extra pounds, but it was her height that staggered me. She must have been crowding six feet. I was short next to her. Not petite, just smaller than when I was next to my girlfriends while waiting to be seated for lunch.

Lorraine, in particular, was short and borderline cadaverous, despite her assertions that one could never be too rich or too thin. If it hadn't been for those false boobs of hers, she would have been lucky to hit one-hundred-pounds.

On the walk over to the dining room, Bev brought me up to speed on the daily routine. This included the meals, or lack of them, and the personalities. She also did a complete hatchet job on the center manager.

"We call her Chalky behind her back."

"Chalky?"

"Yeah, C. Hawkie equals Chalky. Plus, the woman looks like a stick of the stuff and has the emotions to match."

"You think she's had Botox?"

Stopping in her tracks, Bev looked at me with eyes wide. "I've had better reactions from cinder blocks."

Because it wasn't far from my room to the dining room, she then gave me the condensed version of her life up to that point. Coming from a remote farm, she had been at boarding school from age seven. By the time she left at eighteen, she'd been well on her way to being obese. This was thanks to comfort eating to counteract misery and a menu that was in the basement of the food pyramid. The one thing that had stopped her from being bullied had been her size and her being "the best damned shot putter that school had ever seen."

She had been married to Stan for five years and with the way her eyes lit up, happily. She deemed herself lucky to have snagged a man who could see past her weight. Her confidence in herself and her husband filled me with envy.

"But if Stan is happy with you as you are, why are you here?"

She looked sideways at me as we continued on to the dining room. "Because I want to live until I'm old and crotchety. I want to be a nuisance to his kids."

I understood this. People often saw the extra weight as

negative in terms of appearance or not being Insta-friendly. It was so much easier to avoid the issues around health. Not that being scrawny meant you were healthy, either.

Bev opened the doors to the dining room with a flourish and stood to the side to allow me to enter first. I would have preferred it to be the other way around. While not inept in social situations, I was more of a follower.

However, on stepping into the room, I couldn't see a thing, which somewhat soothed my nerves. It was brighter in here than outside, thanks to the wall opposite being floor-to-ceiling glass.

"Sorry, should have warned you to keep your sunglasses on."

Bev tapped her own, which had me sliding mine back down off my forehead and waiting until I could make out the other people in the room.

There were three tables of four, and a testament to the boutique nature of the establishment. One table was empty, while at another, there were four women who wouldn't recognize a steak if it bit them on the ass. They had the coloring of those for whom the sun and protein were anathemas.

Perhaps the biggest disappointment was that I didn't recognize any of them, and I knew my celebrities thanks to the women's magazines. The way Chalky went on about confidentiality, I had expected to see someone off the B-List, at the very least.

There wasn't even an early disqualification from Dancing with the Stars. The poor sod with a lagging career. The one with two left feet that the production team always contrived to include for giggles. It was a pity, as I had been looking forward to catching up on showbiz gossip over meals.

The remaining table had two larger ladies sitting there, intent on their conversation, with both dressed in double-wide ninja outfits that matched Bev's. I suspected it wouldn't be long before I joined them in the clothing malfunction department.

The lack of reaction from any of the other diners rendered us invisible, a state I was okay with. Bev had no such issues, making her presence known by walking over to the table of two, pulling out a chair, and slumping into it.

Unsure whether I should join them or take a seat at the empty table, I didn't move. I was dithering when Bev told me to get my skinny butt in the spare seat.

Skinny, she called me skinny! I hadn't been called that in a long time. Comparison was a wonderful thing.

I wasted no time in doing as she had suggested. No, that wasn't a suggestion, it was an order.

"Marilyn, I'd like you to meet Tee and 'A', your fellow AGENTS OF FAT."

Much laughter from the other two met this introduction, and I couldn't help but chuckle to myself. It was so refreshing to not have to avoid the elephant in the room, often me.

"It's Tallulah," said the woman introduced as Tee, quoting in the air with her fingers, to show that it was her alias. "The problem is, when people call me by it, half the time I don't know they're talking to me. Still, it's better than my real name."

It didn't take someone from MI5 to spot that our aliases started with the same initial as our real names, at least, so far as I had heard until then. Keeping my voice down, I asked, "What's your real name?"

Tee glanced over her shoulder at the table of pale women and then through the hatch to the kitchen before eyeballing me. "Promise you won't laugh?"

I nodded instead of voicing my agreement. I mean, what was more unusual than Tallulah?

"Teophania."

I couldn't stop the snort that escaped. "Sorry. You must have copped heaps about it at school."

"You will never know."

Tee was also from the country, although not from farming stock. Rather, her parents had opted for the commune life, which went some way toward explaining her off-the-wall name. Maybe it was the name-calling at school that drove her to seek solace in food, or that her appetite was rampant and there had been lots of food on hand. Either way, she was a big girl. There, any similarities to Bev ended.

Bev glowed with good health, and there was also evidence of muscle underneath her cushiony covering. Tee, by comparison, looked unhealthy. Her skin was blotchy, her breathing labored, and her breath told of food having hung around in her system for longer than was required for normal digestion.

She also had the air of a crazy cat lady about her, doing nothing to bolster the picture she painted of saving herself for the right man. I suspected they'd come out of hiding while she was in here. Heaven help me. I would do anything to avoid ending up like that.

On turning to the fourth woman at the table, I raised an eyebrow. It was enough. More than enough. Angela, known as Angel—an alias so similar why bother—was a motor-mouth. Ange to her friends. She didn't waste time with full sentences. She spoke in fragments. Forty-five. Nurse. Four kids. Divorced. On Tinder. Sick of clothes not fitting.

She didn't breathe once during this data dump, leaving me breathless and thankful we weren't in shared accommodation. Mealtimes would be more than a challenge. After a quick peek at the occupants of the other table, I leaned forward. "Where are all the celebrities? I thought there would be one or two in residence."

Tee burst out in booming laughter. "Hah, celebrities. Yeah, fat chance of seeing one of them. They keep the celebrities well away from us riffraff. I've been here five weeks and the only stars I've seen are up there." She jabbed her forefinger skywards before continuing. "Hell, they even sneak them in through the back somehow."

Five weeks? I couldn't work out what horrified me the most. That she was still this size after being here for that long. Or worse, that she had lost no weight at all. I hoped it was the former.

She'd filled her lungs to speak again when the tinkling of small bells filled the room, the upmarket version of the bog-standard gong.

For someone as big as she was, Tee could haul butt. She was the first to collect her tray at the kitchen hatch, allowing me to check out what was on offer when she passed me on her way back to our table.

Horror washed over me. The last time I saw that much kale was in the fruit and veg section at the supermarket. If doused in oil, oven baked, and sprinkled with sea salt, I might have coped.

Unfortunately, in its current state, it was as nature, and the compost heap preferred it.

Even though I knew this would be the case, the confirmation that the menu was indeed vegan disappointed me all the same. After that scouring at the service station, and being sick halfway up Flays Road, my last proper meal was a long way back.

As I looked down at my tray on my return to our table, I had to give the kitchen crew credit. However, even with the rabbit food displayed as it was in award-winning restaurants, experience told me it would do nothing to quell my raging hunger.

As I dutifully chewed the first mouthful, I longed for a creamy dressing. The lemon vinaigrette they had used erred on the side of citrus, with my lips resembling a cat's ass after the first mouthful.

The bells ringing followed by a disembodied voice from the

kitchen announcing our protein shakes were ready, dashed any hopes this was a starter. This saw everyone gathering up their plates and cutlery and filing over to the hatch, with Tee even faster to collect this part of her meal.

All this self-service was odd, given how much I was paying to stay here. I had expected waitress service, but maybe they saved that for the celebrities wherever they were hiding.

I slid my tray across the counter to a small weasel-like—and way past retirement age—chap who was collecting them for washing. His job was straightforward, with our plates licked-clean.

Shuffling along, I took the tall, brown shake that the next weasel slid over the counter in my direction. At first, I thought I was seeing double. A quick peek back at weasel number one confirmed they were twins. So unusual to see older twins. I had always thought of them as something that happened at elementary school.

On the return trip to the table, I sniffed my protein shake, latching onto the aroma of chocolate like a pig searching out truffles. A second sniff and I picked up undertones of roast pork.

It just went to show how hungry I was that I didn't care if the drink was a crazy blend of chocolate and meat. If the Mexicans could make that combo palatable, who was I to argue?

Even less obvious was how this could be low in calories. However, the speed with which Tee, Bev, and Ange were sucking down their drinks conveyed it tasted okay. A tentative sip confirmed this.

It was delicious, something that took me by surprise.

Creamy and sure as hell not like any diet food I'd ever tried. It also had more substance than I'd expected, something that had been lacking with any meal replacement I'd had to date.

"What's in it, apart from chocolate?" While waiting for an answer, I stood my straw up in the middle of the glass. It didn't surprise me when it stayed upright unaided. The damned shake was even firmer than my belly fat.

There was a gurgling of dregs being inhaled through an extra-wide straw before Tee answered me. "We don't know, and we've given up asking. I'd kill to get my hands on what goes into it."

Sunup the next morning, and the speakers in the ceiling of my room crackled to life, emitting an OM chant that was well past annoying. A soothing voice followed this, instructing me I should prepare for my cleansing.

So soothing was the voice that I nodded off again, at least until the word coffee roused me. Thinking about breakfast, I realized how hungry I was. I hadn't been this empty in living memory, if ever.

Because I'd unplugged the bedside clock radio during the night—the glowing red numbers keeping me awake—I didn't know what time it was. I'd check the time on my phone, but had agreed not to break out my stash unless I was desperate. As it was, even thinking about looking at the device would be draining the battery.

Unable to ring room service for a full-English, those blocks of Dark Ghana were so close. Just one square. To take off the edge. And it was close at hand, with my bag delivered to my room the night before while I was at dinner. Other than removing my intact toiletry bag and pajamas, everything else was where it had been when I packed.

A hard rap at the door while I was still crouched in front of my case, saw the clothes drop from my now nerveless fingers. I shut the lid for fear of discovery by whoever was standing less than a a couple of feet away. Even with a wall between us, I wasn't risking my stash for anything.

Before I could stand and open the door, Chalky barged in, a surprise both from a manners standpoint and given the hour.

"You should have finished your cleanse and evacuated. You should be ready for yoga. You're not even dressed."

At last, I get a decent reaction out of her, and it's a dressing-down because I'm running late. Flustered by the first reprimand since David shuffled off, my Pavlovian response kicked in hard enough that all I was missing was a flea collar.

"I'm so very sorry. I'd normally set the alarm on my phone."

This did nothing to calm the waters. Chalky's nostrils flared even wider. "And what, may I ask, is wrong with the alarm clock we provided?"

While her voice was calm, her expression shrieked with anger. Now was not the time to remind her she'd said there was no need to keep track of time while I was in here.

I shrank into myself before stuttering out, "The light was keeping me awake. I suffer from insomnia."

"I want you in that bathroom as soon as you are able. It isn't fair to hold up others because of your beauty sleep, now, is it?"

My head bowed in submission, I whispered, "No."

When she shoved something at me without warning, my arms shot out to the sides, before wrapping about the plastic-wrapped bucket. The atmosphere in the room didn't warm with her departure. Damn it, the last thing I needed was to rush my first enema. My sphincter muscles were already in a knot, without performance anxiety added to the mix.

I concentrated on relaxing my shoulders, closed my eyes, and tried hard to imagine myself walking down a white-sand beach and into sparkling blue water. My bikini was tiny, my tits were not. A couple more breaths and I enjoyed a virtual frolic in the surf.

As always, I was with a faceless guy with a body often seen in men's fitness magazines. After leaving him to his swim, I got up and walked into the bathroom. It was time to get on with my new life.

I was relieved to find the floor warm to my bare feet. I had worried that with the cabin being solar powered, it wouldn't be the case this early in the day.

I ripped the plastic wrap from the enema kit, shoving it into a tiny wastebasket under the vanity unit. After setting the components of the kit on the counter, it was as if I was preparing for surgery.

This was enough to have me back on the toilet for a nervous

pee and something to minimize the enema's action. Nothing was forthcoming: that session at the motorway service station had done a job on me.

The kit had everything. A lubricated soft vinyl tube, a clamp for one-handed operation, a red rubber tube and last up, a sachet of coffee. I hoped it wasn't decaf. A skim through the instructions surprised me by how simple it all looked, although this didn't calm my nerves.

With the correct temperature pre-programmed, I got the hot water running. Next, I emptied the sachet of coffee into the bucket and topped it up with water from the tap. Any dreams of cappuccino drained away when I connected the hoses to the bucket as per the instructions.

It was reading the next bullet point that had me aware of the hooks down the back of the bathroom door. The top one held the supplied bathrobe. The others marked at various heights were for an altogether different purpose. I peered to see which one I was supposed to use.

This crap just got real. Well, it soon enough would. Five minutes and half a tube of lube later, I regretted all those yoga classes I'd avoided over the years. The brunches and coffee mornings I attended in their stead had done nothing for my flexibility.

Something else that was making it hard to concentrate was the sound of the extractor fan whirring from time to time. It sounded too much like the zoom on a camera for my paranoia to subside enough to make the exercise easy. Not helping was my imagination conjuring an image of me kneeling like this on the boardroom table at David's lawyers.

Why did my mind come up with these humiliating scenarios? Did I hate myself that much? After this, the coffee wasn't even good for drinking.

I was struggling to my feet, wondering if toilet paper would work as a filter, when a soothing voice filled the room. "Remember, ladies, the red tube connects to the bucket, the PVC tube connects to the douche nozzle."

Are you freaking kidding me?

Rereading the instructions, I stopped my cussing about black and white instruction sheets. When I looked at the diagram again, I saw it was clear. Unless you weren't panicking about feeding a liter and a half of top-quality Columbian in through your back door. Dumping the coffee down the toilet, I binned the rest.

Thoughts of phoning and asking Chalky for a replacement cooled my blood. As I stood frozen in the middle of the bathroom, the soothing voice once again filtered through the speaker. This time it reminded me there were more kits in the closet.

New bucket in hand, I hunkered back down on all fours on the bathroom floor. This time I had a towel under my knees because despite the floor being warm, it was not soft. When I followed the instructions to the letter, the session was a success and not as bad as I had imagined. I wouldn't be avoiding yoga while I was there, though. Flexibility was the key.

The little tap was easy to turn on and off, allowing me to

control how many espressos I got through in the half-hour the session was supposed to take.

Hmmpf, last time I saw a tap like that was on a box of wine in my student days. Imagine the bladder from one of those hanging from the back of the door.

I snorted.

This turned into full-on guffaws, jet-propelling the douche nozzle from my rear end at a rate of knots. I'd sprayed coffee all over the bathroom before I got it under control.

After this, my chief concern was parking on the toilet before this short black incident turned into something with Grande in the name. So much for thinking I was empty. Just went to show you how long a backlog of fine dining and chocolate could stick with a girl.

I was hovering outside the bathroom door, waiting to see if it was worth getting dressed, when static emanated from the speakers. Slowing my breathing, I waited for the next instruction from hell. None was forthcoming.

The sunrise yoga session was a distant memory before my ass had run out of ammo, and it was okay for me to leave my room. On the plus side, my stomach had never looked flatter.

This was more like it.

I was on my way to the dining room when I ran my hand over my tummy. I shouldn't have. After spinning on my heel, I walked stiff-legged back to my room, all the while giving my sphincter the workout from hell.

I didn't make it in time.

At this rate, I'd be out of clean clothes in no time. The thought of parading around in one of those butt-ugly ninja outfits didn't sit well. And neither would I. I vowed to wash my clothes in the shower and dry them on the towel rail before submitting to that indignity.

In the end, I didn't have a choice, with the clothes I rinsed out during the day being whisked away whenever I turned my back. Despite laundry being part of the package, there wasn't a chance I wanted someone else scrubbing away at my enema-induced skid marks.

When I'd told Chalky that I was running out of clean clothes, she'd assured me that once the team disinfected them, I'd get them back.

She'd also made me feel like a toddler who'd failed toilet training. But that had been three days ago. Long enough they could have boiled them in disinfectant and line-dried them by now.

Then a piece of carrot cake I'd scoffed at Lorraine's birthday lunch messed up my last pair of clean yoga pants. Cleaning myself off in the shower, my tears joined the water sluicing down my body. They rained down on my crappy yoga pants, huddled in a heap on the floor of the shower stall.

This wasn't what I'd signed up for. No matter how hard I

tried, I couldn't envisage myself back on that imaginary beach without the handsome hunk bent double with laughter.

Six months of beta-blockers were looking better all the time.

I didn't bother rinsing the pants, rather leaving them in a filthy heap on the shower floor. Let the phantom clothes collector deal with them as they were.

11

With my tears and body dried, the quandary I was now facing was what on earth to wear? Yes, the place was a woman-only establishment, but there were men on staff. Men who I wasn't happy to flash any bits to, especially the creep who had driven me here.

I emptied my suitcase article by article, and it wasn't until I was at the very bottom that I found a solution to my current dilemma. While it hadn't been on the list of required clothing, something that took me straight back to school camp days, I'd packed it, anyway.

After wrapping it securely around me, I dumped everything else back in my suitcase. I then marched over to the admin building with my anger cloaking me. If it weren't for this, my sarong-yoga-top combination would have had me feeling naked from the waist down.

It wasn't the right apparel in which to tell Chalky I had had enough of being turned inside out and that I was going home. It would be Weight Watchers and horse-strength beta-blockers for me from now on.

Soon enough, things were as pear-shaped as me.

"We can't do that. I'm sorry, Maisie." Her tone said she was anything but.

"I beg your pardon?" I said this not because I hadn't heard her, but because I didn't comprehend what she meant.

"As per Clause 97 of the agreement you signed mere days ago, you committed to staying with us for the full six weeks. Your rehabilitation is our priority, even if it isn't yours."

Rehabilitation? Was she kidding? It was chocolate, not crack cocaine.

I was trying to assemble a reply when she swung around in her seat and collected a pile of plastic-wrapped packages from the credenza behind her. She slid these across her desk, and my heart dropped. That damned Vale logo was easy to read with the outfits inside folded in such a way as to have this dead center.

"What about my own clothes?" Annoyed that I had stuttered, I still pressed on, determined to stand up for myself, for once. "They should be clean by now."

"Yes, about those. We find it best if all our guests dress the same as it puts everyone on an even footing. We'll keep hold of your garments until you check out."

I opened my mouth to complain, but she stopped me with a look. "Clause 37."

Damn, damn, damn, I should have read that horrid contract before signing it.

My anger escalated with every step of the return trip to my room. It was an emotion I had suppressed for a very long time, but finding my suitcase open and gutted, anger turned to fury in a nanosecond. Any clean tops I had left were gone. The only things left in my suitcase were my lacy bras.

I dumped my plastic-wrapped Vale outfits on the bed and dropped to my knees in front of the case. Running my hands over the inside, I found what I was looking for, and my head dropped back in relief. I then voiced a silent prayer to the gods of electronica and cacao.

I could do with some chocolate to help me deal with the shock. Lots of it, and the darker, the better.

Static from the speakers, followed by the whirring of the extractor fan in the bathroom, and I froze. My hands dropped away from the Velcro-sealed pocket and I looked over my shoulder, surprised to find no one behind me.

The temptation to self-medicate was strong, and the whiff of 70% proof chocolate when I dropped the lid on my suitcase had me close to succumbing. If not for the strange sensation of being watched, I would have given in. The ninja outfits awaiting my presence were cause enough to scoff both blocks.

I struggled up and onto the bed, where I flicked through the assorted items of clothing. I wasn't sure if I was relieved, or not, when I found a multi-pack of underwear. Commando was never a good idea when Downward Dogs were on the menu.

Misery, thy name is Candida.

I didn't bother with dinner that night, instead giving into my abject misery of being stuck in this place for the next five-odd weeks. What on earth had I gotten myself into?

The image in the full-length mirror after I struggled into the assorted items of Vale branded gear the following morning enforced my despair. Great, I scored free gear, and it was as ugly as sin and several sizes too small.

In my favor was my boobs still being the size of a pre-pubescent teen. I didn't stretch the Vale logo beyond recognition like the others. Shame the same wasn't true for the waistband of the ninja-equivalent of yoga pants.

Could I force myself to leave the room looking like this?

In the end, hunger drove me out. Well, that and a blood-sugar level hovering around zero. It would also be the first time I'd made it to breakfast. At least I hoped we got breakfast. The thought of another one of those chocolate shakes made me speed up.

I couldn't hear myself think over the scratching of the fabric rubbing together between my thighs. I eased the door open, unsure of what sort of reaction I would garner. It wasn't what I had expected.

Bev looked annoyed before picking up a piece of toast and slamming it down on Tee's plate. Ange looked ticked off, too.

By the time I grabbed my breakfast at the serving hatch and sat down, Tee was the proud owner of two extra pieces of toast. They were so thin that if you were to gobble them, you'd risk lacerating your throat.

What on earth? Did bread have a street value in this place?

Tee was quick to gloat about winning the sweep on how many days I could hold out before being stuffed into a Vale uniform. "You must have been backed-up to hell to get through your gear this fast."

I wasn't sure what shocked me the most. That she was discussing my bowel functions at breakfast, or that she was doing it on purpose to put me off my two wafer-thin slices of wholegrain. Woe betides anyone who got between me and food when I was this hangry.

I kept eye contact with her and took a large bite of toast, soon bemoaning the fact it was free of spread of any kind. Ange and Bev laughed with delight, although it was Bev who commented first.

"Hah, she's got you, Tee. You're not gonna put her off her tucker that easy."

So, I hadn't imagined it, something I dwelled on while I chewed my toast.

And chewed.

And chewed.

Good lord, the stuff had the consistency of cardboard, although I suspected cardboard would have more flavor.

It was a while before I could swallow without risking a spontaneous tonsillectomy. The mouthful went down like a golf ball before dropping into my empty stomach. I knew the booming echo was down to my vivid imagination. Still, it was appropriate.

I dropped the piece, and it clattered about on my plate before settling next to its mate. Hell's bells. I hoped my jaw was up to taking care of this lot.

I would just bet chewing the stuff burned more calories than it contained.

Still, if it was this or nothing, I'd push on.

A sip of green tea, bursting with antioxidants but lacking in flavor, cleared my throat of any residual gravel. There was no way you could describe them as crumbs. I grabbed my piece of toast for another bite.

Before I could do so, Ange picked up her one remaining piece of toast and slammed it down on Tee's plate.

"Damn it, I didn't expect you to manage more than one bite." Ange looked down at her empty plate before licking her finger and clearing up any remaining crumbs.

Bev looked at me with admiration and even a tinge of pride. "I told you she's made of sterner stuff."

By the time I had chewed through a whole slice of cardboard, Tee was down to one slice and Bev had three. Some of this was down to carbohydrate wagers being won and lost. Others because they'd chewed their way through a slice or two.

Ange, whose plate was pristine, looked at my second slice and I took pity on her, with it not as if my jaw was up to chewing it. The very thought of two slices exiting after tomorrow's enema had my sphincter clenching in terror.

Piles?

What piles?

With breakfast over, they left us to our own devices until the pre-lunch yoga session, something I hoped to attend. Between trips to the bathroom and rolling around on my bed dealing with stomach cramps, it would be my first one. At least, I hoped to make it.

Bev slid her tray across to one of the kitchen twins. "You want to go for a walk around the property, M?"

I couldn't look at either twin without Bowie's Laughing Gnome jingling in my head. They were too weedy to be labeled Tweedle Dum and Tweedle Dee, and they were gnome-like in appearance. Give them each a fishing rod and a pointy hat and you would have the perfect garden ornaments.

"A walk sounds nice." Fresh air would also be a welcome change from the stench of antiseptic spray, backed up by more organic undertones.

"Mind if I tag along?" said Ange, dashing any hopes of a quiet commune with nature.

"The more the merrier." Bev didn't show any signs that Ange's presence wasn't welcome. "Tee, you up for a stroll?"

The large woman was quick in her refusal, hurling rapid-fire excuses to the point Ange held her hand up to stop the ever-growing list. "Chill, not our loss if you get caught breaking the rules."

Despite the website boasting that the resort covered twenty

acres, most of them were off-limits. This was down to the impenetrable bush behind the property and the drop-offs at the front.

These were such that my stomach did somersaults every time we got near them. I couldn't decide if it was vertigo, or the toast beating the living daylights out of my stomach acid. Either way, it wasn't pleasant, and I kept well back. It was no easy feat with me having to fight their magnetic pull with every breath.

I slowed my steps. "What was that about Tee breaking the rules?"

"Chalky doesn't like it if we stay in the dining room. Says it leads to temptation." Bev's resultant laughter soon got the better of her.

"Temptation?"

Was she for real? There wasn't a chance my gut could handle any more of that plywood, masquerading as toast. The idea of being tempted by it was laughable.

"Yeah, temptation. Someone broke into the kitchen at night. Drank all the chocolate protein drinks. A whole bucket of the stuff." Ange's tone was one of incredulity at whoever managed this feat.

"What? Wait? A whole bucket of it? As in a bucket, bucket?"

Ange nodded briefly, and then again for emphasis. "Chalky has been strict about security ever since."

It didn't take a rocket scientist to work out who was behind it. Bev, shaking her head, left me wondering if she was disappointed about missing out, or upset at Tee for the break-in. Or could it be at Chalky for not identifying the woman as the culprit?

"It's a bugger. It's put a stop to any late-night incursions. We've been hungry ever since." Ange's pout following these complaints wouldn't have been out of place on a two-year-old.

Wait? Tee wasn't alone in raiding the kitchen? It was a wonder Ange could keep quiet long enough to sneak in anywhere undetected. My gaze caught Bev's and her shrug confirmed she had also been in on the raids. This place was too much like a school camp for my liking.

Continuing our walk, no make that stroll, I perceived what my days would be like over the next five weeks. One good thing was that, like a blazing flame, Ange's chatter soon spluttered and died, leaving us to enjoy the birdsong.

As we worked our way around the back of the accommodation units, we passed by several paths that were marked STAFF ONLY. To further emphasize we should back off, NO ADMITTANCE appeared in smaller type underneath.

However, by following the tree line, we soon came to a path that we could use. Mesmerized by the rhythmic crunching of our steps and the beauty of the dark bush enveloping us, when Bev stopped, I bumped into her.

"Sorry, wasn't watching where I was going."

Bev spun on her heel with military prowess, facing me. "This is as far as we can go."

On peeping around her, I saw why. The high hurricane wire fence, with its razor wire topping, stretched tight across the path. And while the path continued to meander its way through the bush on the other side, we were stuck right where we were.

I cocked my head to the side, trying to pick up what was wrong. "That's strange?"

"Maybe it was part of the old army base," said Ange, who must have heard the same story as I did.

Bev jerked her head at the wire barrier. "It's for security. Keeps the pigs out. Nasty things, they are."

I shook my head before speaking. "Not the fence. Chalky told me about that. I'm talking about the birdsong."

The other two joined me in listening. Bev even closed her eyes to concentrate, and I followed suit, focusing on my hearing. It confirmed I hadn't imagined it.

It was as though someone had hit Mother Nature's mute button. Not even the quietest cheeping was audible. The swishing of the ferns and the occasional creak of a branch were all we heard. It took a second to remember where I'd experienced this before. The day I'd waited on the edge of the bush for Lance to collect me.

Could his presence be what silenced the birds?

After opening my eyes, I took in the expressions of the other two. This told me I wasn't alone in thinking it was strange. We were still staring at each other when a scream shattered the unearthly quiet, and my scalp did its best to scurry off my skull.

"What the hell was that?" I then scrubbed my head, doing my best to rid it of that awful crawling sensation. It didn't work, leaving me frozen on the spot. I did my best to locate the source of the shriek, waiting for a follow-up, but none was forthcoming.

"I don't like it. That didn't sound like any bird I've ever heard," Ange wasted no time in stumbling back down the path as though pursued. In a heartbeat, I was on her heels, followed by Bev.

After bursting into the open, I swung to face the bush. "What the hell was that?"

Bev was pale, the fine sheen of sweat on her forehead out of kilter with our stroll. " It might have been a Long-Tailed Cuckoo?" Her words were tentative and lacked conviction.

"Creepy as hell is what it was." Ange shivered like a dog left wet after a bath.

While we didn't hear another scream, there was movement deep in the bush. To hell with staying here.

I took off, with Ange and Bev also showing themselves to be up for a burst of speed. None of us slowed until we were back in the dining room. Tee didn't appear to have moved since our departure and was looking guilty at being caught still lounging.

While I wanted a large brandy, green tea had to do.

"Sheesh, what's up?" After this, Tee's mumbling got so bad that I moved closer, hoping to catch more. It was then I spotted the toast crumbs caught at the corner of her mouth. Her tongue flicked them away with such speed, I thought I must have imagined them.

"Tee, what have you done?" Bev's shout got my heart chattering double time.

"You promised!" Ange also had her volume cranked right up.

The guilty party's face turned from an unbecoming mushroom to the rhubarb side of the florid spectrum. After gulping, she crumpled under the scrutiny of the others. "I know, I know. But it was just one piece."

One piece, that wasn't so bad. Was it?

I looked at Tee as the others berated her. I felt sorry for the woman until I spotted her ninja top wasn't sitting as smoothly as it should. "What's that?"

While the others didn't hear me over their haranguing, Tee did, hunching her shoulders to hide her carbohydrate contraband. I said nothing else. It wasn't my job to police toast consumption in this hellhole. If rations were this scarce, I'd be in a similar position in a day or two.

Tee slammed her hand over her heart—and the hidden toast—before stumbling to her feet and fleeing. The one remaining sign she had been there was a single slice of wholegrain cardboard on the floor. Bloody hell, how many slices did she have stuffed inside her bra?

"Three-second rule!" Ange dropped to the ground and nabbed the piece of toast before Bev had time to react.

This had me wondering how long it would be before I was desperate enough that I would eat off the floor? One week? Two? Would I even last that long?

More and more, I thought that starving to death would be the easiest way to escape this place. Or was that the only way?

12

The yoga class was a shock on several levels. The first was that Anton, our yoga instructor, thought I could fold myself into the positions he showed. The second was his being blessed in the anatomical department.

His singlet was so loose and so thin that I didn't know why he bothered. Meanwhile, his Lycra pants were form-fitting to the point he wouldn't have needed to remove them for a prostate exam.

If he was wearing undies, I'd eat mine.

A snort escaped at the idea of munching on the utilitarian pair I was wearing. It was something that had him swinging in my direction and I didn't need a mirror to know I was an unbecoming shade of pink.

There I had it. The only thing between me and a naked man for the first time in over a year was elastin in nature. A lot like the man himself. He walked in my direction and I tensed. Which led to wobbling. I was nowhere near ready to process the ton of testosterone he had on board. And it didn't matter that he played for the home team.

My relief when Tee demanded help in achieving the posture was immense. My relief was short-lived. Anton bent her into the correct position, being none too gentle about it. She over-balanced, crashing in a heap, taking him down.

Then it was all I could do to avoid a code yellow.

Ange wasn't so lucky.

Free of Tee's embrace, Anton showed the next position as though nothing had happened. When I saw how complex the pose was, it was obvious he had taken our laughter to heart. That would teach us to get the giggles, although watching him extricate himself from under Tee had been funny. Even the vegans had trouble keeping their mirth under control.

I was halfway through getting myself into the position when I became conscious of a skittering sensation working its way up the back of my neck. I looked up, expecting to see Anton glaring at me for my non-existent yoga abilities.

However, it wasn't him.

It was Lance.

He was standing outside, looking at me through the large picture window. However, there was no censure in his eyes, as there had been last time. It was something much darker, with this only amplified when he ran his tongue across his bottom lip.

Not wanting to keep eye contact, I dropped my gaze, with

the alternate view no better. He had his hands shoved deep in the pockets of his filthy jeans, as if groping for something. I doubted it was the keys to the Hummer.

I spent the rest of the day avoiding thoughts of Lance ogling me during yoga and food in any form. While delicious, the vegetable broth masquerading as lunch hadn't hit the spot, or even come close. More than this, it didn't even hit the sides as it rocketed through my empty digestive tract. My belly button and spine hadn't been this close since I was in the womb.

The one thing that had stayed with me was the scene in the bush. It was easy to think what we'd experienced was a flight of fancy, but I had my doubts. I had always prided myself on being pragmatic, down-to-earth, and not given to the vapors.

Mid-afternoon and Bev suggested another walk, but I declined. Despite it being a beautiful sunny day, I was shaking and cold, with my blood-sugar levels destined to drop as the afternoon progressed. Huddled under my duvet, I tried to sleep to pass the time. It was a pointless exercise, with the gurgling of my gut and hunger gnawing away at my insides, making it impossible.

It was a long time before dinner rolled around. Except there were no dinner rolls, just more sodding kale salad, followed by another chocolate shake. A lack of anything hot to eat did nothing to help rid me of the shivers that rolled through my system at regular intervals.

I finished chewing another piece of kale to the point I must have looked as though my ancestors were rabbits. I was dragging it out, hoping to fool my body into thinking it had had more sustenance than it had in reality.

I was therefore not even halfway through my minuscule salad when the bells rang announcing that our protein drinks were up and ready to go.

I had to finish pulverizing a mouthful of kale and celery before I could speak. "Could one of you grab mine when you're up there?"

"Not allowed," said Ange, looking down at me with pity.

"For goodness' sake." I dropped my fork amid the detritus of salad and stood.

Tee shook her head. "The rule is you have to return your plate before you collect the second course."

"Are you kidding me?" I said, as she departed.

She didn't answer, and neither did Bev, before also wandering over to the serving hatch.

Once again seated, I shoveled down another mouthful of green and set to chewing. I would stick to their stupid rules, but if they thought I was bolting the rest of this child's portion, they were wrong.

Tee once again took her seat and was halfway through her drink before she spoke. "I'd hurry if I were you."

"Why?"

Ange siphoned the rest of her drink up the extra-wide straw before answering me. "Because if you don't collect your shake pronto, they'll bin it." She sucked on her straw again, ensuring she got everything on offer out of the glass.

It was the first I had heard of this stupid rule, this explaining why they had been so eager to finish their salads. "How long do I have?"

Bev likewise vacuumed up her dregs before speaking. "Two minutes tops."

I didn't bother with any further discussion, shoveling the rest of my salad down as if kale was on the brink of extinction. Something I wished was true. I didn't bother chewing the stuff as much as recommended. Not if it meant missing out on the chocolate drink.

I was still working on the last mouthful when I slammed the plate down on the kitchen counter. My hand closed around the glass a second before that of one of the laughing gnomes. Holy moly, had that growl come from me? It must have been, if the speed with which the gnome snatched his hand away was any measure.

Back at the table, I pushed my drinking straw into the depths and was about to take my first slurp when Tee put her hand on my shoulder. "Better mix it up first. It's separated."

"Separated?" I tilted my head to see if I could sort out the constituent parts, hoping to replicate the recipe when I returned home. It surprised me to see the top layer was darker than it had been moments before. Meanwhile, the sludge at the bottom had a yellow cast. Yum, banana was my favorite, after chocolate.

I slid my drinking straw to the very bottom of the glass and took a tentative sip. Nope, my theory was all wrong. If I didn't know better, I'd say it was pure fat, and bacon fat at that. How was I supposed to lose weight if I was subsisting on what equated to chocolate-flavored gravy?

After dinner, we wandered over to the yoga studio, although not for another session with the half-naked Anton. No, tonight was movie night, and I was hoping for a romantic comedy, or something light. Even the four women from the corner table joined us. However, they did so without uttering a word, which was weirder than weird.

Falling back beside Bev, I slowed my steps to match hers. "What's with that lot? They haven't spoken once since I got here."

"Idiots have taken a vow of silence," snorted Ange, over her shoulder, telling me I hadn't spoken as quietly as I'd thought. She hadn't bothered to whisper, either.

"Something to do with that crazy meditation retreat they're on." Bev didn't bother keeping her voice low, either. It was as if she thought the group's hearing was out of action, like their speech.

A glower thrown in our direction told me she was so very wrong.

Tee's booming laughter sliced through the twilight like a laser. "Careful, Bev. I reckon they're hungry."

This teasing of the mute crew didn't sit well with me. Call it what you will, it was still bullying. Of course, I thought they were stupid for keeping quiet for however many weeks it was they'd signed up for. But was I giving them a hard time about it? Well, not to their faces.

This had me wondering what the collective term for mute

vegans was. A Mugan? A Mutgan? A Megan? The Megans! That worked, and it wasn't like they could tell me their real names.

The transformation in the yoga studio was a pleasant surprise. While not Gold Class Cinema, the bean bags scattered in haphazard rows across the bamboo floor appeared comfortable. The large screen, until now hidden behind shoji panels, was state-of-the-art.

Tee struggled into a beanbag in the back row, leaving me to question the appropriateness of the seating on offer. It was as though Chalky had chosen furniture to emphasize how overweight we were. First the ghost chairs and now these beanbags.

I was careful when I dropped into the beanbag next to Tee. The last thing I needed was for it to burst, leaving me covered in polystyrene balls and looking like that tire company's mascot. After that, I kept as still as I could, something that negated any comfort offered by the squishy thing. While we waited for the movie to start, I carefully twisted to the side so I could speak to Tee.

"There must have been a heap of people through the place while you've been here." Part of me still clung to the hope of mingling with a famous guest. Even someone from the C-List would suffice.

Tee didn't turn to me when she answered, keeping her eyes glued to the still-blank screen. It was as if she didn't want to miss a second of whatever was on offer. "Sure, a stack of them," she puffed before continuing. "Lightweights couldn't hack the pace. And I didn't even get the chance to give them hell about it."

I speculated on the nerve of the toast-stealing woman, able to see why the spa kept its elite clients separate from the likes of us. With Tee's disappointment as large as she was, I wondered what had stopped her from haranguing anyone who checked out early. And more to the point, how the heck had they managed such a thing? "Why didn't you? Give them hell about it, that is."

"They all left in the middle of the night. Every single one of them."

On a very familiar intro bursting from the large speakers on either side of the screen, it denied me the chance to grill her further. So much for something fluffy. That night, we were to watch back-to-back episodes of Weight Loss Warriors.

The evening was a wash-out apart from me spotting a couple of episodes I'd missed. Not that I didn't like the show. It was more that I usually watched it with wine and chocolate on hand. Comforted that I wasn't as big as the poor shmucks being put through hell week after week. The challenges becoming ever more absurd as ratings inevitably fell.

It always made me feel slimmer, although this wasn't the case that night. I needed to roll onto all fours before I could get to my feet, and I was more conscious than ever of the gravity-defying pounds I was lugging around.

Sleep was elusive. Each time I was about to drop off, my mind swirled with images of me at the fat camp from hell in a strange half-awake nightmare. In it, I was stuck exercising in workout clothes that made the Vale uniform look runway-ready in comparison.

Abandoning sleep, I turned on the light and grabbed my eReader off the bedside table. I suspected the only reason Chalky let me keep hold of it was because it was the most basic model.

Luckily for me, I had ordered twenty books online before leaving the hotel. It was a shame that only fifteen had downloaded, with the other five lost somewhere in the ether. Besides these, there were other old favorites I could read if I ran out of new material. I also enjoyed rereading a book with many of these like old friends.

A loud knock on my door coincided with this very action in the Stephen King I was reading. I shrieked. My heart rate went through the stratosphere, and my eReader was last seen flying over the side of the bed.

Upon opening the drawer in the nightstand, the radio alarm glared back at me. It was just after midnight and not an appropriate time for visitors. The horror story still haunted me, and I was undecided on whether I wanted to answer the door when it opened.

It was Chalky, dressed as always in her demon dental assistant's get-up.

Lord, didn't the woman ever sleep? More to the point, didn't she need to be invited in?

I knew that was the accepted practice with vampires.

"Trouble sleeping?" she asked. Without waiting for me to reply, she walked across the room and put a tray down on my bedside table. It held a tiny French press of herbal tea that was the color of three-day-old pee and would doubtless taste the same.

"Maisie, an important part of weight loss, is ensuring you have quality sleep. This should help." Without asking, she pushed the plunger on the tea and poured me a cup, holding it out. This left me with no option but to struggle into a sitting position and take it.

Wetting my lips confirmed any tasting notes on the packet should include the word urine. While it looked as if I'd swallowed some, there was no way I'd drink that muck. I had to fake a couple more sips before she was happy.

On leaving, she paused in the doorway, holding the handle in readiness to shut the door. Soon enough, her gaze dropped to the floor next to my bed. "Best you turn your device and the lights off."

I didn't argue for fear she would confiscate my eReader. She reminded me too much of that prison warden on Orange Is the New Black for me to relax my guard. Under her watchful gaze, I put the cup down on my bedside table before leaning over the side of the bed and retrieving the eReader. I was fumbling to turn it off when I noticed the bar at the top stated ITEMS DOWNLOADED.

I didn't dare check to see what they were, instead shoving it in the top drawer and shutting it. Only then did Chalky appear happy I had complied. And while she pulled the door to behind her, she didn't shut it completely. Nor did she move away, with her presence outside having an ominous edge to it. It was something I dwelled on while lying in the dark, waiting for her to leave.

I was having difficulty coming to terms with any friends of Lorraine's putting up with this crap. But with them returning every year, as she had said, they must have. It was a full five minutes before Chalky left, doing nothing to soften her footfalls when she clomped down the front steps.

If I'd been asleep as she apparently wanted, the noise would have woken me for sure.

13

An hour later and I wasn't any closer to sleep. As tempting as it was to drink the cup of urine Chalky had delivered earlier, I couldn't bring myself to do so. I was doing deep breathing exercises to calm my mind when I noticed movement outside my unit door.

The door handle then turned in small increments, which was unusual because it wasn't like Chalky to be quiet. Damn it, why didn't they have chains on the doors like at hotels? It was all I could do not to laugh nervously when she couldn't open the door.

I still wasn't sure why I'd shoved the desk chair under the door handle after her earlier visit, but I was glad about it now. There followed a stage-whispered exchange and while I expected to hear Chalky's American twang, when Lance, the chauffeur, responded, I was stunned.

"Can't you break in?"

"You think those knock-out drops of yours are up to that kinda ruckus?"

Knock-out drops? The tea! There was a brief pause before I sensed a faint rustling outside the window near the headboard. Had I secured it properly? It was too late if I hadn't.

Anxiety gripped me, my heart pounding and filling my ears with the sound of rushing blood. Behind me, the window creaked open a sliver, sending quivers down my spine and intensifying my fear.

Without the glass to muffle him, Lance's curses were loud. Whatever was in that tea was supposed to incapacitate me in a big way. He tried sliding the window open again, putting enough effort into it that the window came close to lifting free of its track. I didn't get it. Why couldn't he open it? He was trying hard enough.

Then I remembered the piece of bleached wood I'd found the day before. The one that looked lovely on the windowsill. Hopefully, it would work in the same way as a broom handle in the frame of a sliding door. At least to stop him from opening it enough that he could climb in.

My eyes widened. My gaze darting about as if searching for a solution. It would be easy enough for him to reach inside and grab the piece of wood. On hearing further movement on the other side of the blackout curtains, I faked a cough. Rather than getting a reaction, silence met my little piece of theater.

I then made a good show of tossing and turning, as though

trying to find a comfortable spot. For good measure, I backed this up by mumbling and even thumping my pillow. This last act, more than any of my other theatrics, would let them know I was awake.

While many would have turned on the lights, wrenched the curtains open, and confronted the pair, I wasn't one of them.

Even though I didn't hear them moving away, my gut told me Lance was no longer there. After a decent interval, I slid my hand up underneath the curtain and closed the window, relieved when the catch snapped tight. Who knew what would have happened if the beautiful bone-shaped piece of wood hadn't been sitting on the sill?

With my heart engaged in a weird polka, complete with missed steps and dips, there wasn't a chance I could sleep after this. After slipping out of bed, I took the French press off the tray, stepped over the beam in the bathroom doorway, and poured the contents down the toilet.

Best Chalky believed I had drunk the damned stuff.

I couldn't face yoga the following morning. Not on an hour of sleep. I felt like hell and from the reactions of the others at breakfast; I knew I looked like it, too. I waited until we were all on our second slice of plywood before broaching the subject.

"Has Chalky ever tried to drug any of you?"

"Drug!" said Tee, spraying me with toast crumbs while she was about it.

A peek at the hatch through to the kitchen showed the laughing gnomes were looking at us.

"Shhh!"

My warning was too late, but I worried she, or the others, would speak without thinking. This had me reinforcing the need for secrecy by placing my finger over my lips and keeping it there until they all nodded.

I then leaned toward the center of the table, with the others quick to copy, allowing me to whisper. "Late last night. I was reading when I got a visit from Chalky."

"No surprises there. Woman's nocturnal." Ange's lips had barely moved during this assertion, the low volume making her words difficult to catch.

"She came armed with a pot of tea. Said I should drink it because sleep was important in achieving weight loss. I only had a sip, but it was awful."

Bev looked first over one shoulder and then her other. "Awful is how you feel in the morning, too."

Bev's paranoia escalated my own. I popped my head up, eyes darting around the dining room and over to the hatch, before I dropped back into the huddle. "What do you mean?"

"It's like you've been running for hours. And everywhere hurts." Bev's color intensified when she shuddered and added. "And I mean everywhere."

If I was in any doubt, she pointed through the table toward her crotch, confirming she meant everywhere.

"You think that's weird? Once, I woke to find fresh sheets on my bed." Ange looked both impressed and disgruntled. "Don't remember an effing thing."

My gaze darted around the table, with me even looking at

Tee, despite her having said nothing since reacting to my first question. "How many times?"

"It's every second or third night for me." Bev's whisper was hoarse.

"Same for me," whispered Ange.

As if on cue, we all turned to look at Tee. "Only once a week for me." For once, she appeared relieved to have had less of something.

I addressed my next question to all three women. "Why do you keep drinking the tea?"

"And risk the wrath of Chalky by leaving it? Don't think so," said Ange, through a muffling mouthful of toast. "I was ready to up sticks and leave. But she waved that effing contract in my face."

"Yeah, me too," added Bev. "Kept going on about Clause 37B. As if I knew what the hell that was. Plus, if you don't drink it, the bitch halves your rations."

Bev followed this up by finishing her second piece of toast, as though expecting Chalky to sneak up and snatch it away.

"Hang on." Ange tapped the side of my plate. "If they didn't drug you, how did you get away without drinking it?" Ange looked intrigued at my avoiding the nasty brew and yet still being the proud recipient of two planks of toast.

"After they left, I stepped over the beam and chucked it down the toilet."

Tee's face dropped in disappointment. "Damn, I was hoping it was something we could do."

It was then I comprehended these ladies couldn't clear the beam in the bathroom door because of their weight.

"Oh, sorry. But hang on, why didn't you chuck it out of the window?"

"Tried that the first time," said Tee. "Opened the curtains to find Chalky staring back at me. Thought I was going to have a heart attack."

Ange and Bev's solemn nodding confirmed they had experienced the same.

Fearing interruption, I made quick work of telling them how I had shoved my desk chair under the door handle. "Lance would have climbed in the window if I hadn't had a piece of wood jammed in it."

The color drained from Ange's face, leaving her looking ready to pass out. "He was there?" Her words were as weak and pale as her face. "Excuse me." She staggered to her feet and tottered out of the room.

"What's gotten into her?" I turned to the other two, hoping for clues.

Tee slapped her hand over her mouth before stumbling to her feet. If I didn't know better, I'd think she was about to puke. She was gone before I could ask if she was all right. The sounds of retching from outside confirmed she wasn't.

Bev stayed where she was, but she wasn't happy either. "At least I now know why I wake up feeling like I've taken part in a porno."

I didn't ask what she meant, instead rolling my hand in the air, urging her to press on. She nodded and leaned forward. I followed suit until our heads were inches apart. The more she told me, the happier I was that I'd barricaded myself in my room last night.

As automatic as it had been to scream holy murder when Lance tried to get in through the window, I was now glad I hadn't. This way, I could pretend I had consumed the tea and been unaware of Chalky and Lance's attempted break-in.

As a background to this saving grace, my thoughts were of how I could have been stupid enough to get caught up in something like this. The sort of women Lorraine knew would never condone this sort of behavior. Would they?

Unless they'd stayed in the more upmarket part of the complex? Hadn't Lorraine said The Vale might not take my booking.

Either way, I had to get out of here. And soon. But how?

Even if I could walk into town, there was no getting over that vicious fence. The same was true of the front gate, with this also topped with that vicious razor wire. Plus, if I confronted Chalky, she would only wave that stupid contract in my face, like she had with the others.

I was every bit the prisoner that I had worried I would be on arrival. And if Chalky was prepared to drug us for whatever nefarious reasons, then she wouldn't appreciate being confronted.

No, however we dealt with this, we'd need to be careful. To wait until we got out before we said anything. Perhaps more upsetting than knowing I was stuck there, was knowing David was in hell laughing.

Laughing that I'd been dumb enough to sign a contract without reading it. Even beyond the grave, he was telling me, "I told you so."

On entering my room after breakfast, I noticed the desk chair was missing. A glance showed my beautiful wooden souvenir from the windowsill had also vanished. This confirmed two things.

One, they were trying again tonight.

Two, I needed to join the others on their walk.

Drained after my sleepless night, I had opted out of this. I hoped they had taken the same route as last time, except for the path where we'd heard that scream. I wasn't in a hurry to go back there. A quick mental calculation and I knew the best spot to intercept them.

I didn't bother closing the door behind me. What was the point? I aimed for the far corner of the compound, bypassing the raised boardwalks in favor of going cross-country. It took ten minutes of serious trudging for me to find them, and when I did, they were far too close to that creepy path for my liking.

"Hi, guys, I ... had ... to tell ... you."

"Crap!" Ange spun in my direction, her hand clutching her crotch, doubtless to make up for a lack of pelvic floor muscles.

"Bloody hell!" Bev seemed as shocked, although she was clutching her throat.

It wasn't as though I'd snuck up on them. Nor had I been quiet when walking through the ankle-high grass that had done its best to trip me at every opportunity.

"You scared the crap out of us." Ange still had her hand

between her legs, suggesting her preventative measure had been in vain.

"Sorry, I wasn't trying to sneak up on you."

"Something moved." Bev's hand dropped from her throat to her side. "Deep in the bush."

Ange briefly sniffed her fingers and shrugged, before adding, "On this side of the fence."

"I didn't think there was anything out there." The map in the welcome pack showed this part of the property as being dense bush, with no buildings or paths. Although we had already proved that wrong. "I hope it wasn't a pig."

Bev never took her eyes off the bush, her gaze intent, like that of a hunter. "I hope not. Nasty beasts they are." Her voice wasn't much above a whisper.

"There!" said Ange, keeping her voice low despite her excitement.

I saw it, but only because she had pointed me in the right direction. It wasn't a pig, unless the local population was human-sized and had taken up wearing camo. Thanks to my corrected vision, I could even make out the smears of paint on his face. There was also no missing the diagonal strap across his chest, the barrel of his gun towering over one shoulder.

Seeing someone armed with what appeared to be a military assault rifle shocked me to the core. Was Chalky that keen on stopping us from escaping? And wasn't it illegal to have a gun like that in New Zealand? I thought that kind of gun was exclusive to the military.

Reality then slapped me in the face. Chalky didn't care

about breaking the law. She had proved that when she tried to drug me. She had more than proved it by drugging the others and letting Lance loose on them. But why did she want to, and why hadn't any of Lorraine's friends said anything about it? Or was it they enjoyed it?

The only thing in our favor was that the guy doing his best to hide in the bush wasn't looking in our direction. However, that could change at any second.

Next to me, Bev stiffened. Had she spotted him? Or had she readied herself to face down an enemy of the porcine variety? Her backing away while whispering, "Let's get out of here before he realizes we've spotted him," said she must have seen what I did.

I agreed with her about getting away. Anyone trying that hard to stay out of sight wouldn't want us waving and saying "hi". And after last night's potential intrusion, I was gun-shy on the gung-ho.

This had the three of us sticking to an unspoken pact to keep quiet until we were well away from camo-boy. Even that wasn't enough. We said nothing until there was a building between us and him. For once, even Ange kept quiet.

Only then did we slow. We were on the far side of the compound and behind some trees before we discussed what we'd seen. The guard patrolling the perimeter, being armed to the teeth, was a worry.

We couldn't go to Chalky about this because the chances of her not knowing about it were slim to none. Could it be that because she was American, she was okay having guns on the property? It wouldn't have surprised me. It would have been different if he had been on the other side of the razor wire. However, his presence on the property told us a lot, although not as much as we'd like.

We had gone from being rooted to the spot, to wandering without a goal before I remembered why I had come out there to find them. My knowing what lurked in the native bush, protecting myself from nocturnal visitors, was a priority.

"They confiscated my chair. And the lovely piece of aged wood I had on my windowsill. I came out here to replace them." Without them, my room was as secure as your average hiking tent.

Ange looked at me for a heartbeat. "Hate to break it to you, but I don't think you'll find a chair out here."

There was a solemn edge to Bev's nod before she spoke. "She's right."

"I know that. But I can find another piece of wood to keep the window closed. I'll also look for a smaller piece I can jam under the door to stop them from opening it."

Ange appeared to think about it for a second. "That's not a bad idea. If I'm out for the count, I'd rather know that creep can't get to me."

"You've got that right," said Bev, shuddering. "I'll grab a couple of bits myself." She then scanned the bush, as if looking for likely spots or more armed guards. Her body language said she hadn't spotted either when she turned and looked at me over one shoulder. "Where did you find the last bit?"

My hand went up to my eyes to block out the worst of the

sun, and my gaze swept the bushes that cloaked the perimeter, all while hiding the fence. On spotting the Rata tree that marked the narrow path, I started forward, relieved we were nowhere near where the guard had been patrolling earlier. "This way!"

14

I made a beeline for the Rata tree, soon picking up on the faint, but unusual perfume of its scarlet flowers. After a quick look about, I shot down the path and into the dense bush that encircled the large tree. The others were right behind me.

Close to the fence line, I found another piece of wood perfect for securing the window. Relief swamped me as I held it up in a victory salute. I then continued looking for something to use as a doorstop.

"Ah, Marilyn, I hate to break it to you, but that isn't wood." For once, Bev's voice was reedy.

Ange looked up from where she was kicking the undergrowth. "Holy crap!"

I dropped my treasure before wiping my hand over and over down the leg of my Vale uniform. Ange wasn't as squeamish, retrieving it before it could settle back amongst the ferns. "Part of a femur."

Bev murmured, 'Hmmm,' in agreement. "It's definitely not bovine." She examined it a little longer, all the while slowly shaking her head. "I don't think it's deer, either." There was a grim quality to her words that didn't bode well.

Five minutes later, and all we could see of Ange was her backside. Buried deep in the ferns, she was rummaging through the bone pile as if she was at a Black Friday sale. "I'd say they're all female."

Because she was a nurse, I didn't question this assertion. The other thing I now knew was that it was no Long-Tailed Cuckoo we'd heard screaming the day before. It was a woman, and she'd been in pain. Lots of it.

As with everything else that had happened in the last twenty-four hours, I was having trouble coming to terms with it. Why were all these women killed? Or had they merely starved to death? Merely? How could I even think that?

Unable to deal with the horror we were facing, all I wanted to do was go back to my room, curl up in a ball, and cry, but I couldn't. And anyway, it wasn't as if my room was some sort of haven. Anything but.

Bev scanned the depths of the bush before leaning over to speak to Ange, careful to keep her voice low. "How many do you reckon there are?" Before Ange could answer, Bev spoke again. "Holy moly. Look at that." She then pointed at something I couldn't see. It was something I didn't want to see by the sound of things.

Ange now peered into the bush as intently, her brow crinkled in confusion. "What is it?"

"You see those regular marks on the bone? That's evidence of knife work. Last time I saw that was after we had a beast at the farm home-killed." Despite Bev's words being measured, her disbelief at what she'd just said was clear.

"Oh, gross." Ange stumbled out of the ferns, crashing in a heap in the middle of the narrow path. "Maggots!" She followed this up by flicking her hands around.

Revulsion flooded my system. Maggots freaked me out in a big way. And if a nurse was looking green, there was no hope for me. I got out of there, with Bev hot footing it behind me.

"But why? Why would they shove the bodies in there?" I thought about it for a little longer. "If they threw them over the cliff, the pigs would take care of them, wouldn't they?" I turned to Bev, suspecting she was more up to speed on porcine behavior than I was.

"That they would, but they'd also make one hell of a racket while they were about it. That might be why the remains are on this side of the fence."

Ange joined us and she wasn't happy, crouching down and wiping her hands repeatedly on the grass to rid them of any remaining gunk. After scrutinizing them to check they were clean, she took a deep breath. "Damn it, I can't believe we have to keep quiet about this."

It was ironic that it was the chatterbox saying this. "Yeah, I figured as much." Even in agreement with her, I couldn't believe we had to sweep this travesty under the ferns. However, it was our only option if we didn't want to suffer the same fate as those women.

"And who would we tell, anyway?" said Bev. "Whether they died of starvation or something else, Chalky has to know about it." Her lips tightened briefly. "I'm glad this place is vegan, considering those knife marks." She was still staring into the bush when she said, as if to herself, "We can't say anything to anyone else until we're out of here." She paused for a beat. "And we especially say nothing to Tee."

In unspoken agreement, we beat a hasty retreat, getting ourselves as far from the spot as we could. We only slowed our pace when we were well away from any buildings or trees, free to talk.

As I gazed out over the sea of trees that lapped against the front of the property, I struggled for the right words. "Damn it, when I signed my life away with that blasted contract, I didn't realize the monochromatic cow planned on following through."

Bev snorted before speaking. "They're called Holstein-Friesians, and I never met one I didn't like. Unlike that bitch."

As we continued discussing our options, we indulged in the occasional burst of rapid-fire laughter. Anything to avoid looking as if we'd just discovered a pile of cadavers hidden in the bush.

However, it didn't matter how we looked at it. We were up to our necks in trouble. The place had been a challenge as it was, without adding potential death to the mix. Sure, I'd tried killer diets in the past, but none that came close to actually delivering.

Yet again, my hand strayed to the back of my neck, smoothing the fine baby hairs. And yet again, the gesture failed.

Next to me, Ange wrung her hands together in a virtual scrub. "I guess this explains their 100% success rate."

"Don't do that." Bev's voice was low when she whacked Ange's hands hard, stopping the scrubbing motion in an instant.

Unable to squelch the sensation that someone was looking at us, I casually glanced at the admin building. "How much longer are you guys in here for?"

I was well aware five long weeks stretched ahead of me before I escaped through the metal gates, but wondered about my friends. And they were friends, too. Despite our brief acquaintance, I was already closer to these two women than any of my so-called friends back in the city.

I was at ease in their company, not worried about saying the wrong thing, or constantly comparing myself to them physically. I didn't need to pretend to be someone I wasn't. I could truly relax, although not right now.

"Three weeks for me." Bev looked relieved to be halfway through her stint.

"Three and a half for me." Ange, too, looked to be counting the days.

Great, I'd be there on my own for a couple of weeks unless Ange and Bev could convince the cops to raid the place. "Hang on, what about Tee? She'll be out in just over a week. Can't she go for help?"

Bev rolled her eyes and shook her head before responding. "She could if she wasn't in here for the duration."

"The duration?"

After another burst of canned laughter, Ange answered for Bev. "Not leaving until she's lost two-hundred-pounds."

Given the rate that Tee was inveigling extra rations out of the laughing gnomes in the kitchen, she'd be there for life. The question was, how long would that be?

What was it they scrawled on those chalkboards outside cafes? That's right.

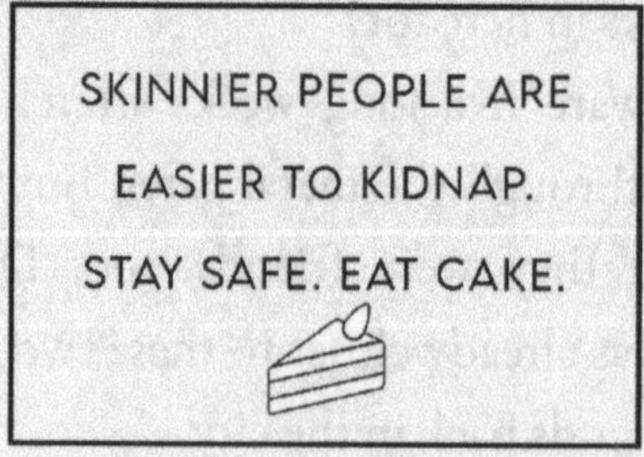

Not so sure it would keep you safe from being murdered, but it would sure make it harder to dispose of your body.

The rest of the morning crawled by, with Bev, Ange, and me acting the part of the carefree, which involved more effort than I'd have thought. We kept ourselves busy fitting in an extra yoga session and completing further loops of the property.

The idea of keeping up this pretense until Bev escaped was

agonizing. Three weeks before any chance of help. As intense was the thought that when Bev left, I'd be saying goodbye to a new friend.

As we avoided rotting corpses and the spot where we had seen that armed guard, we foreshortened our loops. This had us passing the sheer drop-offs more times than I would have liked. In the end, I decided I would rather face those than the other obstacles on offer.

It was at lunch that we hit a snag. It was bone broth. A dish that had no place appearing on a vegan menu. If they'd served this up before we stumbled across the human remains, I would have beaten Tee to the serving hatch. As it was, I hung back, with Bev and Ange beside me.

Thanks to Tee's habit of blurting everything out at volume, we couldn't even warn the poor woman not to touch it. Nor was there an opportunity, with her gulping down the mug of broth while on her way back to our usual table.

I wasn't sure which turned my stomach more. That Tee had inadvertently turned cannibal, or that my tummy rumbled in response to the broth's delicious aroma. Muttering something about needing to fast, I legged it with the other two right behind me.

After a thankfully kale-based dinner, I was getting ready for bed when I realized I'd never gotten a wedge for under my door. The window wasn't a problem. I just needed to make sure I locked it properly. But without a key, I wasn't sure how I'd secure the door.

At nine o'clock, there was a knock. It wasn't unexpected, but I was still loath to answer it. Not a problem because Chalky walked in uninvited, holding a tray with another French press of pee masquerading as herbal tea.

"How thoughtful of you." My opening gambit threw her off her stride. It was as though she had expected me to argue about drinking more of the drug-laced urine.

"I slept so well last night." I cast my eyes briefly skyward. If you could get struck down for out-and-out lies, then there was a bolt of lightning with my name on it.

Her eyes narrowed a fraction, although she said nothing.

I was unsure if this was down to my passable acting skills or an udder's worth of botulism toxin swirling around inside her face.

Walking across my room and placing the tray on my bedside table, she continued her examination of me. She then straightened and waited with arms folded for me to drink the toxic brew.

"It looks lovely. As soon as I've had a quick shower and let it steep, I'll drink it tucked up in bed."

Her mouth opened as though to argue about this course of action. "Don't let it get cold, it doesn't work, ah, taste as good."

I fought my reaction to her slip, busying myself with pulling the covers back in readiness for bed. "I'll just have a quick sluice off." I smoothed the sheets and plumped the pillows, all the while stalling. "It should still be hot by the time I hit the hay."

Hit the hay? OMG, when had I ever said something that hokey?

Turning, I found her gone. Those ankle boots, while clunky, allowed her to move almost without sound when it suited her. Almost, because if I hadn't been blathering about hitting the hay, I would have been able to hear the rubber souls squeaking. As was her habit, she hadn't bothered to shut the door, leaving me to do so while wondering how I'd secure it.

A moment's contemplation, and I realized I was staring at the answer. By jamming the toe of one flip-flop under the door with the other wedged underneath that, I would have a passable door stop. Whether it would be enough to hold the greasy cretin at bay, I would soon find out.

Ablutions and dumping of the disgusting brew over, I climbed into bed. A quick flick of the curtains behind the headboard confirmed the window was closed.

But when I touched the clip to make doubly sure it was fully engaged, it became clear someone had tampered with it. In its current state, it couldn't keep a cockroach out, let alone Lance, the biggest cockroach of them all. I'd even be okay with there still being a femur on the sill if it would stop the window from opening. Short of using my own, there was nothing else to hand.

Biting on my thumbnail, I scanned the contents of my room, hoping for something I could use to stop the window from opening. Or booby-trap it such that if Lance tried to open it, all hell would break loose.

I stared at the desk to the point it was out of focus before the perfect solution struck me. Although only if I could remove the drawer.

There were fresh flowers on David's grave, doubtless put there by the Mini Me. I stopped jumping for a moment, taking delight in kicking the vase. That was weird. It shouldn't have made that much noise.

I couldn't stop the scream, ruining my plan to pretend to sleep through any racket. This time, Lance's exit wasn't as quiet, even if there was an element of stealth to his muttered, "Fuck."

I had two options: I could turn on the light and let them know I was awake, or I could keep it off and feign a nightmare. In the end, the need for light won out. If Chalky confronted me, I'd tell her I'd had a bad dream.

"Hell, girlfriend, you look like crap." Tee's assertion was as audible to me as it was to everyone else within a twenty-foot radius. Her loud persona grated this morning. "Anton wanted to know where you were."

Anton? Oh right, the half-naked yogi. This was the second morning I had missed yoga, and I imagined my breakfast rations would reflect this. While not a fan of that cardboard toast, having seen what happened to those who didn't eat, I'd chow down. Even if it meant a visit to the dentist for veneers when I got out of here.

I slouched in my chair for a moment before responding. "Thanks, Tee. I feel like crap, too."

Bev dropped her elbows on the table and leaned in, her face clouded with concern. "What happened?"

Ange too shimmied forward in her seat to get closer. I hadn't uttered two words when any others stuck in my throat. Chalky stood inside the doors to the dining room, her gaze glued to me. I dropped my head to stare at the table, but I was all too aware she was walking in our direction.

She stood by my side, her foot tapping in a manner I couldn't ignore. I peeked up at her. "Good morning, Chal—Candice." Hell, that was close. No need to piss her off more than her body language already said she was. No need to piss her off when I knew what she was capable of.

Or at least what she'd let slide.

"Maisie, I'd like a word with you. In my office."

It took concentration to get rid of the golf ball stuck in my throat before I could speak. Despite this, my "Now?" had a strangled quality to it.

"No, after breakfast will suffice." None of us spoke until she'd left, and then it was all at once, with everyone, except Tee, keeping their voices down. Tee wanted to know what it was about, but on seeing Ange and Bev's expressions, I steered clear of our grisly discovery.

Tee's booming voice would make it impossible for her to keep it a secret, no matter how hard she tried. Instead, I muttered about not being able to get back to sleep after Lance had tried getting into my room at two a.m. The late hour doubtless to give the drug time to work.

"But why would Chalky want to speak to you about that?" Tee had trouble getting her words out around the large mouthful of toast she was working away at. It made me realize I hadn't yet collected mine. Knowing I couldn't dodge my visit to Chalky, I nipped up to the counter and grabbed my toast and a mug of peppermint tea.

I'd only just parked my rear end when Ange spoke. "Tee has a point. Why would Chalky bring that up?"

Bev's cogitation kept her quiet for a moment before she also questioned the reason for the visit. "Yeah, it makes little sense."

Desperate to find another reason for Chalky's summons, I said the first thing that came to mind. "Maybe it's because I've missed yoga for a couple of days in a row?"

Tee tapped my plate with its two slices of toast. "Can't be that, otherwise you'd be down to one slice."

"What if it's about that, ah, other thing?" Bev's face then creased with worry. "Maybe I should come with you?"

I'd be lying if Bev's offer to accompany me wasn't tempting. And while her concern warmed me, I'd rather she stay here than risk censure.

"I'll, I'll be fine." I was about to add, "What's the worst that can happen?" but I knew all too well.

Ange stopped chewing on a hangnail long enough to add, "Are you sure? You really shouldn't go there on your own. It's got to be serious to warrant a visit to the principal's office."

On hearing this term, I experienced a flashback to my first

day of school. Another girl had pulled my hair hard, with me smacking her around the head in retaliation. It was something that saw me sent to Mrs. Shield's office. It was my first and only visit.

Any thoughts of standing up for myself after that were smothered by the fear I'd suffered while waiting. The officious woman kept me sitting there for an hour, my legs numb from hanging over the edge of the hard chair.

On facing her, my teeth were chattering thanks to the wind whistling down the empty corridor. It was the loneliest place in the world for a five-year-old.

15

After refusing yet more offers from my friends to accompany me, all too soon, I was over at the main office. I'd been unable to finish my two slices of toast thanks to a throat that had been anaphylactic. My cardboard toast hadn't gone to waste, though, with Bev and Ange going halves on it.

This pissed Tee off, but they'd soon enough quashed her argument that she had more body to sustain. Bev's pointing out she'd wait until after breakfast and get extra helpings from the gnomes like she always did, had soon shut her up.

I didn't know whether to be relieved when, on opening the sliding door to the main office, I found Chalky waiting for me. No sitting in the cold to think about my sins on this visit to the principal. This time, I gained an immediate audience.

Despite this, careful theater still guaranteed I was uncomfortable. Gone were the Barcelona chairs with their crisscrossed metal frames. Instead, I sat opposite her, the smooth surface of her desk all that separated me from her and my fate. That the chair I sat on was the one from my room didn't bode well.

Chalky made a real production of flipping through my notes, tapping the pages with a pen to highlight my lack of progress on the weight-loss front. She hadn't said a word when one of the laughing gnomes arrived with a tray. On clocking the contents of the French press, my eyes dilated.

Coffee! No way? Bet it's bloody decaf.

No sooner had he placed the tray on Chalky's desk than she gave a curt, "That will be all, Simon." He made no secret that her brusque wave of dismissal irked him, although only if you were looking at him as I was.

The aroma of dark Colombian soon filled the room, with my mouth watering in anticipation. I knew I was getting a cup because there were two on the tray.

"Hmmm, your progress hasn't been what we'd have hoped for."

Chalky was right. Even possessing the world's cleanest colon and having ingested more kale than would be required to make a bunny nauseous, I'd lost a measly five pounds. And I suspected most of that was down to backed-up lunches.

The biggest insult, however, was my damned blood pressure being even higher than it had been at check-in. And all thanks to what I'd endured since my arrival. At this rate, I'd be stuck with the boobs of a twelve-year-old boy for the foreseeable future.

Could escape from this hellhole be as simple as being kicked out? What if my lack of progress was enough to have me ousted from the program? The thought of being driven back through the front gates and returning to my normal life soon took hold.

My normal life? It wasn't as if that was brilliant either, with thoughts of what a mess I'd made of it consuming me. Anxiety at not being given the chance to put things right shot through my veins, making my palms clammy and my heart race. The walls of Chalky's office were closing in on me.

"You'd be a perfect candidate."

Mired as I was in thoughts of how badly I'd screwed up my life, I had to ask her to repeat herself. It didn't help. While her words were concise, I wouldn't have a clue what she was talking about.

Chalky examined me, her eyes full of speculation as she lowered the plunger in the French press. She then poured two cups, pushing one in my direction. I savored the first mouthful but had guzzled the rest before she'd even finished stirring two heaped teaspoons of sugar into hers.

"It's something we reserve for our celebrity guests."

I was still in the dark, but refused to play her stupid game, instead keeping quiet and forcing her to do all the work.

"We have a special program."

Again, I said nothing.

"It's the Sleeping Beauty Program." As if finally understanding I wouldn't respond, she pressed on. "Yes, well. You keep saying in your daily weigh-ins that you'd do anything to lose the weight. The question is, do you really mean it?"

My answer in the past would always have been a resounding 'yes'. Now I wasn't so sure. What if being thin also meant being dead?

I wouldn't need new boobs then, would I?

In the interests of staying alive, I hedged my bets.

"Within reason."

At any other time, I'd have been in full agreement. However, my survival instinct hammering away in my chest at full throttle had me fond of my extra pounds.

She did her best to lift an eyebrow before continuing with her sales pitch.

"When you're a guest in the Sleeping Beauty Suites, you're lightly sedated. This means we can cut right back on your calories, with you sleeping through any hunger pangs. There are daily massages, and we use neuromuscular electrical stimulation to keep your muscles working. Our celebrity clients swear by it."

Until two days ago, this would have been my idea of bliss. As it was, there wasn't a snowball's chance in hell I'd put myself in her hands like that. "Can I think about it?"

She smirked at me, before responding with a bald, "No!"

I was wondering what she meant by this when I noticed something was off-kilter. It took longer than it should for me to realize I was the one tilting to the side, and not her.

I didn't so much wake as clawed my way back to consciousness. On arrival, I wished I'd stayed where I was, the comfort of the void winning hands down.

Whatever Chalky used to drug me, it was strong. I didn't have the faintest recollection of the trip from her office to wherever I was now. If I was to hazard a guess, I'd say I was somewhere in the ex-army base rather than anywhere you'd find a celebrity.

Indeed, the linens on the enormous bed were more akin to rubber than anything you'd find at a 5-star establishment. The lights illuminating my body were as bright as any seen in an operating theater. Sadly, they weren't so blinding that I couldn't see a multitude of cameras on the periphery of the room.

Even without lifting my head, I knew I was naked. There was also no need to try moving my arms and legs to know someone had tied me down. That this was in such a way that my legs were wide didn't bode well.

On my finally breaking free of the effects of the drug, panic coursed through me, my heart skipping beats and my breathing too fast. The room was suffocatingly hot, tension hanging heavy in the air. My mind raced as I tried to comprehend my situation. I was at their mercy, with no way out that I could see.

I struggled against my restraints, but it was in vain, with this only intensifying my feelings of helplessness. I tried again and again. But my attempts were futile, the bindings restricting any freedom I might have gained.

The knowledge someone had deliberately tied me down filled me with a sickening mix of fear and dread. It had to be Chalky. It couldn't be anyone else. She'd drugged me, but why? Wouldn't it have made more sense to poison me and be done with it? Maybe that's what happened to all those women whose bodies we'd found?

Even amid my fear, a flicker of determination ignited within me, one I'd usually have extinguished, but no more. I refused to succumb to the paralyzing grip of terror. I vowed to stay alert, to regain control of my fate.

It only took one word to disabuse me of this newfound resolve.

"Lance!"

The command being nasal and New York and there was no need to twist my head around to know who'd issued it. I had assumed the headboard was against the wall, but this didn't appear to be the case. Probably something to do with camera angles.

It took every ounce of my concentration to slow my breathing, to fight the panic waiting to pounce. It was this stillness that allowed me to appreciate that while the voice had come from behind me. I was alone in the room.

But not for long.

While Lance's dress sense was deplorable, it was better than his current state. He stood naked and without shame at the end of the bed, showing himself to be harder than my ex on his way to the morgue.

To avoid looking at him, I instead focused on the ceiling. The dipping of the mattress under my legs confirmed my worst fears. Unable to stop myself, my gaze met his. There wasn't a spark of compassion.

"It's gonna be fun screwing a live one," he hissed, before poking at me.

"Please, please don't do this," I snotter'd out, my sinuses evacuating in sympathy with my tear ducts. "I can pay. I have money, lots of it." I made eye contact with him, mouthing any further entreaties to avoid them being picked up by a microphone.

He stilled, and a small beacon of hope flickered to life in my chest.

"Lance, the client is waiting. You have your instructions!"

Client?

His grin as he continued crawling up the bed had an insane edge to it, with not an ounce of humor showing in his eyes.

My shrieks of pain when he slammed himself deep inside me were the cause for cackling laughter from a speaker overhead. As I panted to cope with the agony of the assault, this laughter only intensified.

The attack continued until I was numb to the pain and lay there, staring blindly at the ceiling. I didn't even have it in me to cry anymore.

"Cut!" screamed Chalky.

I closed my eyes and gave into whimpering before understanding this was a directorial command and not a call for Lance to get the knives out.

A stream of cold water then shocked me into full sentience, the ultimate insult. I opened my eyes but soon closed them when Lance sprayed me full in the face, water filling my mouth and nose, choking me.

Sluiced down like a side of beef in an abattoir, Lance gave parts of me more attention than they deserved after the last half hour. I tried for oblivion, but it remained as out of reach as ever.

"No passing out. You're on again!" An unfamiliar male, whose clipped accent marked him as South African, barked at me.

My eyes flashed open, and I looked up at the man. At any other time, I'd have found him handsome. However, when my gaze locked with his, there was no missing a sinister edge, one that told me he'd have no compunction about hurting me. Another look and I knew he'd enjoy it.

"Piers, you have your instructions," came from the speaker above my head. There was barely a pause before Chalky drawled. "Annnnnd, action!" The only thing missing was the bang of a clapper board, with this doubtless unnecessary thanks to it being a live feed.

The hours of torture turned into what I thought might be days, blending into a living nightmare with only just enough sleep and nourishment to survive.

There was neither rhyme nor rhythm to when the studio lights flared into life. The speaker above my head emitted accents as varied as the time zones they likely represented.

They didn't feed me any solids to make cleaning me easier. Instead, I subsisted on those chocolate shakes. Soon enough, even their delicious flavor turned my stomach to the point I spewed up as much as they could force-feed me, resulting in yet more icy hose-downs.

Then everything stopped. It was as though I'd been voted off the island and they'd moved on to torture another contestant. I'd even decided I was okay with this when it hit me like another bucket of cold water, that it could be Ange, Bev, or Tee.

It was awful when it was happening to me. The thought of my friends being hurt was enough to have me in tears. For the first time in what felt like decades, I had loyal friends. Friends I cared about.

After this, every time I heard a woman screaming, I stilled my breathing, desperate to see if I could recognize it as one of my friends. Any relief at no longer being the center of attention, canceled by bone-deep guilt. The other thing that was canceled was those chocolate shakes, their absence leaving me faint, even though I was lying down.

I therefore thought I was imagining things when I detected scratching from somewhere off to my left. Dropping my head to the side, I faced the Venetian blinds I'd thought concealed a window into another room.

There it was again.

Even knowing the consequences, I yelled for help as loudly as I was able. This wasn't any great shakes, with my voice unused for days and nothing to drink for at least one of those. But it did the trick. I made out the words 'get help' before silence returned.

The relative peace was short-lived, with Lance, and then Piers, thundering into my room. Both of them were naked.

Oh, crap.

I didn't have long to think. If they knew there was someone outside, then we'd all be dead.

"Cockroach, there's a monster cockroach!" I threw as much energy into this declaration as possible, adding to my apparent terror by twisting against my bindings in a vain attempt at escape.

"You stupid bitch, you fucking interrupted a triple." Lance backhanded me across the mouth, hard enough that my vision sparkled before I passed out.

17

It was a sense of malevolent evil inveigling its way into my subconscious that ruined my familiar dream where I frolicked on that golden beach. My eyelids fluttered open, and I saw Chalky next to the bed, looking at me. The speculation in her gaze was unsettling.

I didn't know what to make of it when she held a cup with a straw next to my mouth so I could take a drink. I didn't care what was in the plastic cup. Anything that would help rid my mouth of the gum accumulated from a lack of fluids would suffice.

I'd managed several deep swigs of what tasted like tap water before she snatched the cup away. I wasn't sure if she did this to stop me from overloading myself or if she was being her usual bitchy self.

My money was on the second and, before I could stop

myself, I let fly with a satisfying gob of spit that was just this side of tenacious. My reward was that it stuck to the front of her pristine smock in a satisfying manner. Not so gratifying was the look of pure venom she speared me with.

But what the hell, it wasn't like I was getting out of here alive. Unless whoever it was at the window arrived with the cavalry pretty damn smart.

"You'll regret that, Marilyn."

"Hah, you don't scare me!" Despite my bravado, this was complete rubbish. That she'd used my real name didn't bode well.

"Did you think we'd just let you slip away?" Her laughter had that same tinkling quality often associated with fundraising events. Fake to the core. However, when she continued, her voice had none of this subterfuge. It was raw and unfiltered. "It's amazing what our clients enjoy watching and how much they'll pay. Even the ultimate sacrifice has a price."

There was no need for her to go into detail, as my imagination was more than capable of coming up with what I would be facing. My subsequent death would be neither easy nor cheap, a thought that had me shutting my eyes to the room, and especially her.

I couldn't stay like that though, the silence pressing in on all sides, enough to rouse my curiosity. My eyes snapped open, ready to face whatever I had to. However, I was on my own again, with only my thoughts for company.

Those thoughts were reaching Stephen-King-level crazy when Lance stomped back into my room. He was no longer naked, and he didn't look happy. When he pulled a gigantic knife out of a sheath strapped to his leg, I whimpered in terror. My demise wasn't far off. I was about to find out if David made it to heaven or hell.

I squeezed my eyes shut, unable to watch my death, and was therefore stunned when, rather than disemboweling me, Lance hacked through my bindings. He then threw me like a sack of grain over one shoulder and made quick work of striding out of the room.

After trudging down a long corridor, we entered another room. The space, even when viewed upside down, appeared set up for only one purpose.

There was nothing gentle about how he dumped me onto the unforgiving concrete floor. My muscles having atrophied to noodle status, there was nothing I could do to soften my fall. My cries of agony bounced off the concrete walls and ceiling. Rather than tip my head back and slit my throat, Lance shoved me with his foot and I sprawled on my back next to a drain.

My startled gaze latched onto a series of meat hooks hanging from the ceiling, letting me know my time was near. The years of loneliness despite being married, my failure to become a mother, all of it flashed before me. What a waste.

I was busy preparing to meet my maker when, rather than bending over and killing me, Lance made a show of unzipping his filthy jeans and dragging his penis free.

This was weird. It was more common for him to arrive, pre-fluffed and ready to go. My eyes widened in horror when I realized that the way he was holding his member had more to do with accuracy than stimulation.

With my mouth and eyes shut tight, I turned my head to the side as far as it would go. Despite this, I still copped an earful of urine that reeked of asparagus. This splattered up at me from the cold concrete. But it could have been worse. My relief was short-lived when, on turning back, I saw Lance stepping aside to make way for Piers. It also confirmed the golden shower wasn't a freebie.

To hell with this!

"Pencil dick, pencil dick, can't get hard without a stick. Pencil dick, pencil dick, can't get laid without a trick." I sang this stupid rhyme at the top of my voice, rewarded by a sharp intake of breath coming from a speaker in the ceiling.

Piers looked confused, thinking I was directing my singing at him, but there was no point in emasculating him. It was better to go to work on the pay-per-view jerk, living in his mom's basement, who was forking out for the performance.

"Pencil dick, pencil dick, can't get hard without a stick!"

I was working through yet another refrain when there was a burst of static from the speaker. Chalky then spoke, her tone clipped and dripping with wrath.

"That will be all. Thank you, Piers."

He didn't stay long after Chalky stormed in.

She barely slowed, instead striding across the room and without warning, kicking me in the kidneys. "That's for us having to give a refund!"

The pain was excruciating. I dry-retched, with even those

hideous shakes refusing to make a comeback. Throwing up all over her was out of the question, so I made do with screaming at her with as much volume as I could muster. "You botoxed, skinny OLD bitch!"

It felt good. Not since I had dealt with that bully on the first day of school had I experienced this sense of identity. Of standing up for myself and refusing to play the part of a doormat.

My euphoria didn't last past Chalky kicking me between the legs. It made smashing into my bike seat child's play by comparison, but it didn't shut me up, even if there was a forced quality to my words.

"Botoxed, skinny OLD bitch! Botoxed, skinny OLD bitch!" I didn't stop until Chalky bent over and punched me in the nose hard, with blood spraying in all directions. My mouth soon filled with O positive, and I took delight in spitting it out as hard as I could, ruining a crisp, white smock that looked fresh on. I was laughing like a maniac when Pencil Dick started screaming.

"Get rid of her, get rid of her!" He'd then snarled, "I'll watch!" He was quiet for a moment before adding, "But I'll be damned if I'll pay!"

Cold water then assaulted me, with Lance hosing the room down at the same time as me. Lifted, dripping wet, he threw me over his shoulder for the return trip to what I thought of as my room. No sooner had he flung me back on the bed than a tinny voice said, "I want to see that bitch fucked until she snuffs it."

Presumably, this was Pencil Dick himself, looking for

another go-round. I was readying myself to sing, when Chalky stormed into the room, holding a power drill aloft like it was an Oscar's statue. Oh hell.

"Hurry, hurry," said Pencil Dick, apparently having worked himself into quite the lather over what was about to happen. Thoughts of him distracted me enough that Lance had tied me down with new ropes before I comprehended what was going on.

Then all I could focus on was Chalky making a show of putting a spade bit into the power drill. Theatrical is how I'd describe it. My laughter about that sort of drill bit more commonly being used to put holes in than take them out, filled the room, with no missing its manic edge.

For all, Chalky acknowledged it. Too busy with her running commentary. It was one that guaranteed I was cognizant of what she intended doing, although I thought this was more for Pencil Dick's edification than mine.

"Not getting any younger here," came a snippy instruction from the speaker, spurring Chalky to abandon the theatrics and get on with proceedings.

Expecting Lance to take care of this task, it shocked me when he slipped out of the room, with Chalky unaware he had left. Not until she swung to where he'd last stood did she exhibit any surprise, or as much as her paralyzed wrinkles could muster.

She didn't bother calling for him as I'd expected. Rather, she smiled and turned in my direction, whirring the drill for maximum terror ... or was that pleasure?

She'd positioned herself between my feet when the Hummer roared to life outside. The unmistakable sound of gravel being scattered courtesy of a quick departure followed this. Chalky's brows knotted as if she was trying to give birth to last night's nut burger, but her confusion didn't last.

Once again, she smiled broadly, conveying the show would go on even without his presence, and that she'd doubtless enjoy every second.

I did everything I could to distance myself from what was about to happen. I tried for my happy place, but it remained elusive. The drill was now so close that there was a breeze on the inside of my thighs.

Tied up as tightly as I was, I couldn't get even a inch farther away. I whimpered like a beaten puppy, but there was nothing I could do. Closing my eyes, I waited for the pain, thinking of babies I would never hold.

"Cut, cut!" screamed Pencil Dick, his voice more high-pitched than ever.

I surrendered, knowing this was it. It would all be over soon and I could lie on that beautiful beach for eternity. With the breeze now cooling my very core, I knew Chalky was close to gutting me, or whatever the gynecological equivalent was.

"Dammit! Argh!! Stop!!! Stop!!!"

Chalky was so close with the drill bit that if they'd left me any pubes, I would have lost the lot by now. As it was, the drill stopped, my relief coming early as it would appear Pencil Dick had.

With terror still having me in its grip, his rescheduling for the same time tomorrow almost went unnoticed.

18

A hand slapped over my mouth was all that stopped me from screaming. At the sight of Ange, tears of relief sprung unbidden. Relief that she was here, and relief that she looked to be okay.

"We need to be quiet. This place is crawling with scum."

Because she'd whispered into my ear, her words were loud, although not as loud as the bong from out in the hallway. Without bothering to check what it was, she made quick work of my restraints thanks to a serrated bread knife she'd picked up from somewhere.

She then took her time easing me into a sitting position, but it was still too fast. Faintness swamped me, and I had to lie back to avoid passing out.

Ange bent over and again whispered into my ear. "When did you last eat?"

I shrugged. I wouldn't have a clue how much time had passed. It could have been days or even months. Okay, not months. If it'd been months, I would have been on the menu in a maggoty all-you-can-eat buffet in the bush by now.

Ange shoved a granola bar into my hand before steering it toward my mouth. "Eat!"

I took a small bite, and my taste buds exploded with gratitude before the mouthful landed like a brick in my stomach.

Once I knew the food was staying put, I asked her the question that had been buzzing around in my brain since I heard that scratching at the window.

"How on earth did you find me? How did you even know to look?"

Ange looked over her shoulder at the doorway before turning back to me. "You're our friend. We knew you would have said goodbye if you were leaving, so we followed Chalky. Nasty bitch was being sneaky as all get out, so we knew something was up. Eventually, we followed her here."

The second bite of granola bar tasted as good as the first, and despite the desire to bolt it, I took my time. I didn't want to choke or puke right now.

"I'll be back in a second." Ange moved from my side, with blind panic clawing at my throat, threatening to choke me.

Don't leave me!

It was all I could do to stop myself from calling out. However, she didn't go far, stopping in the doorway to peek out into the hallway, first one way and then the other. When she disappeared, the sense of abandonment was excruciating.

With the granola bar half-finished, I dragged myself into a sitting position and waited for the wooziness to disappear before struggling to my feet. First, I needed the headboard for support, but soon enough, I found my equilibrium, standing unaided.

This was how Ange found me when she returned with her arms full of clothing in a bright green often seen in medical dramas. She dropped a pair of poo-colored rubber clogs on the floor and then laid the surgical scrubs on the bed. I needed her help to dress, having to sit and put my head between my knees once or twice to avoid passing out.

"Are you ready?" She looked at me, her worrying that she'd have to carry me on full display. I wasn't sure she could. This had me wondering where Bev was. Bev would have no trouble hefting me.

No sooner had I nodded confirmation at being as ready as I ever would when there was another loud bong from out in the hallway.

Bev appeared in the doorway a second later. She was holding a large, heavy-duty roasting pan above her head in readiness, but lowered it when she saw Ange and me. My stomach rumbled in eagerness when the aroma of roasted meat hit my nostrils, followed by me gagging when I thought about what kind of meat it was.

As if understanding my reticence, Bev held the roasting dish out. "Go for it. It's lamb. I checked."

While there were a few large dents in the pan, the meat scrapings, along with a scattering of crispy potato, appeared untouched by human cranium. This saw me gobbling everything down before handing Bev's weapon of choice back to her.

"Come on, let's get you outta here." Ange threw one arm around my middle and dragged me into a supportive embrace that proved she was stronger than she looked. Without her help, I wouldn't be going anywhere.

Moments later, we were in a big industrial kitchen where Bev tentatively touched the handle of a cast-iron frying pan sitting on the stovetop. "It was too freaking hot before." Soon enough, she'd dropped the roasting dish in preference for her new weapon of choice.

Unarmed, my vulnerability intensified when Ange inched open an outside door and we faced a large gravel parking lot. We'd need to navigate that and a gravel driveway before we'd reach the cover of the bush.

Never had gravel underfoot sounded so loud to me, meaning that rather than sneaking across, we traversed as fast as we were able. I knew I was slowing the others down, making me grateful that they stuck to my side. They helped me move quicker than I could have on my own.

Within a few feet of entering the bush, we realized we weren't ready for such thick vegetation. Apart from not having the right equipment, we sure as hell didn't have the knowledge to deal with the conditions.

As tempting as it had been to rush down the driveway, this

would have left us vulnerable to recapture. Despite how unprepared we were, there was no way I was heading back into the open. The bush was our only option.

While nightfall was yet to arrive, spotlights soon burst into life on all sides of the building, their effect on my flight-or-fight reflex paralyzing. This quadrupled when a couple of dozen men in camouflage gear burst out of the door we'd just used.

They must have been at dinner when we were making our escape. The freshness of the meat in the roasting dish and Bev's frying pan, still being hot, pointed to this.

These soldiers, or mercenaries, were the first I'd seen since that guy Ange, Bev, and I had seen hiding in the bush. And even he was mild compared to the battle-hardened men spreading out and advancing in measured steps toward the bush in an ever-widening arc. They carried assault rifles across their fronts, at the ready.

Lance and Piers made up two of their number, identifiable by their smaller stature. Despite them always frightening me, they had a look of weekend warrior about them when compared to the others.

What started as a slight tremor soon developed into a full-body shake. It was enough to have my legs giving out, with me dropping to the leaf litter underfoot in a heap, taking Bev down with me.

Meanwhile, Ange stood at attention, peering through the bush at the approaching men. "We need to get out of here," she gasped.

I shook my head. While I didn't disagree with her, I didn't know if I was up to moving yet, and not as fast as required.

Bev grabbed my head, forcing me to look at her. "Do this. If we go back there, we all die." Her hissed words broke through the terror that threatened to swallow me, with our surroundings once again snapping into focus.

After her scary-as-crap pep talk, she stood and dragged me to my feet and pointed me in the direction Ange had already taken through the bush.

"Put your feet where she puts hers," whispered Bev. "Don't think, walk."

It was a sound strategy, even if on a couple of occasions, this had me tripping when Ange did. As long as I was tripping in the right direction, I didn't care. We hadn't stumbled far when we encountered the pig fence. On looking up at the angled razor wire barrier towering over me, I knew this was it. They had us trapped, like rats.

"I'd rather face the pigs than those murderous thugs behind us." Ange dropped to her knees and started digging terrier-style at the base of the fence. Bev soon joined her, with them grunting loud enough to wake the dead.

However, in short order, they'd both ruined their nails and created a good-size gap, although nowhere big enough for us.

I fell to my knees next to them, not to help with the excavation, but because my legs had given out.

"The gap's too small."

"Marilyn, you are going through."

I was having trouble seeing Bev's face in the relative dark of the bush, but her voice was a clarion call that this wasn't up for discussion. Her hand on the back of my neck, she shoved me toward the gap, confirming her eagerness to get me moving. This also had me face-planting the undergrowth, my mouth full of leaf litter and who knew what else.

After getting down to my level, she patted me on the back. "Sorry, love, but they're getting closer. If we stay on this side of the fence, we die."

This, more than her comforting touch, mobilized me. Bev was right. We couldn't go back, and we couldn't stay here. The only thing I was unsure of was my fitting through the gap the other two had created. For that to happen, I'd have to have been without food for a lot longer than I had.

19

I was halfway under the fence when I became stuck. I knew the gap was never coping with my ass, as I'd told Bev and Ange. The wire caught at my clothes, and even my skin, determined to trap me.

My friends, however, weren't ready to give up on me just yet. While Bev wrenched up on the bottom of the wire fence, Ange shoved me forward with all her might.

I hadn't long escaped the tender embrace of the fence when the ground gave way under me. I dropped a couple of feet, the air in my lungs shocked free. A second later, and I was sliding, with the leaf litter proving as slippery as any ride at a water park.

There was nothing covert about my descent, with me gathering speed by the second and making a hell of a racket as I mowed down anything in my path. Despite grabbing at anything and everything, nothing slowed me.

The other two weren't far behind, with all of us landing in a tumble at the bottom of the ravine, up to our waists in freezing water.

The only plus in all of this was that my being winded meant I hadn't been able to scream my head off. Might it be our pursuers put our ruckus down to the local pig population?

Ange was on her feet in a heartbeat. "Come on, move ya butt." She shoved at me from behind, urging me to stand.

Meanwhile, Bev moved in front of me, and between them, they hoisted me upright. I was so tired that I was hallucinating. A wild pig approached. It was walking upright, like a man. It was too much, and Bev had to slap me hard to stop my screaming. No sooner had I stopped than Ange took up, earning her a smack of her own from Bev.

Ange pointed, and Bev turned to find the pig now within striking distance. She didn't bother screaming. She smacked it hard across the snout with the frying pan she'd somehow kept a hold of.

Rather than knocking the porker out, this sent it flying, with it landing in the creek with an enormous splash. However, it didn't attack us. It spoke.

"Will you crazy bitches shut the fuck up?"

While not a knight in shining armor, the blood-encrusted man glaring at us through the half-light would do. Happy in the knowledge we'd been rescued, I allowed the darkness that was nudging at my consciousness to take over.

A pungent stench interrupted my dream, rousing me. If I didn't know better, I'd think I was sharing the bed with a large block of Stilton cheese. I coughed, hoping to clear my airways of the noxious presence, but it was no good, and I woke fully, opening my eyes to see how I could escape.

Right in front of my face was a pair of size elevens, wrapped in wet wool socks that molded to arches and ankles alike. I yanked my head backward in search of clean air and smashed it into a wall. A couple of items hanging on rusty nails above me fell and whacked me on the side of my head.

"Ow!" My yelp of pain was loud in the small hut, but not so loud that I roused the large man whom I was topping and tailing with.

A quick look at my new surroundings showed a basic hunting shelter, cobbled together out of fallen logs and bits of scrap wood. A plastic tarpaulin topped the structure, giving the interior an eerie glow that turned our rescuer's blond hair a bright blue. However, there was nothing Smurf-like about the guy from what I could remember of last night.

Ange and Bev were sleeping top and tail in a cot on the other side of the hut, and I took solace in how relaxed they appeared. Them not being tied down also added to my peace of mind.

Unable to get up without climbing over our erstwhile rescuer, I took the easy option and rolled over to face the wall. A small breeze snuck its way between the ill-fitting logs, and this freshness encouraged me to sink back into sleep's sweet stranglehold.

Next time I woke, it was because I needed to pee, and there was no ignoring it, with this working better than any alarm clock. I rolled over, pleased to see the cheesy socks had gone, along with the size elevens that owned them, making it easier for me to try getting up.

"Look who's awake." Bev smiled at me before tending to what smelled like bacon in the frying pan. The pan was the same one she'd armed herself with yesterday. At least I think it was yesterday. Funny, but thoughts of eating left me cold.

Ange bustled in with a battered pot, sloshing water onto the packed dirt floor of the hut. She placed the aluminum container on the small wood burner alongside the frying pan.

"Where's ...?" I asked, struggling into a sitting position.

"Johnno? He's out on a scouting mission to see what's up with the neighbors."

The casual way Ange said this would make you think the neighbors were up to nothing more than over-zealous trimming of boundary hedges. Or growing dope in their backyard rather than torture and lethal pay-per-view?

Before I could ask more, Johnno stormed into the hut. "Kill the fire!"

I was questioning this random instruction when Ange opened the front of the small wood burner, chucked the contents of the pot in there, and closed the door. No doubt a plume of smoke had shot up the chimney, but nothing more. If we were lucky.

"You," said Johnno, pointing in my direction, "On your bloody feet! Now!"

So forceful was his command that I was standing before I was even aware of getting up. He wasn't the sort of guy you argued with. He was what my mum would describe as rough around the edges. And if he was on edge, by rights I should be, too.

A minute later, we'd left the hut, crossed a small stream, and were trotting single file down a narrow track. Bev was in the lead, with Johnno at the rear. He held a knife that would have had Crocodile Dundee looking like a pansy. The pig was slung over his shoulders like a bloody, hairy backpack, its feet tied together to form shoulder straps.

Scared as I was, I couldn't stop a strained smile when I saw Bev had maintained a firm hold on the cast-iron frying pan. And, because of the residual heat, the bacon was still sizzling. Thankfully, there was a strong breeze, meaning our pursuers wouldn't get a bead on our location, although I got a waft now and then. Nope, still didn't appeal.

Could it be my full bladder putting pressure on my stomach that was taking the edge off my hunger? Appetite had never been an issue in the past.

"Stop here!" hissed Johnno from behind me. Bev, Ange, and I didn't so much freeze as solidify, not daring to blink. He, however, kept up his pace, storming past us, and coating me with boar bits. If I'd had anything in my stomach, I'd have barfed for sure.

Lucky for us, Ange's muttered "Gross," had Bev turning to see what was up. Her reactions, being better than mine, had her whipping the frying pan well away from pork products of a fresher variety.

Prizing my gaze away from the frying pan, I didn't grasp what was missing. How can a hulking big bloke with a pig on his back disappear like that? It was at least thirty feet before the track turned a corner, and he wasn't moving that fast.

"Move it!"

A blink later, I worked out where this terse instruction had come from when I saw Bev advance on what looked like a solid wall of green. It was one she parted with the frying pan before disappearing. Ange followed in her stead, and I wasted no time stumbling after them.

On the other side was a different world. The foliage formed a tunnel, which Johnno was marching down, leaving us to keep up as best we could. My blood-sugar levels were now protesting louder than ever, and I knew I wasn't alone when I saw Ange whack herself on the side of the head. The light-headedness was getting to me, too, with more and more shaking required to clear my vision.

Soon, even this wasn't working, and it was all I could do to place one foot in front of the other and keep up. My relief was immense when Johnno ducked into a cave off to the side of the track. I arrived in time to witness the boar being dumped on the floor of this sanctuary with a sickening squelch and blood seeping from every orifice.

No amount of gulping could keep the bile down, and I darted outside to spit it into the undergrowth. It was an action that saw me come close to peeing my pants.

Unable to hold on any longer, I staggered behind the nearest tree. Desperation to untie the knot on my borrowed drawstring pants had me all fingers-and-thumbs. I was then unsure if my relief was down to emptying my bladder or not having had an accident while I was about it.

I arrived back at the cave in time to see Johnno departing, a "You lot wait here while I cover our tracks," hissed over one shoulder. Not weighed down by an afternoon's work for a butcher, he covered the ground in long strides.

Back in the cave, I dropped to the sandy floor, as far from the carcass as possible. I was one step up from comatose, but revived when Bev waved the cast-iron frying pan under my nose.

Knowing I needed the sustenance, I forced myself to eat a rasher, unsurprised to find it tasted like sawdust. The second wasn't much better. If anyone had told me a month ago that I'd be eating so soon after spitting up all that bile, I'd never have believed them.

"Any more?" Ange's words roused me from my semi-coma, both with their volume in the cave and the hope that sprung into my stomach that the answer would be no.

"Two rashers," said Bev, "and I'm saving those for Johnno. We owe him big time."

Before Ange could complain, Johnno stormed into the cave, picked up the boar and threw it over his shoulders as though it weighed nothing. Despite his actions speaking louder than words, he still put his finger to his lips, showing there was a reason for his haste.

I needed both Bev and Ange's help to regain my feet. Upright, I was anything but steady, with head spins in the realms of those experienced after a real bender. At first, I balked when they led me deeper into the cave. They were heading in the wrong direction, weren't they? But then I heard Johnno moving ahead of us.

The deeper we went, the darker it got. To the point, I doubted there was any light reaching us at all. Ange, Bev, and I kept hold of each other in unspoken agreement, sliding our feet along the floor of the cave to avoid unseen obstacles.

Now and then a husky 'left,' 'right,' or 'middle' would filter back to us from the black beyond. Without these instructions, we'd have gotten lost, for sure.

Minutes felt like hours. Then I latched onto the slightest increase in light, my pupils shrinking in response to sunshine filtering through the foliage covering the opening ahead. I couldn't see what was beyond that, but one thing was certain. Johnno and Piggy were no longer in the cavern with us.

"I hope he hasn't done a runner!" Bev's voice was loud, bouncing off the walls and battering us from all angles. The echoes were in their death throes when we heard a sibilant, "Shut the fuck up!" from the other side of the green curtain. Our guide was still with us. Maybe because Bev had his share of the bacon?

The closer we got to the exit, the faster the three of us walked, no longer bothering to slide our feet along the ground as we had been. If Johnno was worried about us making noise, then our escape wasn't a fait accompli. For all we knew, those pursuing us could have flashlights.

The pain of a stubbed toe registered only as I slammed into the floor of the cave, winding myself. Stunned, I knew my fall hadn't been quiet, and neither was my desperate fight to get air into my lungs. I was still struggling to breathe when Johnno man-handled me off the ground, slung me over his shoulder, and jogged for the exit, with Bev and Ange in tow.

The one positive from the rough handling was that I got more air back in my lungs. However, I came close to losing the bacon when I saw how close my face was to Johnno's gore-encrusted back. Before I got a chance, he dumped me next to the pig he'd abandoned to come back and grab me.

We were outside the cave on a ledge that was a couple of yards wide. Beyond that, it was a sea of treetops and open sky, with an uninterrupted view of the coastline in the distance. If the ledge were wider, someone would have built a holiday home on it by now. One with what would be million-dollar views.

Helped back to my feet, I was no more prepared now than I had been in the cave earlier. I focused on Johnno taking the frying pan from Bev, with this helping me keep my balance. He gobbled down the last two rashers of bacon and then sent the pan out into the open like a cast-iron Frisbee.

A very porcine squealing radiated from far below us. With Johnno in their midst, the local pig population didn't stand a chance. His latest victim hoisted back over his shoulders, he bolted up the track, all the while pulling its makeshift shoulder straps into place.

Bev and Ange took off after him, but soon appreciated I was stuck where I was. With standing a challenge, there wasn't a hope in hell I could keep up with them. My chances of sticking to the track weren't good.

Swaying, I was a couple of steps away from the edge, a couple of steps from oblivion and the horrors facing me. It would be so easy, so simple, and so peaceful. Even my life back in Auckland sucked. No friends, only frenemies. Barren. No love life, no backbone, and fat.

I'd committed to a leap of faith when Bev shattered my dark reverie. Grabbing my shoulders, she spun me away from the drop-off and bent in front of me, with my world view soon turned on its head. Yet again, she showed me how strong she was. Reverse our positions and I'd never have been able to return the favor.

What followed was a stomach-churning forced march along the track that skirted the cliff face. One I'd never have managed without Bev's intervention. If I'd had my way, it would all be over now, barring the memorial service, the wild pigs voiding the need for an actual burial.

On reaching the safety of the bush, the unmistakable sounds of a dead pig hitting the dirt met us. This at least showed us we could rest, with me soon enough snuggling up to the carcass.

"Why can't this useless bitch walk?" Johnno looked down at me with a level of disgust previously reserved for my late husband. It was enough to once again have me looking longingly at the drop off.

20

If Ange was worried about losing our guide, she hid it well, getting right up in Johnno's face. "Because those monsters at The Vale raped, tortured and starved her for two weeks, that's why, you prick."

Johnno's eyes widened as he continued to look at me. "You're shitting me? I thought you were on the run so you could go grab some takeaways?"

Bev's expression as she looked at him had 'YOU MUPPET' writ large across it. "I wasn't serious when I said that last night."

Johnno opened his mouth but then closed it again, as if unable to come up with the right response, opting instead for safer territory. "We need to keep moving if we want to stay ahead of those dickheads."

He'd then stared through the bush at the track that bisected the cliff face all the way back to the cave. While his stance was relaxed, he appeared alert for signs of anyone exiting the trail of vines that concealed it.

It was obvious the second he saw something. This had me doing my best to clamber onto my hands and knees in readiness to stand. I didn't get a chance, with him grabbing me from behind and swinging me to my feet so fast I came close to blacking out. I was still swaying when he hooked my hands around his neck and said, "Climb on."

Much as I wanted to escape, I recoiled at being up close and personal with that much blood, gore, and a sweaty bloke. I was still dithering when Bev shoved him out of the way. "I'll take her. You grab the pig." It was with indescribable gratitude that I struggled up onto her back.

Johnno's relief at not having to abandon Piggy was funny, but my smirk disappeared when I saw six guys in army fatigues jogging in sync along the cliff track. With rifles at the ready, I felt a lot like Piggy must have yesterday when Johnno was stalking her through the bush.

Of more concern was where the rest of the guys were that we'd seen spewing out of the Sleeping Beauty Suites the night before. There had to be at least as many others around somewhere. Did we risk running into them coming from the other direction?

Right then, though, the chief concern was those we could see, and Johnno wasted no time in setting off again. Not far along, the track split, and he forked left, then right, and a couple more lefts. Everyone with their feet on the ground had been sticking to the side of the track, allowing the leaf litter to absorb footprints. Ange, who was at the back, was even dragging a dead palm frond behind her, obliterating any unwanted evidence.

Without warning, Johnno took a hard right, walking into the bush itself. But it was an illusion. While the main track led straight on, we were traveling down an offshoot. It was one so little used that unless you knew about it, you'd never see it. On looking back, I saw Ange stomping up the track for a bit to create a false trail. She then cut the corner, joining up with us again.

She shrugged at my look of enquiry. "I saw it in a movie once."

This time I smiled, even if it was lackluster.

I wasn't sure how far we'd gone when I came to with a start, horrified to find I'd been drooling. "Oh, I'm so sorry." I dabbed at Bev's shoulder, but all I got in response was a grunt. "You can put me down now."

She didn't, nor did she slow until Johnno did. At the first glimpse of the hut through the foliage, my relief was immense.

Any luck and there'd be beds and food on offer.

"Welcome to Hemi's place. It's crap, but better than ..." Johnno's words petered out. "Forget that. It's just crap, but we can rest here for the night."

Night?

I guess it had to happen, but it'd still snuck up on me. Bev lowered me to my feet, not letting go until I'd steadied myself. "You need food, but not too much, or you'll be sick," she said.

There was no need to answer. My stomach did it for me, lending truth to her words even if I didn't feel hungry in the slightest. By rights, even the pig should look good, and with my appetite of old, you could have put an apple in its mouth, and I'd be gnawing on its ass by now.

I took in the small hut in front of me. What was it about people in this part of the world building stuff out of corrugated iron? Ramshackle it might be, but the perfect place to crash for the night when out hunting for a couple of days, or even if being hunted, yourself.

Johnno wasted no time getting stuck into the carcass with that lethal knife of his, with any ideas I had about eating running for cover. Moments later, Piggy was missing part of a shoulder strap.

Johnno wiped his knife clean by running it across the leg of his jeans, first on one side and then the other, leaving tram-tracks of blood in evidence. "Hell, lady, sit down before you fall down, will ya? There's a bed of sorts in the hut."

The scent of roast pork cut through my nightmare, unleashing me from my bed in the Sleeping Beauty Suites. It also shattered the image of Lance driving himself into me at the behest of a jerk glued to a laptop. The one thing worse than being able to see him was when I couldn't, his sweat dripping on my back.

It'd be a good long time before I had sex again, if ever. I was quaking at memories of Lance and Piers shuddering all those times, when the aroma of pork became too strong to ignore. Only then was I freed from the remnants of my nightmare.

Even rested, I took my time getting to my feet, with my

blood-sugar level doubtless deserving of a 5-star rating. However, it wasn't so low that roast pork was appealing, and especially not after having seen it in its raw state earlier.

Imagine my relief on sitting next to the fire and Ange handing me a bowl of porridge. "You can start with that and see how your tummy copes with it."

The porridge was lumpy, and there wasn't any cream. It did, however, have a thick crust of sugar coating the surface. It was about as unappealing as food could get, but I knew I needed to eat something if I was keeping up with the others tomorrow.

I dipped the battered camping spoon into the gloop and tasted it, ready for more cardboard. It was better than I'd expected, if you didn't count the ants.

After ingesting a couple, I tilted my bowl to the firelight and picked them free of the sugar, flicking them off into the undergrowth.

The others chewed on roast pork while I worked my way through the porridge, with this as nectar now that my taste buds had reawakened. In between mouthfuls, we brought Johnno up to speed on what'd been happening at The Vale.

It was a relief that I didn't have to recount my own experiences, with us instead sticking to being drugged and finding the bodies in the bush.

"But that's my land. They can't kill people on my land."

"Your land?"

I asked this in tandem with Ange and Bev, our skepticism obvious to even the most obtuse.

Johnno had to finish a mouthful of pork before he could

respond. "Hey, I pay tax, which makes it mine as much as the next blokes."

Bev put a voice to the very question I had been thinking about myself. "We were on government land? You had a hunting permit, right?"

Johnno shrugged, with this answer enough. Could this be why he was hunting only using a knife and feral cunning? A quick glance at the butchered pig didn't show any bullet holes. I was no closer to a decision when I heard rustling from the bushes on the other side of the clearing.

"Hah! They'll run outta chicken at KFC before that one forks out for a license." This rejoinder, booming out from the dark of the bush, elicited cries of alarm from all but Johnno. He was relaxed, as though he had been expecting someone, unlike Ange and Bev, who were holding up lumps of unburned firewood. They looked ready to deck anyone who so much as looked at them funny.

After lots of crashing, hacking, and foul language, a mountain of a man stumbled into the clearing. A smaller bloke then wandered through the wide swathe created by his mate. Without preamble, the big man threw himself down next to the fire. "Name's Hemi," said the new arrival from his position beside me.

When he relaxed into his pose, his gut flopped out from under his worn bush singlet and spilled onto the ground with a soft wobble. When he leaned forward to snag himself a hunk of roast pork, the armhole of his singlet gaped, leaving me feeling more flat-chested than ever.

His companion couldn't be more different. He'd squeezed himself in between Bev and Ange, showing he wasn't so little after all, just small compared to Hemi.

"What's this about people being killed around here? Name's Horse, by the way."

It was all I could do not to spit my mouthful of porridge back into the bowl. What he'd done to deserve that nickname, who knew, but I decided I'd rather not know.

After introducing ourselves, we repeated what'd been going on at The Vale for the benefit of Hemi and Horse, with each retelling making it sound even more unbelievable. Again, I kept quiet about my starring role in the pay-per-view side of the operation. I doubt I'd ever be ready to share details of that, unless it was with a professional.

"The blokes chasing you have made themselves at home down at South Junction Hut," said Hemi, around a greasy mouthful of pork. I checked to see how Ange and Bev reacted to this before putting a voice to my major concern. "How many were there?"

Horse looked off into the middle distance as he thought back about their earlier encounter. "Around half-a-dozen, I guess. A couple of scrawny blokes and four or five big mothers."

"Hah!" burst out Hemi. "They were all scrawny so far as I'm concerned."

I looked at Bev to see that she, too, was carrying out some mental arithmetic. She had another slurp of her tea before speaking. "Better keep your eyes peeled. When we took off, there were at least a dozen, maybe more, of those jerk wads on our tail."

"That many! Fuck me."

Despite Johnno's sentiment being crass, I couldn't help but share it. Hemi pushed himself into a sitting position and cut another slice of meat, uncaring that there were bristles still sticking out in places. "Any luck and the lot we saw will get lost in the tracks down that way. Place is a rabbit's warren unless you know your way around."

"Still, I wish we'd known what those bastards were up to when we were passing. We could have made sure they got lost." Horse chomped on a large piece of pork, with any further words or clarification on what he meant by lost, disappearing with the mouthful.

Johnno looked at Horse as if for the first time, a huge grin splitting his face. "Sheesh mate, what's with the clobber? You look like the center-spread in a Hunting & Fishing catalog!"

Only then did I notice everything Horse was wearing appeared to be brand new, to the point there were still creases down the front of his shirt. Likewise, his khaki trousers sported creases at regular intervals from where they'd been sitting on a shelf.

"Yeah, yeah. Whatever, knucklehead. Sharon bitched about me having my hunting stuff at the apartment, so I had to hire a storage unit. When Hemi invited me along, I ripped the effing thing to bits and couldn't find anything, just a shitload of her dodgy online purchases. Reckon she snuck in there when I was down in Wellington for a meeting and biffed the lot."

He ripped a mouthful of meat from the hunk he was holding and chewed on it while still spitting out. "Not keen on me hunting."

Of interest was he looked at Johnno when he said this, giving me the impression Sharon was okay with Horse going hunting, just not with Johnno.

Johnno laughed hard. "Man, she's got you under her thumb. I said this would happen when you got yourself all educated and moved to the city. Never thought I'd see the day when that Missus of yours domesticated you."

Hemi likewise looked across at his fashion plate hunting buddy. "Hunting & Fishing catalog. Yep, he's pegged you, mate." His deep laughter filled the clearing, his eyes twinkling in the firelight, and I couldn't help but smile. There was something infectious about his mirth.

Johnno threw a bit of something he couldn't chew into the fire before looking at Bev, Ange, and then me. "We'll get you lot back out to town tomorrow."

Bev sat tall, her arms crossed tight. "We can't leave yet."

"Not without Tee," affirmed Ange.

Oh, no. Wallowing in my misery, I'd forgotten about Tee. "They're right. We can't leave her behind. She'll be in danger because we've done a runner."

Thoughts of Tee being tortured flooded my mind, ridding me of what appetite I had. I doubted I could force even a sliver of pork down now. However, I knew I'd need every bit of strength I could garner tomorrow. This had me pulling an enormous piece of meat from the bone and stashing it in my bowl for later.

"Could be fun," said Johnno, looking at no one in particular.

Hemi nodded. "Yeah, I'm in." Unable to speak, Horse waved a half-eaten slab of pork around, confirming he was up for it.

"Great, we should leave at first light," said Ange, channeling her inner girl guide again.

Hemi threw the bone he'd been gnawing on deep into the bush and got to his feet with astonishing ease. "No fucking way. We leave now!" Despite what amounted to a direct order, I stayed where I was, holding tight to my bowl of pork and porridge, like a culinary security blanket of sorts. It wasn't one I got to enjoy for long.

Hemi shoved enormous hands in my armpits, lifting me before I could even yelp. The heat from the food seeping through my now-filthy surgical scrubs reassured me I had dropped none of my stash. Although hard up against my chest, if I moved, I'd lose everything. This saw me leaning forward until I felt the food drop back into the bowl, before straightening and awaiting further instructions from Hemi.

The large man moved around the campsite with every action measured. There was no wasted energy, as though he'd rehearsed for this very thing. After rattling around in the hut, he rejoined us, carrying a small ax, a machete, and a cricket bat, which he dumped on the ground next to the fire. "Ladies, choose your weapons."

A chortle escaped me, morphing into high-pitched laughter that continued until Ange slapped me hard, shocking a final hyena impression from me in a gurgled choke.

"Sorry, love, I needed to stop that in its tracks." She rubbed my face to relieve the sting before picking up the small ax with obvious disgust.

The upside of my minor case of hysterics was that it left me holding the cricket bat. No chance of self-harm with that, unless I clobbered myself.

"Right, are we all good to go?" While Hemi addressed everyone standing around the campfire, he focused on Bev, Ange, and me. I tried to nod as emphatically as the other two, but I'd have preferred to stay here than head back to The Vale.

I only knew I'd passed muster when Hemi pulled a machete from the sheath on his leg and flipped it up in the air. He then caught it again without the loss of any fingers. "Let's go have us a little fun."

A little fun? I peered at the machete Hemi was twirling like a juggling baton and doubted being on the receiving end of it would be a giggle. Sure, the blade might be in awful shape and dotted with rust, but with Hemi's brute strength behind it, that wouldn't matter.

I checked to see if Bev and Ange looked concerned that things might get to that point. They didn't appear worried, though, other than with our situation. They remained stoic even when Horse put his hand over his shoulder and retrieved a machete that looked to be as sharp as Hemi's, was blunt.

The weapon's pristine condition identified it as another

recent purchase. New or old, I didn't know if the men's weaponry made me feel safer or not. Were things going to be hairy enough that they'd need to use their playthings?

I hadn't decided when Hemi doused the fire, doubtless in the same way as countless times before, filling the campsite with a whiff of long-neglected public toilets. Plunged into darkness, I was blind to my surroundings. Eventually, though, my sight adjusted to the filtered moonlight sneaking through the treetops, revealing Bev and Ange were standing stock-still, too.

Meanwhile, the men were moving around as though it was midday and not the dead of night. I had always heard Puha, that leafy green the Maori were so keen on eating, was great for night vision. It looked like it worked even better than British carrots, although wasn't that story put about to hide the fact the British had invented radar?

21

We didn't leave the campsite the same way we'd arrived, or indeed via the route used by Hemi and Horse. Instead, we filed around the side of the hut and along another pig track into the dark bush.

Hemi was in the lead. I was behind him, followed by Bev, Ange, and Horse. Johnno—and what remained of Piggy—played Tail End Charlie.

Even with porridge on board, I couldn't keep up with Hemi. This proved beyond all doubt that there was a lot of muscle holding any fat in place.

Aware I was no longer right behind him, he stopped, and I stumbled along, hampered by my bowl and the cricket bat. Eventually, though, I caught up with him.

"Lady, you gonna hold us up all night?"

Unable to see his face and given his neutral tone, I didn't

know if he was angry or not. Before I could plan a response, Bev got stuck into him, reminding him of what we'd been through, before hinting at my own personal hell.

"Why didn't ya say?" Hemi grabbed the cricket bat, turned his back to me, and squatted down. "On ya get."

This time I didn't quibble about manly odors, and it helped that his singlet, while old, smelled of soap and sunshine. I clambered onto his enormous back as best I could, my legs sticking out to the sides like a three-year-old playing horsey with their dad.

I shoved the bowl against my chest and held it in place by leaning into his back. I couldn't get my arms around his neck all the way, having to make do with hanging onto his shoulders.

I squawked when his hands, together with the cricket bat, slid under my backside like a makeshift seat. I kept quiet after that, knowing that I needed his support.

To my tired eyes, our journey through the bush had a surreal Edward and Bella quality to it. There was no way I could have kept pace with the speed now being set by Hemi. The one thing slowing him was my out-spread feet getting caught in creepers or whacking into trees. Soon enough, I tucked them back under the cricket bat.

Not fifteen minutes had passed when Hemi stopped with a jerk, as though he had hit a wall of sorts. He then removed the cricket bat and squatted down, allowing me to slide to the ground. I was quick to take the bat from him, feeling safer holding it.

Conscious of the bowl of food still jammed against my

chest, I bent forward, allowing the contents to settle. We had been standing in the small clearing for a couple of minutes before the sound of the others came from the deathly quiet of the bush.

Despite not being able to see their faces clearly in the half light, I knew Angie and Bev were suffering, their labored breathing proof of this.

"We've got another five minutes before we get there." Hemi's voice was low. "We'd better rest up and eat some more tucker before we go in."

I tapped the small bowl against my chest before jabbing it in Angie and Bev's direction. "But us three... We're staying in the bush, aren't we?" Even being this close to The Vale was doing weird things to my stomach. There wasn't a chance I wanted to face Chalky and revisit the site of my torture and potential hysterectomy again, even if armed with a nice slab of willow.

Horse snorted. "You'll be safer in there than out here." If his ominous tone wasn't enough, his staring into the dark bush convinced me.

Hemi then joined his mate in staring out into the bush, head cocked to the side, listening out. A quick jerk of his head, and I knew he had picked up on the same thing as Horse.

"Is it them?" I had no trouble keeping my voice down, my throat constricted with fear.

Rather than answer, Hemi continued to stare into the bush, the narrowing of his eyes just visible in the moonlight. Despite having only just met the guy, I glued myself to his side, his innate strength drawing me like a magnet.

Likewise, Ange and Bev had crowded next to Horse, Johnno, and even Piggy, with our group now taking up far less square footage than a minute earlier.

I found myself mouth-breathing in the technique of childhood games of hide-and-seek to make myself as quiet as possible. The others followed suit, the ensuing hush smothering us with a quiet rarely found in nature.

"Screw this," hissed Johnno. "I'm not staying here and dealing with those crazy bastards." Without pause, he pitched Piggy into the nearest clump of ferns. "Let's get the fuck outta here."

He was then off up the track at a speed even Hemi would be hard-pressed to match, with Ange, Bev, and Horse following suit. However, Johnno hadn't gone far when he took a hard left into the bush and disappeared, with the others right behind him.

Hemi didn't need to invite me to climb on his back this time around. After tossing the cricket bat in his direction, I flung my bowl into the bush next to Piggy and clambered on. Hemi proved me wrong in my assertion he wouldn't be able to keep up with the others, with those stalking us doubtless proving an accelerant.

When he plunged into the bush as the others had done, I again tucked my feet out of the way and planted my face against his broad back. This had me avoiding the worst of the branches and ferns slapping at us. If they were bothering Hemi, it didn't show with him not slowing. As to our destination, only the men knew this, but I'd trust them over anyone connected to

The Vale.

And better we faced those guys when we could hide behind something that could stop bullets. Out in the bush, they could pick us off as easily as fish in a barrel.

As tempting as it was, I didn't check behind to see if we were still being followed. I didn't want to know, figuring if I couldn't see them, then they didn't exist. And yes, it was childish, but I was hanging on by a thread here.

It was a surprise when we burst into the open, the moonlight bright after the dark of the bush. Rather than stop, we kept going, crossing an expanse of hard scrabble, our goal a dark, windowless lump of a building.

Soon enough, we were around the back and hidden from anyone following us. While not the greatest hiding spot in the world, it would do for now. It was only after sliding off Hemi's back that I discovered my legs would no longer support me, and I dropped to the ground in a boneless heap.

I'd rather be anywhere than back here, with the memories of what happened already threatening to overwhelm.

Bev dropped to her knees beside me, jamming her machete into the soft ground. "Are you okay, Marilyn?"

Ange hunkered on my other side, taking my pulse and fussing about how fast it was. It didn't even feel good to me, despite my being carried here.

"I'm fine. I just want to get away from this place." It was only now that I took proper notice of the bunker next to us. "Where are we?" It wasn't the building Ange and Bev had rescued me from. This had me wondering if it was part of the old military facility. "Are we still on the other side of the fence?"

I hadn't addressed my question to anyone in particular, but it was Johnno who jerked his head toward the bush. "Nah, we're just further around from where you lot crashed into me. Fence only goes so far."

Even with this lack of an obstacle, it was a good thing we hadn't waited until the morning. If we'd exploded out of the bush like we had, there'd have been a welcoming committee.

After scrabbling along the ground on my hands and knees, I peeked around the far end of the building. This revealed a familiar parking lot and gravel driveway. The merest glance at the Sleeping Beauty Suites and a shudder skittered up my spine. I didn't want to be back here.

The only thing in our favor was that there weren't any signs of life. Where were all the mercenaries? If they'd been close enough to us in the bush that Hemi and Horse could hear them, shouldn't they be back here by now?

It must be something Angie was wondering about, too, with her soon peering around the corner. She then dropped back next to me and whispered, "Should we be sitting out here like this?"

This had me nodding toward the bush before hissing. "I am not going back in there, not with armed crazies in the mix." I then settled back against the bunker, as if to reinforce my stance.

Ange settled next to me, chopping a crisscross pattern in the grass with her small ax. "What happens now?"

"We're not doing anything until we've got a plan." Bev's tone, while quiet, had a ring of authority to it. Enough that even Hemi, the alpha male, nodded in agreement.

"We need to check the lower buildings first. See if we can find Tee." Bev yanked her machete free from the dirt and firmed up her grip. "Damn, I wish I still had my frying pan. I hate sharp things." She looked at Johnno, accusation alight in her eyes.

He shrugged as if this absolved him of all responsibilities. "How was I supposed to know ya were decking people with it?"

"Is there a kitchen?" said Horse.

Ange again peeked around the corner, this time pointing to the third door along with her ax. "In there."

"Back in a mo."

Horse didn't make a sound as he crossed the open area. Perhaps it was because he wasn't wearing boots, something I hadn't noticed earlier. Or was it he'd ditched them somewhere along the way? As new as they likely were, perhaps they were squeaking, or causing blisters? His movements were fluid, silent, and blended with the shadows, a Rorschach quality to them. As hackneyed as it sounded, I blinked, and he was gone.

"Will he be long?" Bev again looked at her machete, as if deciding whether waiting was her best option.

"Nope." Johnno threw himself down on the ground. He then reclined and supported his head with his hands, making a lie of the assertion his mate would be quick about it.

Should I be as relaxed as he, Hemi, and Horse appeared to be? I knew what we were facing, and they didn't. Perhaps it was that they were confident in their abilities to beat the crap out of anyone we encountered? I sure hoped so.

I'd come to no conclusions when a Jamie Oliver non-stick frying pan and a rolling pin landed in front of me. I was pondering the choice when Ange buried her small ax in the dirt and helped herself to the rolling pin. "I'll take this. I don't even like scalpels."

Meantime, Bev grabbed the frying pan. "Hmm, it's not cast iron, but if I brain anyone, at least they won't stick." She twirled the large pan by the handle. "And it's easier to swing."

It made me happy to still have the bat. I was on the cricket team in high school but got straight Ds in cooking. This had me much more at ease with the heft and shape of the slab of willow.

I forgot my weapon of choice when Horse dropped a bulging plastic bag of bread rolls and a large jar of peanut butter in front of us. For the first time in a couple of days, I found myself ravenous.

The rolls were fresh and possessed enough gluten to shut down some inner-city suburbs. Combined with the sticky, fatty goodness of the peanut butter, it was ambrosia after all those weeks of nothing but kale and chocolate shakes.

There was nothing sophisticated about our repast. We ripped the rolls open and spread the peanut butter using a dirty hunting knife. While this would have disgusted me in the past, the speed with which I devoured the first roll said I was way beyond that.

A second followed straightaway, leaving me replete and

fuller than I had been in a long time. Before this, hunger was my constant companion, no matter how much food I threw at it.

"Bev, what's this plan of yours?" Hemi raised an eyebrow, challenging her to come up with the goods after she'd quashed his idea of smacking some heads together and having fun.

Bev waited until she had everyone's attention before outlining a plan that was no frills in the extreme. "We find Tee and anyone else still around, and then we get out of here."

Hemi opened his mouth, closed it, then said, "And if we run into any of those murderous pricks? What then?"

It was Ange who answered, not Bev. "Avoid them. Otherwise, we're no better than they are."

Johnno and Hemi snorted, with even Horse struggling to maintain a straight face. My having seen the enemy up close, I was feeling less than charitable about their welfare. I wouldn't mind if some of them got hurt.

After this thought skipped across my brain, I realized that none of the guys owned a firearm. What good were knives against what I believed were automatic weapons? Not much in my limited experience of being forced to sit through action movies by David.

I waved to get Horse's attention, not wanting to call out to him. He was standing apart, and so I had to wait until he moved closer before I could speak.

"Apart from kitchen stuff, did you see any guns when you were in there?" Despite Ange shying away from violence, my preference was to be armed to the teeth.

"Yeah, stacks, but we don't need them."

Bev's head popped up, and she unclasped the frying pan from her chest. "I wouldn't mind one. Stainless steel is okay, but it's better when it's backed up by lead."

"Not for me," said Ange, slapping the rolling pin against the palm of her free hand.

Horse shrugged in response. "Too late. I fucked any I could find."

"I wondered why you took so sodding long," said Johnno, who was prone again, his head supported by his crossed arms.

Bev shook her head before glaring at Horse. "We could have used those against them. I suppose you removed the firing pins?"

"Nah, too obvious. Funnier, to watch them try to shoot us and have the guns blow up in their faces."

Hemi and Johnno chortled at this, as did Bev. Not in on the joke, Ange and I looked at each other, and then the others, as if hoping for clarification.

"I think he means he stuffed the barrels on every gun he could find." Bev looked at Horse and got a brief nod in response.

"Besides, guns make you too much of a target," said Hemi. "Knives are quiet. Hell, even frying pans and cricket bats are quieter than guns."

It was him saying this that had me realizing I might have to hit someone with the piece of willow I was stroking. I didn't know if I had it in me unless I ran into Lance.

If I did, he was going to be getting the first Gray-Nicoll-sponsored castration in the world's history. There was also a boundary shot with Chalky's name on it. It would be nice to see her with an expression for once.

Hemi signaled our break was done when he over-armed the remains of the peanut butter deep into the bush. "Let's go mess 'em up."

He didn't biff the empty plastic bag into the undergrowth as I'd expected. Rather, he scrunched it up and shoved it deep in the front pocket of his faded jeans.

After gaining my feet, I swung the cricket bat around, getting a sense of its weight, and striking out at imaginary balls and foes alike. It felt good in my hands, and I wondered why I'd given up the game I loved so much all those years ago. That's right, David said it wasn't feminine.

Perfect! Any baddies I ran across, I'd think of David and how I let him screw me over. I'd have no trouble hitting them for a six after that.

Who knew? I might even enjoy it.

22

Progress to the bottom of the property was slow, with Horse, the stealthiest among us, out in front. We dashed from hiding spot to hiding spot, waiting for a nod from him before proceeding. If it had been the daytime, we would have looked like idiots, but under cover of darkness, we were furtive enough.

These maneuvers were pointless or successful because we didn't run into anyone. Was it that the men were right, and the mercenaries had settled for a night in the bush, or was it they'd gotten lost? Both options worked for me.

Just as conspicuous by her absence was Chalky, with the place a spa equivalent of the Mary Celeste. It was then we heard furniture-rattling snoring emanating from Tee's room, and relief flooded me she was okay. However, her being snuggled up and unaware of the hell that had descended on the place soon had annoyance replacing this.

Bev was about to open the door when it became apparent there was more than one set of snoring. In silent agreement, we snuck back down the stairs, not daring to speak until we'd skulked around the bathroom end of the building.

"Might be Lance, fallen asleep on the job," said Bev, before slapping her hand over her mouth, as if unable to believe what she'd just said.

Crap! I hadn't thought of him.

"Won't he still be out in the bush with the others?" Ange gestured wildly with her rolling pin toward the tree line, only just missing Johnno's head.

I thought about it for a second. No, I just couldn't see it being Lance. I wasn't sure why. "Maybe it's the kitchen crew in a food-for-favors kinda deal." The images that then popped up unbidden weren't pretty. It wouldn't be something I'd consider, but Tee loved her food.

"Wonder if she's gone for the two-for-one offer?" This time there was no mistaking the laughter behind Bev's hand, with Ange and me soon joining in. It wasn't something I'd normally laugh about, but after the last couple of weeks, it was a relief.

"What if Anton's in there, too?" snorted out Bev.

This time Ange and I were powerless to stifle our laughter, although we tried. Not until I had myself under control was I able to answer. "Not gonna happen."

Ange backed this up by shaking her head and crossing her

legs, her pelvic floor muscles no stronger now than earlier. Bev looked at us. "What do you mean?"

Before we could answer, Hemi held up his hand. "They friend, or foe?" His voice, while low, was loud in the relative quiet.

Not wanting to further disrupt the stillness of the night, I answered with a shrug. He then looked at Bev and Angie next, with them answering likewise.

We arrived back at the bottom of the front steps in time to see Horse disappearing through the now-open door. I hadn't even seen him move, let alone heard Tee's door open, with the guy more spectral than equine in his movements.

He exited a moment later without a murmur from those inside and held up three fingers. He then flattened his hand at waist height and bounced it up and down, confirming for Bev, Ange, and me it was the kitchen twins.

"They're on the staff here," I whispered, before looking toward the top of the property. "Not sure if they're in on everything else. I never spotted them up there." Calming my mind allowed me to think back, although I remained detached, to avoid the worst of the memories.

"Hang on, they must know about it, because one of them drugged the blasted coffee Chalky sucked me in with."

Horse nipped back inside the room without a sound, the other two men soon joining him. I wanted to go in too, to ease any fears Tee would have on waking to find three scary-looking men crowded around her bed. I was miming this to Bev and Ange when the guys returned.

Hemi and Johnno had a kitchen twin apiece, but the captives weren't offering any protest. Rather, they were out cold. At least I hoped they were only unconscious. Anything was possible if our saviors would go pig hunting without guns.

Hemi leaned over as he passed with his prisoner tucked under one meaty arm. "They'll be fine. Just gonna tie them up somewhere less obvious."

I took this at face value until Johnno's hushed crow of, "Yeah, sure we are."

The kitchen twins, on the way to their fate, I hustled into Tee's room to wake her so we could leave. Bev and Ange were with me, with us shutting the door after shooing Horse outside. If Tee was naked, as I suspected, she wouldn't want an audience.

Then again, there was no telling with Tee. If she'd screw that pair of weasels to get her hands on extra toast, there was no gauging what she'd stoop to.

We started by whispering her name, but all that happened was her snoring broke its rhythm before settling down again. A gentle prod resulted in more of the same.

After pulling the curtains tight, we turned on the bedside lamp, and Ange dropped on the bed next to Tee. "She shouldn't be this hard to wake. They must have drugged her."

Tee's pulse wasn't easy to find, with Ange having to ferret around in the rolls of neck fat for the carotid artery. I only knew she'd found it when she angled the bedside clock and her lips moved as she silently counted.

Eventually, she took her hand away and patted Tee on the

shoulder before looking up. "It's fast, but I'd expect that, given her overall health."

With Ange nursing Tee, I took time to open the closet door and have a rummage, soon finding what I was after. A neat stack of plastic-wrapped Vale uniforms which I helped myself to.

Despite weeks of being naked in front of others, after stepping carefully over the beam, I changed outfits in the bathroom. Tee's gear was too big, but this was still better than running around in surgical scrubs covered in porridge and pork fat. The black uniform would also help me blend into the night better than the bright green scrubs.

The other thing I'd noticed at the bottom of the closet was a couple of pairs of sneakers. Helping myself, I was relieved to find they fit okay. Tee had tiny feet for such a large woman.

I was fiddling with the waistband of the pants so they wouldn't fall down when I saw Bev pick up the jug of water off the dresser. However, she didn't grab the upside-down glass next to it.

I was as astonished as Ange when Bev marched across the room and sloshed the whole jug of water in Tee's face. It didn't work, other than to change the loud snoring to a muted gurgling.

"Goodness, Bev, a glass would have done." Ange turned Tee's head to the side, and an alarming amount of water trickled out of the unconscious woman's mouth. "Any more and I'd have had to give her mouth-to-mouth."

The water having failed, Bev put the empty jug on the

bedside table so she could give Tee a head-loosening shake. "What did they give her, a bloody horse tranquilizer?" She shook Tee even harder, to no avail.

"We'll have to leave her here." Much as I wanted to save Tee, the longer we mucked around, the more likely it was Chalky or her crew would discover us. "We can't move her when she's doped to the eyeballs like this. We need to hide her."

Both Ange and Bev looked around the room and its lack of hiding spots before looking back at me as though I'd misplaced my marbles.

"Some of the best hiding places I had when I was a kid were those that were so obvious, people didn't think to look. If we roll her off the side of the bed, we can jam her between it and the wall. Flip the blankets over the top of her. It'll look like she's climbed out of bed and left it like that."

This had Bev looking at me and then down the side of the bed, as if gauging if Tee would even fit, her then slowly nodding answer enough.

Ange also agreed with my rough-and-ready plan, although she had provisos. "We'll need to make sure she's on her side, given how heavily she's sedated."

Bev, already doing her best to shove Tee's dead weight across the bed, stopped for a short breather. "Plus, it'll stop her freaking snoring."

It took all three of us to manhandle her down the side of the bed, with her only just fitting. Ange said this was a good thing as it would make it impossible for Tee to roll onto her back and suffocate.

As Bev had suggested, she'd also stopped snoring, with us once again able to hear the cicadas outside. I don't think I'd ever heard someone snore that loudly. The last thing we did was flip the blankets back, hiding her from anyone glancing into the room.

On easing the door shut, I saw Horse was no longer outside. Either he'd morphed back into the bush or gone to join Johnno and Hemi at the top of the facility.

"Are you coming?" Ange waited for me on the bottom step. Bev was already a good way along the path.

"Not yet." If I could save myself the long walk into town, I would, then I was all for it.

"Where are you off to?" Bev hadn't lowered her voice, eliciting a "shhh" from Ange that was even louder.

"If my bag's still in my room, I can get my spare phone."

Thankfully, it wasn't too far from Tee's. Especially so with us cutting cross-country, like something out of a Pink Panther movie. We were lucky we didn't encounter anyone on our way, although we heard squealing and grunting from the general direction of the cliff. This had me shaking my head to clear it of images of the wild pigs making a meal out of our enemy.

Oh, the disappointment when, on opening the door of my room, I found my suitcase wasn't there. More than that, there wasn't any sign of me at all. They'd wiped me off the face of the earth, with the space given the full Mafia crime-scene treatment.

I doubted I'd find any trace of myself, even armed with Luminol and a UV light.

My heart sank. Never mind the high-end luggage and the phone, there were two family-sized blocks of best quality dark chocolate MIA.

"What the hell's got you all riled?" said Bev, from where she stood casually in the doorway. However, she wasn't looking at me, rather she was watching for any movement outside.

"She said something about her phone." There followed a sharp intake of breath as if Ange had just deciphered the rest of my mutterings. She grabbed me by the shoulders and spun me around. "What did you just say about chocolate?"

I nodded, not bothering to hide my enthusiasm. "Two bars. King size. Seventy percent." I twisted free of her hold and continued searching. If ever I needed a hit of sugar and cocoa, it was now.

"Chocolate!? Why didn't you say?" Bev gave up her lookout duties and stormed into the room, where she started to open and close every drawer and closet I'd just searched.

She was squinting into the dark of the bathroom, eyeing up the cabinet, when I grabbed her by the scruff of her Vale top and yanked her back. "It's not here! It was in the lining of my suitcase." I waited for a beat. "There's also a chance the beam that activates the light triggers an alarm."

This, more than me having a stranglehold on her top, rocked Bev back on her heels. "Those sneaky bastards. I always thought the fan in my bathroom sounded too much like a zoom lens."

Was she serious? As if anyone would be sick enough to pay to watch us using the bathroom. I shook my head to clear it of thoughts of what anyone spying on me in there would have seen. "It'll be because they wanted to see if we dumped that doped tea of theirs."

Bev tilted her head to the side before responding. "You sure about that, M?"

That couldn't be right, could it? How messed up would you have to be to pay to see people going ones or twos, or giving themselves an enema? I'd no sooner rid myself of thoughts of someone watching me pee when I remembered Pencil Dick paying to see Lance and Piers giving me a golden shower.

Really, who'd find that a turn on? I was giving thought to the target market when Ange's, "I bet I know where we can find your bag," had Bev and me looking at her.

"When we were scouting around up the top, I noticed a dumpster through a back window. They could have put your stuff in there."

Damn it. I didn't want to go anywhere near that part of the complex, preferring to leave the dirty work to the guys. If I had my way, I'd be driving the Hummer down the road now, at speed and to hell with the paintwork. Shame the vehicle hadn't been in the small parking lot behind the Sleeping Beauty Suites.

"Come on," said Bev. "If we can find your phone, we can call for help."

"And if we find your phone, we find the chocolate," said Ange, a goofy expression making itself at home.

About halfway to the scene of my torture, I came to my senses. "What about the tofu munchers? Are they okay?"

"Checked out a few days back," said Bev, over her shoulder.

"Yeah, there for the afternoon yoga session, but didn't make it to dinner that night," said Ange.

Bev stopped without warning, and Angie cannoned into her, with me thumping into both of them. "Chalky told us they were taking part in some meditation marathon." Bev's expression darkened, telling me she now saw this for the lie it had been.

"Crap." Ange swung around and retraced her steps, with Bev and me in hot pursuit.

There would be no argument from me about this change of direction. Even if the tofu munchers were less than friendly, there was no way I wouldn't check to see if they were okay.

And heading away from the Sleeping Beauty Suites, rather than toward them, was a bonus.

23

The silent vegans—the Megans—did indeed appear to have checked out, leaving an air of quiet emptiness despite them never having spoken. This remained true until we got to the third room, which was nestled in a duplex with the fourth.

Some mysterious force compelled me to drop to my hands and knees and look under the bed. Did I expect to find one of them in hiding? No. The bed was so close to the floor that, despite their slender frames, they couldn't possibly have fit underneath.

It wasn't a complete bust, though, with me stumbling upon something unexpected—contraband! As a discovery, it challenged my impression of the Megans as holier-than-thou.

Who would have imagined that vegan-friendly seaweed rice

crackers could be so delectable? Certainly not us, but after a tentative nibble, we swiftly devoured the entire pack.

There was only one room left to inspect. I tried the handle and pushed against the door. "Damn, I think it's locked." Turning the handle, the other way, proved equally futile. It seemed Chalky had a knack for locking doors when it suited her.

"Give me a go." Bev, with her superior strength, muscled in next to me, but our combined efforts yielded no results.

"Guys," said Ange, who was crouched next to us, attempting to peer under the door, "there's someone moving around inside."

After listing our options, Bev dropped to her hands and knees next to Ange, where she stuffed a gruff, "We're here to help" under the door like more contraband. She was as quick to promise, "We'll get you out in a jiffy."

I was worried we wouldn't be able to follow through on this, with the door too rock solid for us to smash through it. Solid enough, it might even prove a challenge for the guys if they were around.

Our only choice was to break the large front window.

"I'm on it." Without further explanation, Bev shot into the other room.

Ange, still peering through the window, questioned this. "Won't that be awfully loud?"

She was right, but we couldn't leave the woman stuck in there, waiting for those jerks to finish her.

Bev soon returned from the other room. She had a couple

of pillows tucked under one arm and was holding the drawer from the bedside table like a hard-sided suitcase. "The pillows should muffle the glass smashing and stop any shards from flying in our direction."

This had me down on my hands and knees next to the door, with the woman inside soon matching my stance. After I'd run through our plan, she moved swiftly, jumping to her feet and yanking the curtains closed as a barrier against flying glass.

After dishing out the pillows, Bev stood back, her drawer at the ready. Carrying it by the handle, she looked like a middle manager at a corporate retreat. If our current situation wasn't so dire, I'd usually have been in stitches by now.

But this, and her serious mien, as she looked first at Ange, then at me, squelched any nervous giggles. "Are we all good?"

The pillows mashed up against the glass, Ange and I were as ready as we'd ever be. This saw us keeping our hands clear of the imaginary target at the center of the square of Eiderdown and Egyptian cotton.

After turning my head to further protect my face, I nodded my readiness. Ange must have done the same because a dull thud soon followed, with the glass shuddering under my hands. But the window didn't break. Bev smacked it again, even harder, but the glass stubbornly refused to shatter.

"Screw this." Bev tossed the drawer into the bushes and grabbed a chair from the patio set. She checked its weight for suitability, signaling her readiness for another attempt.

Realizing the pillows wouldn't come close to silencing the impending racket, I dropped mine and moved away. In the realm of Bed, Bath & Beyond, I opted for the third option, retreating with Ange to a safe distance.

The unmistakable sounds of heavy-duty patio furniture colliding with even heavier-duty glass reverberated through the air. However, the expected tinkling of glass didn't follow.

"You have got to be bloody kidding me?" Bev followed this with several quick breaths before another resounding crash. Once again, the delicate sounds of tinkling glass were absent.

Upon stepping back onto the front porch, I saw the glass was still intact, despite large patches of white where the chair had connected. Bev, now holding the chair more like a baseball bat, took another mighty swing at the window, achieving the same results. "Damn. This could take a while."

After half-a-dozen more attempts, she was drooping, so Ange took over, boasting of tennis trophies in the past. "Ladies, stand back."

Even though she might have a mean backhand, it did her no good, with the window refusing to budge.

It was my turn, something that saw me taking a few practice swings with the cricket bat before I got stuck in. If the others hadn't softened up the window for me, I dreaded to think what damage I would have inflicted on my shoulder.

The glass, doubtless bulletproof, bruised my body with each impact, forcing me to slow down with subsequent whacks. It took the combined efforts of the three of us to create a hole large enough for the vegan to clamber through.

That she hugged each of us was a surprise, as all we'd ever

received from her and her friends were judgmental scowls. To be fair, given our teasing, I couldn't blame them.

"I thought you were them. Coming back for me."

"Where are the others?" I had a fair idea, but I could be wrong. Everything I'd eavesdropped on while locked up said the clients preferred their victims to be overweight.

The Megans were as far from that as you could get. Unless the Vale was branching out, with the thought enough to have me shuddering in revulsion. I then had another thought. One that chilled me to the bone.

Could those behind the Vale have targeted the Megans because they knew the jig was up? With the three of us having escaped, they had to know it was only a matter of time before the cops came calling.

The knowledge I might be behind this woman's friends being hurt, or worse, didn't sit well.

"I don't know where the others are. Weird sounds from Gemma's room woke me late last night, and then a man's voice. He sounded angry, so I got up to see if she was okay, but they'd locked my door. When I opened the curtains, I saw them carrying her away."

The woman's next words caught in her throat, and she had to gulp before carrying on. "She was limp, unconscious." A sob escaped her. "I've heard nothing since."

Ange, who was looking through the gap in the window, backed up and straightened. "You need to get out of here. Is there anything you want to take with you?"

"No. No, they took everything I own after the first week here. Said it was to purify my space."

"Assholes," muttered Bev from beside me.

I assessed the woman. She appeared to be in good shape. However, just because you could contort yourself into pretzels at yoga didn't mean you were up to walking into town. "Are you capable of getting out of here?"

Still curled in on herself and her misery, she looked up at me, her expression one of confusion. But then her eyes flared with a fierce determination, and she stood tall, her back ramrod straight. "If it means getting help for my friends, there's nothing I won't do."

True to her word, she sat on the now worse-for-wear wrought-iron seat, and tightened the laces on her running shoes. After zipping up her Vale-issue hoodie, she stretched in preparation.

Before she could start out, Bev put a hand on her shoulder. "You'll need to avoid the front gate when you leave. They'll have it alarmed."

Ange chimed in next. "Sneak into the bush. Dig under the fence. Exit down the road a bit. You should be okay."

At any other time, I'd have agreed with this course of action, but who knew how many mercenaries there were lurking in the bush? "Best if you get out of the bush as soon as you can. If you keep to the middle of the road, there'll be less chance of, ah, tripping."

"Pace yourself," said Ange. "The last thing you want to do is pull something."

"Yes, slow and steady will be your best bet," added Bev.

"I'll be fine. It'll be good to stretch my legs and get back to my training."

"Training?" Maybe my impression that she was whippet-fit was on the money.

"I average three or four marathons a year. The run into town will be nothing." And with that, she was off, the dark quickly embracing her, thanks to her all-black Vale ensemble. Soon, even the flashes from the reflective tape on her running shoes vanished into the night.

The Megan on her way to town, we nipped back into the adjoining room and grabbed a drink from the jug on the dresser. Not having as much sleep as I'd have liked over the past two days, the bed looked inviting, although not enough to tempt me.

What was it they said about resting when you were dead? Given how close I'd been to this state in recent days, even closing my eyes for a heartbeat had flashbacks threatening to claim me.

There also wasn't a chance we were using the bathroom, not if it might trigger an alarm. This saw us taking it in turns to pee in the bushes at the end of the unit. If I was facing who knew what, I'd rather do so with an empty bladder.

A final check on Tee and we assembled at the bottom of the steps.

"Let's go get that suitcase of yours, shall we?"

Ange tipped her head toward the top facility in invitation,

with even Bev appearing keen to get moving. No doubt motivated by the idea of two family-size blocks of chocolate.

I wasn't of the same mind as my friends. If I'd been capable, I would have jogged into town with the Megan. I'd even shoehorn myself in next to Tee if given the choice.

"Ah, well, I guess we should check Chalky's office first." It didn't take a couch and a chat with a counselor to know why I was opting for this. Anything was better than returning to the Sleeping Beauty Suites.

"Good idea. I'd like to get my handbag back if I can," said Ange.

Bev nodded her approval, and I aped her action. It would be fantastic to get hold of my pre-paid dummy phone, although chances of the battery having lasted this long were slim. Worth a shot, though.

We skirted around the shrubs and palms behind the admin building but then came up short. If the lights were on, the cold-hearted bitch must be in there, pawing through our handbags like a fat spider.

It was that, or she was running command central, keeping in constant contact with her private army out in the bush? With my finger to my lips for quiet, I snuck up next to the portable structure until I was right under the window by the sliding glass door. I eased up on tiptoes and craned my head to get an ear as close to the opening as I could.

It was pointless. I couldn't hear a thing over the cicadas. It was then I remembered how effective that triple glazing was at blocking their chirping when you were inside. It also had to be why Chalky hadn't heard us smashing in that window. After crouching back down, I turned to the others and shrugged.

Bev jerked her head toward the sliding door, backing this up by jabbing the lightweight frying pan repeatedly at it. Both women's eyes then widened, and they melted back into the bushes.

We had company.

This had me doing some melting of my own, first down onto my hands and knees, then under the hut with as much stealth as I could. There'd better not be any weta—a New Zealand native akin to a grasshopper on steroids—under here.

Even armed with the cricket bat, if I spotted one of those, I wouldn't stay hidden for long. The outside lights flared into life, turning the gravel area out front into an arena of sorts. It also made my hiding spot as good as useless. I soon threw any caution about spiders and their mates to the winds, slid the cricket bat under the steps, and shuffled in after it.

Now tucked in behind the wide wooden treads, I was invisible to anyone not on the lookout for me. It would have to do because the hut sat on a gentle rise, meaning there was no escape out the back way. At least not without an excavator.

Two pairs of feet landed with a thud on the step right in front of my face, and a squawk of alarm broke free. It wasn't loud, but audible. Sinking flat to the ground, I covered the pale wood of the cricket bat with my body and face-planted the dirt. I hoped that my dark hair and the black Vale uniform would have me blending into the gloom under the hut.

My breathing was now so shallow as to be non-existent.

The loudest thing was my heartbeat hammering away in my ears and threatening to deafen me. One of the pair was Chalky, identifiable by those clunky white ankle boots of hers. But who was with her? Only time would tell.

I waited.

They waited.

"Musta been a pig."

Lance!? Damn, if he was back, did that mean the other men had also returned?

"Either that, or one of those nasty possums."

My scalp pinged with a weird mix of fear at being so close to him and relief he was unaware of my presence. Lance's voice made my skin crawl far more than any weta could manage. I was about to lift my head when something stopped me.

Maybe it was because they hadn't moved since Lance spoke?

My heart pounded in my chest and adrenaline surged through my veins, my hands trembling uncontrollably. My every muscle was tense, ready to react at a moment's notice, even if I was unsure what I'd do if they discovered me.

I was glad I'd stayed put when Lance jumped up and down on the stairs right above my head. Dirt and detritus rained down on me, sticking to my hair and clothes, threatening to choke me.

But despite the overwhelming urge to flee, I stayed where I was, not daring to make a sound. As scared as I was, I couldn't have talked even if I wanted to.

It was a different story when an enormous possum thundered past me and out into the night. My scream, while short, was loud. They'd have heard it for sure. I face-planted the ground, trying my best to become one with the dirt, to blend, to hide in plain sight.

If I'd thought my scream, or Lance jumping up and down, were loud, they paled when compared to the boom of a shotgun going off directly overhead.

"Dammit, missed the little fucker."

"There'll be more, darling."

Darling? Chalky and Lance? Ew. The unmistakable sound of kissing followed. Gross! As if anyone would put their mouth near that man given the choice.

First chance I got, I was rearranging his gonads. Watch the nasty bitch try to ride him then. While my thoughts were down to bravado, they still had me feeling less the victim.

"Did you and the men find any trace of our escapees in the bush?"

"Yeah, but that's all."

"But the team has their instructions, right?"

"Yep, stick to the bush. Kill the lot of them and leave their stinking carcasses for the pigs. That work for you?"

"Excellent. We've come too far for them to mess things up now. It was annoying to have to move forward with our other project before we were ready."

The stairs creaked under their combined weight as they walked down them, pausing at the bottom to swap some more spit. As if this wasn't disgusting enough, Chalky fumbled with the front of Lance's jeans.

I was closing my eyes to block out this travesty when she spoke. "Come now, Lance, we'll need to get you harder than this to satisfy the new client's request."

I was still gagging at thoughts of Chalky being the chief fluffer when they started up the boardwalk toward the Sleeping Beauty Suites. A quick shifty at them, arm in arm, endorsed that they were the ugliest beast with two backs you'd ever laid eyes on.

Only when I knew they weren't coming back did I throw my cricket bat out into the open and wriggle after it. Angie and Bev joined me before I'd stood.

Being back inside the admin building was doing my head in, my scalp crawling as I thought back on signing my life away with that damned contract. Everything looked as it had the morning Chalky had me over for coffee and kidnap, except my Hermès handbag now sat on the credenza behind her office chair.

After slamming my cricket bat down on her glass desk, I reclaimed my handbag, worried to find it was a lot lighter than when she'd taken it off me. Given what I now knew about her, it was a relief to find my wallet tucked inside. I opened it, expecting to find it empty. It wasn't. Instead, the botoxed, expressionless cow stared back at me from my own damned driving license.

It took me a second to get up the nerve to unzip the internal pocket and shove my hand deep inside. Sure enough, when I opened my passport, her resting bitch face sat next to my details.

The she-devil was making use of my identity and, doubtless, my bank balance. Thank goodness the bulk of my funds were now safely offshore. At least I hoped this was still so. I was unaware of muttering under my breath until Bev spoke.

"What's got you so riled?" She didn't look in my direction. She was too busy for that. With her frying pan dumped on one of the visitor's chairs, she was pressing each wall panel at the end of the small room. She was thorough too, taking the time to push the corner of each panel and then the middle.

I stopped searching my handbag for anything else with Chalky's name or mugshot on it. "That skinny excuse of a woman has been using my bag, and even my freaking identity!" I waited for her to look in my direction, but her focus on the wall panels was laser-like. "Ah, Bev, what are you hoping to find over there? It's the end wall."

Finally, she turned in my direction. "When we were hiding in the bushes, I noticed the windows don't go right to the corner, and yet they do in here. That means there's a cavity behind this wall."

Ange, who was next to me, slammed her rolling pin down on the credenza, doing a fair amount of damage. While she might be squeamish about hurting people, there appeared to be no holding her back with furniture. Kneeling in front of Chalky's desk, she opened the top left-hand drawer and started riffling through the contents.

I'd join them in their searches, but I was back checking my handbag to see what else Chalky had appropriated. Frustrated, I upended the contents onto the glass-topped desk, making a hell of a racket and eliciting profanities from both Ange and Bev.

The last item to drop free was the bottle of beta-blockers from the surgeon. Strange, but after experiencing what I had, I was no longer concerned about side-effects, or how long they'd take to work. However, the merest shake of the bottle was enough to remind me how big the capsules were.

I'd never swallow them dry, and was therefore relieved to see there was a carafe of water and a glass sitting on the reception desk. I was about to go help myself when I had second thoughts.

What if they'd drugged the water? The memories of how helpless I'd felt when I'd slid off the seat in Chalky's office had me staying put.

As soon as I found a clean source of water, I'd start the course of beta-blockers. Meanwhile, I returned to flicking through the assortment from my handbag. Everything was there, except for my dummy but still operational phone, and the vintage Rolex that was my dad's. This last hurt more than anything else because it was irreplaceable.

After gutting my wallet of Chalky's paperwork, I stuffed everything back in my handbag. Then I paused. What if some papers were hers and not just mine reimagined? This had me shoving all of it in the side pocket before snapping the magnetic flap shut.

"Bloody Norah, she must be trying to quit smoking or something."

Ange followed this up by pulling bag after bag of gummy bears from the second drawer down, piling them topsy-turvy on the desk.

She repeated the process with the third drawer and then the three on the other side until there was a veritable bear mountain in the middle of Chalky's desk. Sitting back on her heels, she stared at them.

She even ripped open a bag and stuffed a couple of bears into her mouth, chewing while reading the back of the pack. "Sugar-free? Hah! I just got why she's so freaking skinny."

I helped myself to a couple. "Calories burned from all the chewing?" I said around the bears I was beating into submission.

Ange stopped chewing. "No. If you eat enough of them, it has a laxative effect. Like blow the back out of your underpants, laxative." After tipping half-a-dozen of the brightly colored bears onto the desktop, she closed the pack tight. "You should read some of the stories online about this stuff. They're hysterical. Gross, but funny all the same."

After spinning on her knees, she crawled over to the credenza and slid the right-hand panel to the side. "Perfect."

On her turning back, I saw what she was talking about, even if I wasn't in agreement as to its acceptability. It was a hideous orange tote that, while designer, wouldn't have been out of place in the seventies. On the plus side, it was large, and had no trouble holding all the bags of gummy bears. Not too big, not too small, just right.

Bev stopped pressing and prodding the end wall. "Are you serious? You're nicking that evil bitch's gummy bears?"

"Hell, yes, I am. I want that cow as backed up as a 93-year-old who's been subsisting for months on a diet of overcooked meat!"

Ange's expression when she zipped the bag shut was both delighted and grim. I suspected her experience as a nurse meant she knew how backed up this was.

A loud click interrupted my evil thoughts of a constipated Chalky, with Bev's brief yell of discovery all but drowning it out. She swung the panel out into the room with us all crowding around for a better look.

As dark as the interior was, we couldn't see a damned thing. That was until Bev reached inside and, after an efficient swipe up and down the wall, found the light switch.

Despite trying, there was no way we could all fit through the doorway at the same time. Bev, having discovered the space, got first access, followed by Ange, and then me.

With all three of us crammed in there, it was best described as cozy. While the room might measure eight-foot by six, with shelving lining every wall, the free space in the middle felt cramped.

The khaki paint coating every surface said the admin block had been there for a very long time. That it was on site when the New Zealand army was in residence, not in doubt. Silence descended like a smothering blanket as the consequences of what we were looking at dawned.

I retrieved a gorgeous Givenchy handbag from the shelf in front of me, all while taking in the packed shelves around me. "There must be dozens of bags."

"Yeah, and I doubt she's running a high-end leather goods importing business outta here." Bev picked up a bright yellow Louis Vuitton bag from the bottom shelf. From the way it hung, it wasn't empty.

"This is so much bigger than we thought." Ange turned to take in all the shelves and kept on turning, scanning them a second time. "So many women." She quietened for a moment and then shook her head. "It makes little sense." Before Bev or I could ask what, she continued. "The number of bags in here is out of whack with the bone pile."

Bev's hands stilled, the bag she'd been searching momentarily forgotten. "Too many, or not enough?"

"Too many." Ange reached out and stroked a nearby bag as if it were a living thing. "Far too many."

I stared at the shelves chock full of designer leatherwear, surprised to see how many were only available overseas. Could it be the Vale was importing victims? It made more sense than this many New Zealand women disappearing without someone kicking up a stink.

"Here's mine!" The black leather handbag Bev now held wasn't an exclusive brand. But she didn't seem to care, hugging it as she would a lost child.

Soon after, Ange found hers. This too was chain store

quality, being white and closer to pleather than leather. She must have saved for a very long time to afford the Vale's exorbitant fees.

Had I marked myself as disposable by refusing to be drugged and abused? Would things be different if I'd just shut up, lay back and thought of England? There was never a chance I could. I'd already done too much of that during my marriage to want to pay for the privilege.

Or was it because I'd put my lawyer as my next of kin? This had me thinking back to the form I'd completed on arrival. Despite my initial impression it was the same as the online version, there were additional questions in there.

Like the one about living relatives. I'd thought I was doing mom a favor by saying I had none. I didn't want the Vale bothering her when Sue Ng could as easily answer any queries.

Of course, by helping me, Bev and Ange had put themselves firmly in the Vale's crosshairs. Without that, they'd likely have checked out on time, vowing never to return and unaware they were dark net stars.

As it was now, even if people noticed any of us missing, with all the cloak and dagger around the check-in, there wasn't a chance anyone could track us. We'd vanish without a trace, except for replays.

Dammit, when I got out of here, I was going to throttle Lorraine for recommending this place. The grinding of my teeth roused me from my nefarious thoughts. No, even she wasn't that nasty.

It was more likely the people she knew who'd stayed here

were in the celebrity camp. Hadn't they asked her to keep it quiet?

Idiots if they thought that was happening with Lorraine involved.

As well as being a gossip, Lorraine was also dumb as a bag of hammers. When I didn't turn up in six weeks, it would never occur to her to wonder why, or, heaven forbid, check I was okay. Colin at the gas station would notice my absence before that self-centered socialite.

And with my storage unit pre-paid, it would be three months, maybe more, before someone raised an alarm. Perhaps not even then, with it as likely the storage company would flog the contents to recover costs.

Rather than remain weighed down by their handbags, the others tossed them out onto Chalky's desk, next to mine. Thus unencumbered, we started searching the bags on the middle shelf, with these the easiest to reach.

Half-an-hour later, and despite having checked a good thirty handbags between us, we hadn't come across anything that would identify who the bags had belonged to. Nor did we find a single phone, android, or otherwise.

Ange dropped the handbag she'd just searched back on the shelf in disgust. "That horrible woman doubtless has Lance flog them off at the local pub."

I'd moved onto the bottom shelf when I noticed something.

At first, I thought it was my imagination, but dropping to my hands and knees confirmed it. "Do you feel that?"

Ange and Bev joined me on the floor, with Bev skimming her hands over the boards. "Yep, there's a breeze."

"Guys," said Ange, as though explaining to newbie carpenters, "the building's up on stilts, of course there's a breeze."

I shook my head before speaking. "But this is a converted shipping container, so there shouldn't be any gaps in the floorboards like this, and—"

"—the damned building is metal. There shouldn't be any gaps at all," Bev finished for me at the same time as finding the ring-pull she'd been kneeling on.

I scrambled away from a trapdoor that was now as plain as day and waited while she struggled to lift the two-inch slab of wood. There was nothing to see but some utilitarian steps disappearing into the black beyond.

The other thing of interest was how solid the trapdoor was, even being backed with metal. No wonder Bev had trouble opening it. It must have weighed a ton, with its armored nature confirming the military had installed it back in the day.

Bev stared into the void for a moment before speaking. "This must have been how they got you from here up to the Sleeping Beauty Suites without us spotting you."

She had a point. Part of me was also very glad I'd been unconscious for the journey, with the yawning hole giving me the creeps. At first, I thought I was imagining things, but on peering into the dark, there was no missing the beam of a flashlight bouncing around.

On cocking my head to the side, there was also no missing the unmistakable slap of heavy boots on concrete. Heaven knew I'd heard enough of that sound to last a lifetime.

Scrambling to my feet, I jammed myself hard up against the shelves, all while screaming, "Close it! Close it!" I hadn't bothered to keep my voice down, confident that whoever it was, they already knew we were there.

That they were now running proved that.

25

I was relieved when Bev didn't ask for an explanation. Without pause, she threw her considerable weight on the trapdoor, slamming it shut. Although it didn't stay that way for as long as I'd have liked.

Whoever was down there, they were strong, with the trapdoor bouncing violently as they tried their hardest to open it. The only plus was that if the guy had a weapon, the metal-lined trapdoor would protect us. Unless he could get the muzzle of the gun through the gap.

This had me jumping atop the trapdoor next to Bev, with the trapdoor slamming shut with a loud boom. The problem we had was that it was only our combined weight that was stopping him from opening it, although he was still bouncing us up and down a bit. If we moved, we were toast. And not nice toast either, but the sort of hard tack they served in the dining room.

I was still wondering how we could get away when Ange reached into the office and grabbed the orange tote of gummies off Chalky's desk. After dumping it on the bit of the trapdoor not occupied by Bev and me, she reached out and grabbed a large handbag off the closest shelf. "Ladies, let's get a big old pile of handbags going."

Three seconds elapsed before my synapses connected. Bev had no such problem. She was already snatching handbags off the shelves and dumping them on top of the trapdoor. Ange got those within arm's reach and dropped them by her feet despite also being bounced up and down. What the hell was the guy on?!

I was relieved to find most handbags on my side of the room were as over-stuffed as mine often was. From the weight of some of them, they held enough cosmetics to have a pig looking attractive. It wasn't enough. Whoever the guy was, he had to be hyped up on steroids to be as strong as this. But strong enough to deal with us parting his hair courtesy of that trapdoor? I doubted it.

I kept my voice low as I outlined my plan to the others. All we needed to do was stand poised on the hinge side of the trapdoor until he opened it. Once his head was above floor level, if we all jumped on it, he wouldn't be bothering us for quite some time.

As before, Ange couldn't do it, muttering something about the sanctity of life. It was a pity that the sanctity of ours didn't count as much as that of the guy cussing in frustration at not being able to get to us.

After a deafening roar, he doubled his efforts, lifting the trapdoor even with us standing on it. Soon enough, he'd widened the gap to the point he was shoving handbags to the side.

With no time to think, I grabbed Ange and tucked her behind Bev and me. Our plan wouldn't work if she was standing there like a deer in the headlights.

We then stepped back, allowing him to raise the trapdoor until it stood vertically. The second he took his hand away, Bev and I fell forward, landing in a sprawled heap. The guy never stood a chance, with the heavy wood and metal panel having smashed into his head with a sickening crunch.

It took a little longer for me to see the collateral damage.

Maybe, just maybe, if the man's hand had been as vibrant as the scorching hot pink of the handbag it was resting on, I might have missed it. A lot like the guy who was now screaming with an intensity that left my nerves raw.

As his screams continued, the knot in my stomach tightened, and a queasy feeling settled in. His dismembered hand, sitting inches from my face, had me the first to throw up, with Bev and Ange not far behind.

For a while, the guy who could no longer count to ten continued at full belt, although he soon quieted. Whether this was because he'd succumbed to blood loss—something Ange thought was a possibility—or us stoving his head in, we didn't know.

Either way, we weren't lifting the trapdoor to find out. To ensure he stayed put, we tipped one of the shelving units over and jammed it in place. There wasn't a chance he could get to us now, at least not through the trapdoor.

The only thing we couldn't escape was the three of us wearing more chopped carrot than we'd eaten since check-in. It took all my willpower not to look at the others or down at myself, knowing that if I did, I'd be sick again.

"Chalky's room is the closest." After this assertion, Ange was soon next to the door marked PRIVATE on the other side of the reception area. She tried opening the door, but it wouldn't budge.

"Stand back, I've got this." I didn't bother trying to break the locking mechanism. I got greater satisfaction from smashing through the paper-thin wall next to the door with my trusty cricket bat.

Damn, I needed that.

Ange followed me through the gap, not slowing until she'd ripped her top off and was rinsing it under the shower in the attached bath. I was quick to follow suit, not caring that I had to put my top back on wet. Well, damp, with the petroleum-based fabric almost impervious to water.

While Bev rinsed her top, Ange and I helped ourselves to Chalky's mouthwash, with this soon having us feeling human again. This wasn't the only self-care I indulged in. After grabbing a clean glass from the cabinet above the vanity, I filled it with tap water.

Since I was never going on another diet, ever, I needed to

start that course of beta-blockers pronto. So keen was I that when I returned with the bottle of pills, Bev was still rinsing her top under the shower.

Despite my eagerness to dose myself, the borderline-suppositories weren't easy to swallow. They were still making their way down my throat when Ange exclaimed. "Why on earth does she need a walk-in closet? All she ever wears are those butt-ugly white shift dresses."

It was an observation that had me less worried about Ange knowing the Heimlich maneuver and more interested in checking out what she'd found. Back out in the bedroom with glass in hand, I saw that rather than being inside the closet; she was stock-still in front of it.

"Aren't you going to open it?"

Ange turned in my direction. "No handle."

After dropping my empty glass on the bedside cabinet, I grabbed my cricket bat off the end of the bed. I was getting ready to swing when I realized it was a pocket door, although one without a handle. After propping the bat against the wall, I placed my palms flat against the door and slid it to the side.

Surprise, surprise, there wasn't a white shift dress in sight. Instead, we were facing a bank of monitors and more switches and dials than would be required to run the Enterprise.

Ange and I stood shoulder-to-shoulder as we stared at row upon row of small screens. She stabbed her finger at the second screen along in the middle row. "Damn it, that's my bathroom. I recognize the wonky tile at the bottom of my shower."

Next to this screen, I found a low-level shot of mine,

distinguishable by the slight scratch on the bottom of the vanity door. There was only one reason they'd want a camera pointing in this direction.

Sheesh, butt-hole-cam anyone?

I dropped into the office chair in front of the main control board, with Bev, who'd now joined us, leaning over my shoulder. "Who on earth would pay to watch that?" She hadn't said this for long when I spotted a screen that chilled me more than my damp top.

While the layout of the screen was the same as most online auction sites, there any similarities died. With the emphasis on died. My hand trembled as I pointed to the third auction down. Almost as sick as what the individual was requesting was Chalky being complicit.

It was when I clicked on a COMPLETED AUCTIONS tab I saw the true extent of what was happening. "Oh, hell." I wasn't capable of anything more, with Ange and Bev likewise dumbstruck. And while we weren't talking pages and pages of completed auctions, there were a couple with it showing over forty women had died. Meanwhile, hundreds more had experienced being unknowingly humiliated for the perverse pleasure of some sick individual.

Ange dropped to the nearest flat surface, not caring she was atop the keyboard that must control things. While the first two rows of monitors showed bathrooms, the bottom row showed the yoga studio, Chalky's office, and a few other rooms I was unfamiliar with. Stuffed if I'd let that bitch use this setup to track our movements from here. I jumped to my feet and grabbed my cricket bat from outside the door. "Stand back, you two. I'll take care of this lot."

With them out of the way, I was about to take delight in smashing everything within reach when I stopped. I couldn't destroy it all. Much as I wanted to, if I did that, I'd be destroying potential evidence. I could, however, make it impossible for Chalky and her minions to track our progress. At least from this control room.

"I'll smash all the screens. The other stuff is too important."

With Bev and Ange in agreement, I set about destroying every screen and even the keyboards. The multi-button mouse proved itself to be sturdier than its furry counterpart, but I obliterated it soon enough. Mission accomplished, we grabbed our handbags and made for Tee's room.

This took longer than it should have. Even though we were still moving under cover of darkness, in unspoken agreement we kept to the bushes at the edge of the property. I didn't care that this had us close to the bodies hidden in the bush. I'd face dead people over men with guns any night.

Another reason to keep well away from any paths was Lance being finished with his performance and on his way back to the admin building with Chalky. Just thinking about what he might have been up to had me shaking in disgust. Another unknown was who the victim was, with this not listed among any of the auctions I'd looked at.

On arrival at our friend's room, I smashed every camera and any motion sensors I could find. Something made easy now that I knew what I was looking for. The hardest part was destroying everything as quietly as I could. As tempting as it had been to let fly, we were nowhere near home free, yet.

The other thing we found was dry tops, with none of us wasting time changing. Despite the rinse off, there'd been no avoiding the smell of regurgitated food. Ange and I then checked Tee was still okay stuffed down the side of her bed.

One plus with her current position was that, as hoped, it had stopped her snoring, lowering the odds of her being discovered. And with the kitchen twins out for the count, or so I hoped, they couldn't blab about her location.

The one thing we knew was that when we escaped into town, she wouldn't be with us. If we took her along, we'd guarantee they caught us.

After flicking the covers back over Tee, I turned and looked at the other two. "The thing I don't understand is them wanting those three tofu eaters in the Sleeping Beauty Suites. It makes no sense."

A quick shake of my head to clear my thoughts, and I carried on. "From the little I overheard, the clients are paying to watch overweight women being humiliated, screwed, and abused. Not skinny ones."

Could my theory that our escape had Chalky going off script be the right one? I truly hoped not. I was already feeling guilty about Bev and Ange being mixed up in this.

Stillness cloaked us as we pondered what was happening to the three Megans. If the pain and starvation inflicted on me were anything to go by, I didn't like their chances. At least I had body fat in reserve.

Despite only having just reclaimed our handbags, there wasn't a chance we were heading up to the top facility weighed down by them. This had us stuffing them in the closet in Tee's room before leaving for the Sleeping Beauty Suites, again sticking to the bushes that skirted the fence line.

Our reluctance was such that we were soon hiding amid some shrubs, the final cover between us and the path to the Sleeping Beauty Suites. In front of us lay an enormous expanse of what passed for a lawn at The Vale. It would be one that left us out in the open for longer than we'd like.

And if we made it across there safely, we'd once again be closer to the suites than any of us wanted. Especially me.

"We know they'll be there." Bev's voice was heavy with resignation.

"Much as I'd like to leg it into town, we can't leave them behind," said Ange.

"Once we let the guys know about them, we can leave." I all but crossed my fingers behind my back.

"True." Bev peered in the general direction of the buildings obscured by the bush, "but we've got to find them first."

"Find who?"

"Argh!" I swung the cricket bat before I could stop myself. Lucky for Horse, not only could he move without a sound, he was also fast. Especially when he was about to have his hair parted by a slab of willow. "Sheesh, Horse, don't sneak up like that."

Once over her own shock, Bev smacked him hard on the shoulder with her frying pan. "You idiot."

Ange reined in her response to tutting and shaking her head.

My heart slowing, I looked up at him. "We were just coming to look for you. There are three more women locked up somewhere. You'll need to look out for them."

"Where you gonna be?"

"We're walking into town, but we're leaving Tee in her room, so if you could keep an eye out for her, too." With my piece said, I turned, ready to retrace my steps.

However, Horse was having none of it. "I wouldn't be doing that if I were you."

It turned out that, as well as throughout the property, the guys knew there were cameras mounted on trees along the road.

"We thought the military just left them up rather than waste time taking them down."

This had me thinking back to the day Colin, the chatty taxi driver, dropped me off. A moment's consideration, and I discarded my theory.

There couldn't be any cameras overlooking the parking spot. If there were, Chalky would have known I hadn't brought my vehicle with me, rather than demanding to know where my keys were.

Or was it that Colin's taxi being out of commission had them believing my lie that I'd gotten a ride with a local? No matter how we looked at it, it wasn't safe for us to walk into town. To do so would be to risk a bullet in the back from a mercenary not taken out by our rescuers.

Would I live to escape this place? I was having doubts.

26

If what Horse said about the cameras dotted along the road was true, what were the odds of the Megan making it into town in one piece? Let's hope she was as fast as she'd made out. If she failed on either count, we'd never see the cavalry bursting through the front gates.

Deep in thought about what had befallen the woman, it was only seeing Horse out in the open that had me realizing he was no longer next to us. This had me racing to catch up with him and then sticking to him like glue. Soon enough, the other two were with us.

In a flash, we were next to the flax bushes that concealed the track. Of concern was the deep breath he took before he parted these. Was he expecting company? I hoped not.

On us starting up the path, I couldn't believe how quietly he moved. Despite putting my feet where he put his, I made a racket in comparison, and the other two were as loud. Horse stopped without warning, and I had to slam on the anchors to avoid crashing into him. Turning, he whispered, "We need to hurry."

Hurry was an understatement. I hadn't moved that fast since the regional finals or when Hemi carried me. On reaching the safety of the shadows afforded by the buildings that made up the Suites, my lungs were ready to explode. Listening to the other two, I knew they were in a similar state.

"Give ... us ... a ... moment," panted Bev.

I couldn't speak, more interested in getting as much air into my lungs as I could. Ange was in a similar position to me. Bent double, hands on knees, gasping.

"Sheesh, you lot are unfit. Isn't that why you were here?"

None of us could respond, and Horse didn't wait for a reply, nor did he wait for us. Rather, he nipped along the wall and disappeared around the corner of the building.

It wasn't until we'd all caught our breath that we followed. If the situation weren't so serious, I'd think it was funny, the way we were all running full-tilt while looking in every direction possible. What we'd do if we ran into any bad guys? Who knew?

We found out when, on rounding the same corner as Horse had just disappeared around, we ran into two men. With her frying pan momentarily forgotten, Bev punched the guy nearest her in the gut, his lungs emptying with an explosive oomph.

Meanwhile, Ange, overriding her usual reticence around hurting people, did her best to smack the other guy with her rolling pin.

I was no use at all. Even if not paralyzed with fear, if I was to try hitting either of the men with my cricket bat, I'd risk hurting my friends.

The women's apologies, when they realized it was Johnno and Hemi, followed with the same swiftness as their attack, with Bev patting Johnno on his back. "Sorry, mate, thought you were someone else."

Ange spun her weapon of choice. "Yeah, sorry Hemi."

It was a few seconds before Johnno could stand up straight. That must've been one hell of a blow that Bev landed, with his expression wavering between disgruntled and impressed.

"Bugger me, lady. That's one hell of a right you've got." His words had a huffy edge to them, as if he still hadn't got his breath back.

Bev shrugged as if it was no big deal. "You don't last long on a farm unless you build up some muscle."

While I didn't know the truth of this, I knew strength would be our friend if we had to face Chalky and her evil minions. "Where's Horse?"

"Bet the bastard's asleep somewhere," said Johnno, his longing for that state obvious as he stared across the open at the bush.

I nudged him with the cricket bat to get his attention. "But you must have seen him. He was heading this way. He was just ahead of us."

It was an observation that had Johnno turning back to look the way they must have come. The moonlight showed his face to be covered in sweat. Upon dropping my gaze, I saw his shirt was stuck to his chest. What had he been up to?

On closer examination, Hemi was as disheveled. This made little sense, with the night not that warm. There was no way these two should be in this state without them having put in a serious effort.

I waved my free hand around like a game show hostess, gesturing to each of them. "Did you run into some, ah, problems?"

"Yeah, we did." Hemi's expression was grim, leaving me well aware of what those problems were.

Not so long ago, thoughts of people being laid out would have upset me. Well, apart from David, that was. But having been at the mercy of these thugs, I no longer gave a damn about their wellbeing.

Ange proved more squeamish, although she didn't get very far in her whispered lecture on the sanctity of human life before Hemi interrupted her.

"Bill and me went way back. Them talking about killing you chicks by slitting your throats and chucking you over the cliff like they did to him, yeah?" He paused for a moment before adding, "He looked out for me when I was a kid. More than my old man ever did, that's for damned sure. It was me who found him." He took a calming breath before carrying on. "When I realized they were behind it, I snapped."

"So did they when they hit the bottom." Johnno laughed without humor before carrying on. "He was a nice old bloke. He didn't deserve what happened to him."

"Pigs will take care of them." Hemi's expression was forbidding, and I didn't rate the chances of anyone else we ran into.

Before we were further sidetracked, I brought Hemi and Johnno up to speed regarding the three missing women. "That's three we know about, although the pile of handbags says there are more, like heaps more."

Hemi rubbed his hands together. "Right, let's go get them."

I was gripping my bat in readiness when I thought of something. "Guys, Chalky talked about medical staff when she thought I was out cold. Best if you don't lob them off the cliff. We'll need them, for sure." I'd rather we didn't, but who knew what state any others we found would be in?

On rounding the next corner of the building, we came across a door that was slightly ajar. It must be here that Horse entered. At least, I hoped this was the case and that it wasn't a trap of sorts.

Fortunately, with Hemi and Johnno going first, I felt safe enough following them in. However, once inside, the flight part of my sympathetic nervous system started up, yelling loudly enough the others would surely hear it. It got even louder when Johnno suggested we split up to cover more ground.

Unfortunately, he was right. From the little I'd seen, the buildings were a veritable warren, with passages meandering, only to finish in dead ends. Or, failing that, rooms leading into yet more rooms. Grand Designs would describe the architecture as organic. I'd describe it as creepy as all get out. The dodgy lighting didn't help either, having a lot in common with the emergency variety often seen in public buildings during a power cut.

In the end, splitting up was an anti-climax. Staying rooted to the spot while the others wandered off left me on my own. Bev and Ange hadn't looked keen on splitting up either, but this didn't stop them from disappearing down their assigned hallways. Didn't these people watch horror movies? Didn't they know splitting up like this was NOT a good idea?

Shaking my head to rid it of every terrible scenario, I straightened my back and gawped down the hallway that was mine to explore. It was longer than it had a right to be given the overall size of the building. Despite there only being doors on the left-hand side of the hallway, there were so many it was going to take me ages to check them all.

This had me pulling myself up even straighter, taking a deep breath, and double-handing the bat above my head. I didn't know if this would make it quicker to deploy, but it sure as hell made me feel safer to be at the ready. Unfortunately, it wasn't a stance I could maintain if I was to open the first door.

I was already gripping the door handle when I froze. What if there was someone in there? I put my ear to the door, but all I could hear was the sea.

Speed would be my friend, like ripping off a plaster. All going well it would give me the element of surprise. After getting as much air into my lungs as I'd need, my breathing now had a tinge of hyperventilation to it. Not to be deterred, I bounced on my feet to stimulate adrenaline, although, to be fair, it was unnecessary. I was both on edge and as ready as I'd ever be.

I yanked on the handle and stormed into the room, cricket bat held aloft, ready to brain someone if I had to.

It was a storage space, and an anti-climax after all my prep. I was about to leave when I realized what the neat piles were on the shelves that lined the walls. Surgical scrubs, clean, laundered surgical scrubs. There was nothing like blending in with everyone else, so I helped myself to a set, pulling them on over Tee's Vale uniform. If anyone got a glimpse of me, they'd think I was the new girl, except for the cricket bat, it not being of surgical quality and all.

To further bolster my disguise, I nabbed a plastic-wrapped stethoscope, feeling very Gray's Anatomy when I clipped it around my neck. It also meant I could have a quick listen to what was going on in a room before I entered.

Thus attired, I carried on searching my designated area. Out of one room and into another, and another. Empty of people but full to the gunnels with supplies. There was enough stuff in the rooms I'd searched to keep a survivalist happy for a couple of years.

Given the clandestine nature of the place, they wouldn't want delivery trucks rolling up here every week. With this much in the way of supplies, you'd be lucky to see a delivery truck up here twice a year.

Near the end of the hallway was a single door on the right, opposite the final one on the left. I'd given up hyperventilating and holding the bat above my head in readiness. My search-and-destroy mission was proving as underwhelming as any end-of-year stock take.

I opened the last door on the left, expecting more of the same. This couldn't be further from the truth. An enormous chest freezer opposite where I was standing rocketed my heart into my mouth. The damned thing was big enough that it could hold all three missing women and have room for more.

Unfortunately, there was only one way to find out for sure.

I took hold of the handle and tried lifting the lid, but it didn't budge. As loath as I was, I put the cricket bat on the ground, freeing up both hands. It required concerted effort on my part to fight the suction and the sheer weight of the lid to open it as far as it would go.

I didn't know whether to laugh or cry when I saw the contents. If Tee were with me, she'd be beside herself with glee. The freezer contained hundreds of plastic bottles of that chocolate protein drink. But it wasn't this that grabbed my attention. That would be the stacks of Vale-branded frozen meals.

I picked one up and flipped it over to check the nutritional panel on the back. At a glance, the meal looked super healthy. The only thing not listed was whether it was beef, chicken, or something closer to home.

My next action was one of pure spite. After leaving the lid wide open, I slid my hand down the back and flicked off the power before picking up my bat and leaving the room. "Smell that, Chalky."

There was now only one door left for me to check: the one facing the room I'd just exited. It had a sign on it that said LINEN.

Given every other room that'd held linen hadn't had a sign on the door, I smelled a rat. The other thing that was odd about this door was that it opened out into the hallway. Could it be this obvious? But hey, if hiding in plain sight was working to conceal Tee, then it could work here. They weren't likely to have TORTURE CHAMBER on the door, were they?

It didn't matter that the mundane nature of the search had taken the edge off my nerves. There was no way I was storming in there all gung-ho. Instead, I stepped over to the door and laid my stethoscope against it, listening for any signs of movement on the other side.

Nothing.

After transferring the cricket bat to my left hand, I gripped the handle with my right and turned it in miniscule increments. Despite this, it squealed, and I yanked my hand away as if burned.

"Bloody hell!" I slapped my hand over my mouth a second too late. I knew I'd been loud. The shriek from the door handle was timid by comparison. But had my cuss been audible enough for anyone on the other side to hear? I waited, my breathing shallow, the stethoscope tight against the door. Still nothing.

Part of me couldn't believe I'd gotten away with my outburst. This had me staying put, although this might have had more to do with me getting up the nerve to move than with preparedness.

This time I didn't muck about when I turned the handle. The faster I dealt with it, the better it would be. When I opened the door wide, shock hit me.

It was a linen closet.

I stepped right up to the shelves, then shoved my head inside as far as the piles of towels would allow. It still wasn't enough, with me reaching out and jamming the chest piece of the stethoscope against the back wall of the closet.

Music? No, that wasn't right. Musak would be a better description of what I could hear. Often found in elevators, but out of place here.

An experimental push on the shelves had them pivoting away from me, revealing a sliver of what looked like a hallway beyond. There was no way I was going in there alone. If there was one thing Stephen King had taught me, it was that I needed to find the others, and fast.

Much as I'd like to shut the door and get the hell out of there, I needed to close the shelves before someone saw them and raised the alarm.

I had a firm grip on the middle shelf, ready to pull it back into place, when I heard something that had the blood cooling in my veins. Much as I wanted to move, I couldn't, frozen in place as if I were once more tied down.

27

Fear crashed through my system in response to the familiar squeak of those ugly boots. It was louder than usual, thanks to the stethoscope still jammed in my ears.

"How many times do I need to tell you to close the shelves?" Chalky's nasal New York accent was close and deafening. Only the spontaneous clenching of my sphincter and pelvic floor muscles prevented me from losing everything consumed in the past three hours.

Luckily, I still had them engaged when she shoved the shelving unit back into position. She did this with such venom that I came close to receiving an impromptu nose job and a heart attack.

It was also enough to rouse me from my stasis; the shock unlocking my muscles and allowing me to move. And move I did.

Her continuing tirade hid my actions when I stepped back and closed the door in a rush, even if this proved pointless. On hearing muttering inside the closet, I knew there wasn't a snowball's chance in hell I'd get away without being seen. There wasn't even time to hide in the freezer room across the hall.

This had me nipping to the side of the linen closet door and plastering myself against the wall. At least this way, the door would hide me when it opened. With the cricket bat now held aloft, I was ready for action.

It was as if all my Christmases had come at once.

If it were a stranger, I'd think twice. It was Lance, and he'd had this coming since the first time he did the same.

He crumpled to the floor without a peep, sprawled in front of me, helpless. The tables turned. All I wanted to do was smash away at him until I obliterated every image of him in my dreams, or rather, nightmares.

After easing the door shut, I made the most of him being out cold by kicking his legs wide. I then indulged in a boundary shot that would make sure he never raped another woman, let alone peed straight. There was also the added plus that I'd ruined Chalky's sex life for the foreseeable future.

I stood over him, giving serious consideration to putting him out of my misery, when I saw Hemi steaming in my direction, scaring the crap out of me. Focused on my wicked thoughts, I hadn't heard him coming. Like Horse, he moved without a sound, so I doubted I'd have heard him even if I were listening out.

He latched onto my mood in a flash, making quick work of

taking the cricket bat away from me. Whether this was for Lance's peace of mind or my own, he didn't say.

"Did this creep give you any trouble?"

"Not today."

After assessing my state-of-mind, he handed the cricket bat back before bending down and grabbing hold of Lance's feet. He dragged him down the hallway like a human wheelbarrow with me following in their wake. We rounded the corner and were a good way down the main corridor when I spotted Horse and Johnno over Hemi's shoulder.

Hah, so much for us all splitting up.

Johnno rocked Lance's unconscious form to one side with his boot before allowing the man to flop back down. "Looks like you decked this one good."

Hemi let go of Lance's feet and they dropped to the concrete floor with a dull thud. "Not me. This one."

I squirmed under Horse and Johnno's scrutiny, both of them inspecting me, perhaps on the lookout for slipped cogs.

It was Johnno who broke the silence. "Is this the bloke?"

A sharp nod from me, and he didn't so much nudge Lance this time as put the boot in proper, with a fleshy thump.

"I'll take him from here," said Johnno.

Hemi stepped back, allowing Johnno to drag Lance upright before bending and pitching him over one shoulder. He then straightened and, after adjusting the weight of his captive, walked off. A laconic, "I reckon this fucker will enjoy the view," came back as he disappeared around a corner

Despite knowing what he meant by this, I remained quiet.

While the old me would have pleaded for leniency, the new me was a little more ambivalent about Lance's fate.

Maybe him being dead would stop the night terrors?

It was a chance I was prepared to take.

No sooner had Johnno disappeared than Bev showed up, with Ange arriving soon after.

"Any sign of the tofu eaters?" I addressed this question to everyone.

Bev spoke up first. "Deserted, although I found a room full of clothing and personal effects. Like a modern-day concentration camp." Her expression was one I shared.

"I didn't find squat," confirmed Ange.

Horse shrugged, while Hemi's response was a bald, "Nope."

I turned back the way we'd come, beckoning with my finger for the others to follow. "I think I know where they are."

Back in front of the Narnia closet, I put a finger to my lips to stop anyone talking, for all the good it did.

Ange looked at the door, her brow wrinkled. "Ah, it's a linen closet."

I again put my finger to my lips before rushing to open the door as quietly as I could. With the door open enough for everyone to see, I pushed gently on the shelves.

Again, all five pivoted out of the way before I pulled them back into place. No one said a thing. They didn't need to, their shock clear.

Hemi shut the door to the linen closet without a sound, with not even the squeaky handle daring to defy him. "If we're going through there, we need to wait for Johnno." He leaned into the wall, a repose that shrieked patience.

It was something I was lacking, with my desire to be rid of this place urging me to rush through everything. Of course, it made sense that we should wait for Johnno, but did this make the waiting any easier to bear? Nope.

While we waited, I developed quite the eye twitch, and Bev and Ange fidgeted, all of us eager to do something, anything. Most of all, I wanted to run and never stop. In contrast, Horse had hunkered down against the wall, up on the balls of his feet. He did so with little to no movement, his balance perfect. Such a pose would see me in a heap on the floor.

Hemi was just as relaxed, leaning against the wall opposite, his eyes closed, his breathing slow and regular. I was about to prod him when he pushed himself away from the wall and re-opened the door to the linen closet.

"What?" I looked at Hemi. There wasn't a sign or even a sound of Johnno's return.

Hemi grinned before shoving the shelves out of the way, and with sufficient force to flatten anyone unlucky enough to be standing there. Pity there wasn't a welcoming committee on hand to greet us. It'd have thrilled me if it was Chalky.

"Remember," I placed my hand on his back to stop him, "don't hurt any doctors or nurses. If we find the missing women, they'll more than likely need medical help."

At least, I hoped they'd still need medical help, because the evidence we'd uncovered so far said no one left this place untouched. Unless they were lucky, a celebrity or they worked here.

After nodding, he stepped through the gap and disappeared. Horse followed him, then Bev and Ange, leaving me once more on my own.

After exiting the closet on the other side, they moved off down the hallway to the left. It was strange, but my gut instinct would have been to go right, something to do with shopping psychology, apparently.

It was my hesitation to follow in what I thought was the wrong direction that had me staying put. I was close to legging it and hiding out in the bottom of Tee's closet when Johnno turned up, as Hemi seemed to have expected. The shame of running with an audience was too much for me, and so I held my ground.

My questioning look was all he needed.

"The pigs will eat well tonight."

Bile bubbled up in my throat, burning it, and I struggled to hide my revulsion at how gleeful he was at the prospect.

I needn't have bothered because he looked past me at the linen closet and through into the hallway. "They through there?"

I nodded in answer and, unable to stall any longer, stepped into the closet, then shot through the gap and out into the hallway with Johnno right behind me. I was following in the footsteps of the others when I realized he'd fallen back.

Rather, he was pushing the shelves back into place, the

panel that backed them, showing itself to be a perfect match to the wall.

Moving closer to him so I could keep my voice low. "Is there any point in closing them?" It wasn't as if Hemi had been quiet when he opened them.

Johnno shrugged before edging by me to trail the others. His "Who knows?" didn't inspire confidence. Were he and the others always this lackadaisical?

This side of the operation appeared as deserted as the side we'd just come from, even though I knew this wasn't the case. Screw splitting up with Chalky roaming free.

That things were ritzy on this side shouldn't come as a surprise, with that linen closet, The Vale equivalent of the one in Narnia. The facility we'd entered smacked of a crazy-expensive private hospital and was at odds with where we'd come from.

When I looked down, the opulence of the decor struck me. Rather than utilitarian linoleum, the floor was wall-to-wall marble tiles. Here the lighting was soft rather than dim.

There was no way they were killing people over here. Not to a soundtrack of "The Girl from Ipanema," they weren't.

There wasn't a chance I was heading off to the right on my own. This had me trailing the other five, with an occasional look over my shoulder. In the end, the sensation I was being stalked got too much for me, and a brief tap on Johnno's back had us swapping places.

The high-end finishes didn't last past the first corner. Neither did the music, with a quick look up showing a scarcity of speakers. Here, concrete floors and buzzing fluorescents replaced the marble tiles and soft lighting. The frames of the windows cut into one side of the hall farther along were raw aluminum. Not meant to be seen by celebrity clients from either the inside or the out.

I was wondering what the view would be like when Hemi stopped with a jolt. He turned without a sound, put a finger to his lips, and then dropped to his hands and knees.

For such a large man, he crawled with surprising speed and stealth.

We all followed suit.

As I crawled under the window, I understood the reason for our drop in altitude. When I looked up through the Venetian blinds, I expected to see the night sky. Rather, there was a ceiling that featured a couple of flickering fluorescent tubes. Even with the blinds angled as they were, anyone in the room could see us trooping past.

The temptation to pop my head up and have a look was overwhelming.

I didn't know what I expected to see, but it wasn't this. I got a glimpse of large stainless-steel vats, more commonly seen in boutique breweries. They'd set the room up as a large industrial kitchen, one that was better equipped than that frequented by the laughing gnomes.

Temptation again got the better of me, and I popped my head up to get a proper look into the room. There was no way I could pull my gaze away.

Perhaps it was that the glass made it like I was watching

an enormous television set. A pity the scheduled programming was less "MasterChef" and more "Silence of the Lambs."

Johnno tugged me back down when a bloke in a white cap, overalls, and gumboots walked into the room.

I popped straight back up again. I couldn't help myself.

The stainless-steel bucket the guy was carrying was full to the brim. Mesmerized, I watched him upend the bucket of who knew what into the enormous bowl sitting under a floor-stand mixer in the middle of the room. After clanging the bucket down, he turned the knob on the side of the machine, and the blades whirred into action.

I was conscious Johnno was watching next to me. The others, now past the window, had regained their feet and were already a good distance down the hallway. Hemi disappeared around a corner with Horse right behind him.

I was about to continue crawling forward when another guy entered the room behind the glass and upended a similar bucket into the large bowl. The drone of the motor changed as it worked harder on the extra load. When the new arrival spoke, the clarity was astounding, proving the window wasn't double paned.

"I can't believe those fat bitches drink this crap."

"Hey, if those sad fuckers paying to see them get screwed like them chunky, then this is the easiest way to make sure they stay that way."

I didn't know what distressed me most. How casually they were talking about me and others being drugged and raped on a pay-per-view basis. Or watching how much cocoa powder and sugar they added to the mix?

No wonder I'd had trouble losing any weight.

On the plus side, at least I could tell Tee what the recipe was. Well, I could if I knew what they'd been chucking in there by the bucket-load.

"Yeah, I'd love to see their faces if they knew they were on a steady diet of B-List celebs."

"That lot guzzling it down is sure as hell easier than us having to get rid of it."

They were laughing like drains when a third man arrived, also dressed from head-to-toe in white and carrying yet another stainless-steel bucket full to the brim.

"Mind your backs, more celebrity flab coming through." He upended another bucket of the gelatinous sludge into the mixer.

"Bleeding hell, careful you don't overload the damned thing. Candy will go off her tits if we blow the motor again."

He was right about this warning. The motor sounded as distressed as I was feeling. I wasn't sure if it was my dry retching or Johnno's muttered oath that alerted them to our presence.

Either way, we'd been busted.

28

Also busted were the three guys when Hemi and Horse got to them. Again, the two Maori men startled me with their speed and grace. They were in the room, and their quarry unconscious, without as much as a peep of alarm.

The two men then wasted no time stuffing the unconscious workers into the enormous metal vats that lined the back wall. One criminal per vat, jammed in nice and tight. There appeared to be no need for bindings, with the men unconscious for the foreseeable future. Our saviors were efficient.

Ange and Bev joined the others in the vat room, leaving Johnno and me still in the hallway. He helped me to my feet, looking as green as I'm sure I did. Not until my tummy had settled a little was I able to walk along the hallway, around the corner, and into the room with the others.

What remained of my last meal came close to making a

repeat appearance when I saw what Ange was up to. After turning off the mixer, she was now dipping a finger in the luscious, dark chocolate smoothie.

I smacked her hand away in time, annoying her no end. Not to be deterred, she immediately dipped her finger back into the mix. It was more than my stomach could take, and I projectile vomited all over the mixer. A fair amount found its way into the bowl itself, putting paid to anyone else sampling the brew.

Ange held her hand in front of her mouth, unsure if she should lick it clean or not.

"You don't want to do that." Johnno took hold of her hand and wiped it with a cloth he had found.

He then handed me the cloth, and I made quick work of wiping my face with a clean corner. "He's right. We found out what the secret ingredient is."

After I ran through the recipe, Bev, and then Ange threw up straight into the latest batch of the Vale's special brew. Like me, they were as upset by the vast quantities of sugar and cocoa as they were about the buckets of unwanted celebrity butt and gut.

One thing was for sure, the sheer quantity we had seen thrown into the mixer said there was more than one liposuction operation taking place right then.

If I hadn't been feeling so sick, it would have been funny to see how nauseated Horse and Hemi were when we explained what was in the mix. The last thing Hemi did before we left the room was rip the power cord free of the motor. This put an end to any more mixing in the foreseeable future.

After leaving the mixing room, we soon entered a central hub. From there, three concrete tunnels spread out like the spokes of a wheel. A distinct downward slant showed we were entering the very hill itself.

Anyone up for an army bunker?

Hemi looked stunned. "Hate to say it, but we're gonna need to split up again. We need to cover as much ground as we can before they catch on to us."

And, much as I too hated the idea of us going our separate ways, he was right. Bowie's labyrinth was straightforward compared with what we were facing. Other than unforgiving concrete floors, walls, and ceilings, those dark, dank tunnels had something else in common. Each of them dog-legged after only three or four yards, one to the left and two off to the right.

There was only one way to find out what was around the corners, and it wasn't one I liked. The only plus was that this time I wouldn't be on my own, with Johnno as my assigned muscle. I would have preferred being with Hemi, who made me feel safe, but to reject Johnno would have looked churlish and not been the best start to our partnership.

After fond goodbyes to the other two women, I followed in Johnno's wake. We were off down the tunnel to the left and had only just made it around the corner when we encountered two doors. They were dead opposite each other, in a pattern that was repeated at regular intervals for the length of the tunnel.

Johnno was ready to open the first door when I put my hand on his shoulder to stop him. His expression morphed from annoyed to understanding when I put the stethoscope to my ears and held the chest piece against the door. A quick listen confirmed there was no one breathing on the other side of the slab of wood.

I was right behind Johnno when he entered the room.

Another look, and I decided it was less of a room, and more of a cavern. Spray concrete coated the walls to keep the damp at bay, although the chill in the air said this had been pointless. At not facing a victim, I puffed out in relief, not surprised to see my breath cloud in the frigid air.

With the all-pervading damp, it made sense that the supplies crowding the space were double wrapped in clear plastic. As well as keeping everything dry, it would also make it a simple task to find what you were looking for. The room opposite was a mirror image.

I relaxed, deciding we must be in the warehouse section of the complex. That was until I placed the stethoscope against the next door along.

There was no mistaking the sound of labored breathing. Or the distinctive slap of leather hitting skin. I removed the stethoscope and handed it to Johnno, allowing him to listen in. After a moment's shock, his expression hardened, and he gave the stethoscope back to me and retrieved his knife.

We stormed into the room, not getting far. I shook my head to clear it of what I was seeing. I had been expecting a modern-day torture chamber, not what looked to be a 1950s classroom. It was perfect, right down to the chalkboard and obligatory apple sitting on the teacher's desk.

There, any similarities died. The teacher, one of the tofu

eaters, was naked and hogtied across the desk next to the apple. The studio lights did nothing to hide her injuries.

On her other side, armed with a horsewhip, was a schoolboy. Well, he would have been thirty years ago. Now he was a pathetic excuse for a human being in a school uniform, one acting out some warped pay-per-view revenge fantasy.

Maybe it was how ludicrous he looked, but both Johnno and I burst out laughing, breaking the tension that had held us frozen. The laughter died in our throats when the idiot in the school uniform pulled a gun on us.

However, he didn't look confident, with the piece wavering back and forth between Johnno and me. In the end, he decided the scruffy individual with the big ass hunting knife was the greater threat and concentrated on aiming there.

His gaze briefly flickered above and behind where Johnno and I were standing. And there, right there, all those damned action movies David had forced me to watch came into play.

This had me sneaking a pink cardigan from a pile of schoolmarmish clothing off the chair next to me. I then flicked it up and over the camera, blocking whoever was paying to watch. With luck, they would just think the connection had gone out.

The Axl Rose wannabe in that ludicrous school uniform then swung the gun in my direction, and I came close to having an accident. This was nothing like in the movies. It was scary as hell, but as a distraction, it was perfect.

In a scene straight out of Crocodile Dundee, Johnno threw his knife, and I watched, fascinated, as it buried itself up to the hilt in the schoolboy's throat. The handgun clattered to the ground, followed by its crumpled owner.

Three seconds ticked by before I reacted. It was the first time I had seen someone killed for real, with shock soon winning out, followed by blackness.

I was soon enough roused by screaming, my gaze landing on the heap of dead schoolboy lying close by. However, the agonized cries weren't coming from him, and after scrambling to my feet, I instead focused on the schoolteacher. Untied by Johnno, but still draped over the desk, she was crying out in pain.

"What do we do with her?" Johnno's brow wrinkled as he stared at the woman's flayed back and buttocks.

He had a point. She couldn't get dressed in that state.

"Let me think, let me think, let me think." This mantra was as much for my benefit as Johnno's, with repetition helping my brain to focus on a solution. "I'll be back in a moment."

Leaving an open-mouthed Johnno, I stumbled out into the tunnel, retraced our steps, and opened the last storage space we'd searched. Who could have imagined those first aid courses would pay off like this?

Back in the classroom, I flicked the apple to the side and stacked my goodies on the desk next to the poor teacher. "This might hurt."

There was no point sugar coating it. Whatever I did, it would hurt.

The woman had nerve endings exposed that were never meant to see the light of day. I patted her on the shoulder, the one bit of her back to escape attention. As I inspected her back, I knew she'd carry these scars for life.

I ripped open the industrial-sized container of plastic wrap I had retrieved, pulling long lengths of it free and cutting it on the serrated edge of the box. With Johnno's help, we laid these down her back.

There was no need to pat them into place. The suction effect of all that blood and serum took care of this. We repeated the process, going sideways until I'd covered her in a crisscross of plastic from nape to thighs. We then covered her with another layer, going over her shoulders and around her stomach.

We'd made it as secure as we could, but whether this makeshift covering would stay put when she stood was anyone's guess. Just as well, I had the very thing to help with this.

I'd been so busy concentrating, I hadn't realized she'd stopped moaning. This had me placing my hand on her shoulder and leaning down to her level. "Are you okay?"

I got the briefest nod in response.

"We'll need to bandage you. If we don't, the plastic wrap might not stay put." It didn't matter that the plastic film was clinging as it was supposed to. Tonight, gravity wasn't our friend. The extra layer would also help protect her from the cold, with this cavern being no warmer than the storage rooms. I also worried that some of her shivering was down to shock. "Are you ready?"

Again, I received a tentative nod.

After a deep breath, I grabbed the dark blue fabric hand-towel refill I had found.

Johnno helped her slide backward until her feet touched the ground, while she leaned on the desk with her arms and shoulders. Her torso free, we wrapped the towel around and around her until she resembled a mummy. Only then did we help her stand, albeit with care.

I didn't know her name but recognized her from meal times and yoga. She was having trouble standing, and there was no way we could carry her. It didn't matter that Johnno was strong enough. If we put any pressure on the skin on her back, we would only cause more damage. And perhaps even more important than this, Johnno needed his hands free in case we ran into any of Chalky's team. There was no point being armed to the teeth if weighed down by an unconscious woman.

I dressed her in an outfit that wouldn't look out of place on Miss Jean Brodie. Luckily, the ankle-length tweed skirt had an elastic waist and was loose, therefore not adding too much to her pain.

Upon opening the next cavern, we faced a similar scene, although this time there was no schoolboy. The budget must only run to one. While stripped and tied to a desk, this tofu eater hadn't tasted the whip.

Other than these indignities, she was in good shape and, after throwing her clothes back on, was up to helping her friend. After we found the third of the missing women, we left the two who were able-bodied to support their fast-drooping friend.

Armed with birch rods, horsewhips, and even Axl Rose's gun, they were ready to leave. There were no outward signs of damage to the firearm courtesy of Horse's earlier foray, so we decided it was better they took it, if only as a decoy.

When they were as ready as they'd ever be, we gave the trio directions on how to get out. When they talked about walking back into town, Johnno held his hand up, stopping their gabble of incoherent thoughts.

"No! You don't leave the property. Barricade yourselves in a room and we'll get you when it's safe."

So forceful had he been that they nodded, before shuffling off down the tunnel, soon to disappear around the corner. I would have given anything to be going with them, but now I had committed to the search with Johnno, there wasn't a chance I was leaving. I regretted this when Johnno opened the next door and the smell of death rolled out of the room like a living thing. About to follow him into the room, my cricket bat aloft, he staggered back, stopping me from entering.

"What?" I croaked. I took a second to cobble together his stuttered reply, although it was impossible to miss that the key word was "skinned."

29

My dad had an electric plane like the one apparently used on the woman. Perfect for slicing through wood like butter, but devastating when used on the human body.

All I could hope was that she didn't suffer for long, that the pain allowed her to find solace in the darkness as I had. Unfortunately, I couldn't give in to that right then, instead I was bent double and fighting the desire to faint. If I was to survive this, I needed to stay strong.

Why would somebody pay to see that done to another human being? Of even more concern was who would be sick enough to carry out the request? Anyone capable was certifiable and needed to be locked up, or better still, strung up. No matter how you looked at it, Chalky had tapped into a vein of sick individuals.

Johnno's check of the next chamber was as brief, his

expression grim, with me accepting his muttered assertion that it was the worst home improvement show he had ever seen.

All the caverns checked, we established there was no one left alive. Everyone was beyond help, even the sickos who had paid to see this carnage.

It devastated me that this was the ultimate resting place for these women. Alone and unloved as they must have been in life, if no one had noticed they were gone. I sure didn't remember hearing this many missing persons' reports on the telly. If they even bothered with those these days.

Thoughts of them dropping off the face of the earth without so much as a whimper were closer to home than I'd like. If I got out of this place, I would remedy that. No more hangers-on. No more being a hanger-on myself. Loyalty would be what was important, with me already closer to Ange and Bev than I was to any of my so-called friends back in the city.

If I ever escape this place, I'll even visit my mother down at the ass-end of New Zealand. A week or two each year would be more than enough to keep both of us happy.

The last door closed on its victim, and the atmosphere was back to being innocuous. The only plus was that the caverns being as cold as they were, there wasn't much smell to deal with.

I then spun the cricket bat on its end, grabbing the handle before it could fall over. "We need to find the others."

"You got that right." Johnno shoved his knife back into the sheath on his leg and marched off the way we'd come, with me scrambling to catch up.

We hadn't passed more than a couple of doors when

Chalky's distinctive tones echoed down the tunnel from around the corner. Much as I'd liked to introduce her to my cricket bat, I didn't know who she was talking to. For all we knew, they could be armed.

Cricket bats and knives were useless against guns, although Johnno did okay against the schoolboy. He pulled out his knife and held it up in readiness.

After tapping him on the shoulder, I formed a gun with my hand and pulled the trigger right next to his head. He got the message.

The one good thing about this section of the tunnel was that we weren't short of doors to disappear through. We entered the one right behind us. Sadly, it wasn't one of the storage caverns.

After the briefest glimpse of the carnage, I gave the closed door more attention than it required. Next to me, Johnno had no compunction about staring at the victim, tsking and shaking his head.

After propping the cricket bat against the wall, I slid the stethoscope into my ears and jammed the chest piece hard against the door. It was as if I was out in the tunnel with Chalky and it took every ounce of resolve not to yank the stethoscope free from my ears. She was as loud as if she were right next to me.

"Gad dammit, Heath, move your sorry ass. I don't have all day. Start at the far end with the older ones."

At first I thought the squeaking was from her boots, but there was a rhythmic quality to it I'd not heard before. As it passed the door, I realized it was a trolley, doubtless being pushed by Heath. Concentrating, I detected another set of footsteps in his wake.

While Johnno was handy with his fists, if the guys outside were armed, he wouldn't stand a chance. And what if Chalky was also packing heat? This painted such a ludicrous picture that I had to fight the manic laughter threatening to erupt.

Now what?

Moving as close as I could to Johnno, my gaze never left the door. Only when I was hard up against him did I speak. "Do we wait, or leg it?" I held the stethoscope up to his mouth for him to whisper his reply.

"That tunnel goes on for too sodding long. I don't know about you, but I don't fancy an effing bullet in the back."

Even though he'd kept his voice down, he damn near blew my eardrums, with me only realizing I'd said something when he slapped his hand over my mouth. He didn't take it away until after I'd nodded.

My hand shaking, I put the chest piece back against the door, listening for sounds of discovery. I even gave up breathing for a heartbeat or two.

No sound. No footsteps. No talking. It was all quiet. Perhaps too quiet, with this stopping me from moving.

Johnno, however, was restless to the point I had to grab his arm to stop him from opening the door. I relaxed a little when the squeaking and footsteps resumed out in the tunnel. However, I didn't relax altogether. We'd all watched that scene in movies and I was damned if I was getting sucked in.

Again, Johnno's hand strayed to the door handle.

Again, I stopped him.

There was movement right outside the door with me jabbing my finger at it before putting it to my lips. After this, neither of us so much as blinked. It wasn't until the footsteps carried on toward Heath and Chalky that I slumped against the icy wall.

Good thing we didn't have any plans to leave the cavern.

We couldn't.

While waiting, I realized that our hiding place wasn't that safe after all. What happened if the trolley they were pushing could hold all the bodies?

I whispered this thought to Johnno and even in the dim red light of the room; I saw his eyes widen. A quick scan of the torture chamber showed that short of stacking up body parts, there was nowhere to hide. A quick tally confirmed more than one person had died here.

Was I becoming inured to the carnage? Or was I in a state of denial? With my mouth no longer flooding with saliva at the sight, either option could be true.

All I could hope was that the victims were in their happy places long before they succumbed to the damage inflicted courtesy of pay-per-view.

Meanwhile, Johnno had an ear pressed hard against the door, with him soon signaling for me to get the stethoscope back in place, and fast.

Grunting had replaced the sound of the wheels, painting a picture of a trolley stacked with bodies and spare parts.

When the grunting stopped out in the tunnel, I scooted to the side; the stethoscope left to hang around my neck. No longer able to tell what was going on, I raised my cricket bat in readiness to flatten someone. Johnno positioned himself next to me. The handle turned, and the door opened an inch, with every hair on my body standing in readiness.

"Don't be an idiot, Heath. We're behind schedule already. You can come back for the others after we've processed this lot."

For a horrifying moment, I thought this Heath guy was going to ignore Chalky's orders. While eventually compliant, the way he slammed the door said he hadn't liked the way she'd spoken to him.

The door still shuddering in its frame, I put the stethoscope back against it, listening as Chalky's constant demands for the crew to move faster became ever-fainter. Once her dulcet tones were no longer detectable, I showed Johnno that it was okay to open the door.

The smell that greeted us was reminiscent of that found in a butcher's shop. Fresh meat. Even without the trail of blood bisecting the floor in a sick imitation of the wayfaring signage seen in hospitals, I'd know where they were heading. Chalky having mentioned processing the bodies, there was no need to close my eyes to see that row of meat hooks. That memory was with me for life.

The image of all those frozen meals in that enormous freezer soon followed, with me even happier that I'd turned it off at the wall. To hell with that sick bitch and her minions being paid twice for the victims.

The only thing I was unsure of was where the slaughterhouse was located because I hadn't seen it since being back in the Sleeping Beauty Suites. Neither had I caught sight of the room they'd kept me in. If I had, there would be even more smashed equipment by now.

Without a conscious decision, Johnno and I both kept well clear of the carnage in the middle of the tunnel. Pressed against the walls, we followed the bloodied footsteps of Chalky and her underlings.

This took us back to the hub where the three tunnels joined up. And while the grunting of the trolley pushers was no longer audible, we could see where they had gone. The problem was whether we should wait for the others or keep moving.

While I was still pondering this, someone slapped a hand over my mouth, stifling my scream. When Ange popped up in front of me, I stopped struggling, with Horse removing his hand soon after.

"We've been waiting for you." Ange's voice was so low, I thought about putting the stethoscope back in place and holding the chest piece up to her mouth.

I hadn't done so when Hemi and Bev rounded the corner at the end of the middle tunnel and marched in our direction. A hush fell over us as we all stood back and took in the blood-splattered floor.

Hemi's gaze then followed the trail back to the tunnel I'd inspected with Johnno. "Was it as bad as it looks?"

He'd addressed this question to Johnno rather than me, as

though being a woman, I was incapable of answering. And not too long ago, he would have been right.

Well, to hell with that. I had received too much of that sort of treatment from David over the years. I wasn't sure if it was the constant levels of stress, but I was finding my voice again.

Not giving Johnno time to speak, I held up my hand.

"That cold-hearted bitch is behind torture and mass murder." I waited a beat before continuing. "With power tools. It was like HGTV had bought the rights to Friday the 13th." A hysterical giggle then broke free, with the reactions from Ange and Bev killing any further laughter.

After this, I didn't bother going into my theory about what was happening to the bodies after the Vale team had butchered them.

Hemi was also looking at me sideways, but didn't comment before turning and following the trail of blood. We trooped past the glass-fronted room with its stainless-steel vats and three unconscious lackeys tucked out of sight.

We then filed past the linen closet that would have taken us back to the Sleeping Beauty Suites. I had expected Chalky and the body retrieval team to exit through there. However, the trail of blood led us in the direction I had first wanted to go when we arrived.

We didn't get far before we hit a T-junction with dead ends both to the left and right. Something that made no sense at all. Perhaps even harder to understand was that the trail of blood had disappeared underneath a solid wall. That was until Horse hunkered down and examined the skirting board, where he found a couple of hairline cracks.

They were far enough apart you'd never suspect there was a door there. It must have been at least six feet wide, if not wider. Waving my hand to get everyone's attention, I put my finger to my lips. Re-engaging the stethoscope, I placed the chest piece against the wall, straining to hear what was happening on the other side.

Chalky continued to berate the unfortunate porters, and I listened until their grunting was faint. Not until then did we risk opening up the wall. Horse rose to his feet and pushed against the left-hand side of the panel. Nothing.

Soon enough, Hemi pushed against the right-hand side. Bingo! The panel swung open on a central pivot, smacking into Johnno, who swore to what an idiot his mate was. He wasn't quiet about it. Waiting for all hell to break loose courtesy of his outburst, none of us spoke, instead listening for a reaction. There wasn't one, and there should have been. Dammit, they had taken off on us.

With Johnno no longer playing the part of doorstop, the pivoting panel opened wide, and the six of us marched through. We did, however, continue to be careful to avoid the trail of blood down the center of that new hallway. On the bright side, with that Hansel and Gretel trail, at least we could find our way out again.

We knew why Chalky and the porters didn't react to Johnno's outburst when we turned another corner and faced yet another door. Hemi stopped in front of it, put his ear against it, and held his hand up for quiet. It was unnecessary, without as much as a peep out of us. When he frowned, I leaned in and put the chest piece up to the door.

That was odd.

Even using the stethoscope, I couldn't hear anything. This must be the mother of all doors. "What's it made of?"

Ange and Bev hurried to shush me, but then Hemi talked in a normal voice, too. "No point keeping quiet. I reckon the door is solid steel." He then examined the edges. "And airtight by the look of things."

Despite pushing it all over and looking for a mechanism in the wall on either side, the solution didn't show itself.

Damn it to hell! What now?

30

We were about to retrace our steps when Ange leaned over and looked more closely at the blood trail at our feet. On her straightening, her confusion was apparent. "That's not right."

"What isn't?" said Hemi, also looking at it more closely.

"The blood leading up to the door is fresher. Look at the color."

She was right. On retracing our steps, we soon saw that on rounding the corner, the blood trail changed from a darker red to a brighter hue. There was also a break in the pattern, with it changing from being irregular to something altogether more contrived.

"Those sneaky bastards." Hemi pushed against the wall next to the corner, and sure enough, it opened.

Then all hell broke loose.

It was a good thing Horse had screwed up most of the guns earlier. Even luckier were Hemi's superhuman reflexes, when on spotting the guys on the other side, he'd shut the panel. While this saved us from collateral damage, it did nothing to lessen the noise of their guns exploding, which was deafening.

My ears still ringing, I almost missed the two dull thuds from the other side, following which Hemi turned and motioned for us to stand back. It was something we scrambled to obey.

With the way clear, he slammed the panel open, smashing it hard against the wall opposite. Soon after, he, Johnno, and Horse stormed into the breach, although it soon became clear that storming wasn't necessary.

Both guards were prostrate, their blood splattered over the floor, walls, and even the ceiling. I didn't want to look, but their twitching bodies lured my gaze. Who would have believed a gun exploding in your face could do so much damage? For sure, they wouldn't be using the fast lane at the airport again. Even using the slow lane might prove a challenge. That's if they survived.

Stepping with care over their convulsing bodies, we tracked the blood trail until I realized Hemi wasn't right behind me. Instead, he was busy propping the disabled guards against the revolving panel, stopping anyone from following us.

The guards themselves wouldn't be giving us any more trouble. Not with the remaining air in their lungs escaping through their windpipes in a sodden gurgle.

Hemi then pushed past me, joining Horse and Johnno to ensure all of our strength was upfront. Ange and Bev went next, while I brought up the rear in the safest position of all.

This didn't stop me from checking over my shoulder every few paces. As creepy as this place was, it wouldn't have surprised me to see the guards in zombie form. Everyone knew a through-and-through head shot was best.

The layout of the hallway was anything but straightforward, with it zigzagging its way through this part of the complex. It brought back memories of a school trip to a local hospital where we got to see behind the scenes.

With no conscious instruction, we all kept as quiet as we could. We snuck past a series of viewing windows into operating theaters, with surgeons and nurses cocooned in circles of light. I'd watched enough episodes of Botched to recognize liposuction when I saw it.

Over and over, the surgeon jammed a knitting-needle type device into whomever they were working on. They sucked the offending lumps and bumps out via a clear hose into an all-to-familiar stainless bucket under the operating table.

In each case, the team's concentration was such they were doubtless unaware they were being observed. Nor did they appear to know they were busy harvesting the key ingredient of the spa's popular chocolate shake.

The names on the boards outside each of the three theaters confirmed they had been feeding us Grade-A leavings. Strange, but it had me feeling that bit closer to Hollywood.

The one operation we hadn't seen yet was a boob job. The very one that had seen me desperate enough to lose weight that I had booked in here.

What were these women thinking, undergoing surgery in a backwater like this, and all for the sake of privacy?

It wasn't as if they fooled the paparazzi when they rocked up to an event, minus their love handles. Sure, control wear worked and all, but not enough to mask the removal of a bucket-load of gut.

What if something went wrong? Didn't that famous author Olivia Whatshername die of complications from plastic surgery? Not while she was on the table, but later when things settled.

A hand slapped over my face, shocked me out of my reverie. This time it proved to be foe, rather than friend. Much as I would have liked to fight, the feel of hard steel in the middle of my back guaranteed my compliance.

Even if it was one of those that Horse had damaged, when it misfired, it would still do me irreparable harm. It wasn't a risk I was prepared to take. I did, however, allow the cricket bat to slip from my fingers, breaking its fall with my foot.

I had to hope that the others would see it.

With the gun still jammed hard against my spine, my assailant dragged me backwards into a room. Even without the whiff of familiar perfume, I would have known who was behind the firearm.

People immediately protested our presence, and I swiveled

my eyes to find we were in an operating theater. This one didn't have a glass viewing panel.

Now confident of my obedience, Chalky took her hand away from my mouth, but kept the gun where it was. Then, using her free hand, she slid the bolts shut on the entry panel.

There was no way the others could get to me, although I soon heard their attempts. Much as I'd loved to cry out, "I'm in here," all I managed was a faint whimper. Although not so faint that those in the operating theater didn't hear.

The surgeon voiced his disapproval about us contaminating a sterile area. His admonishment, while short, told me he wasn't a native English speaker. Chalky, waving the gun in his direction, silenced any further complaints. However, when he shoved a gel implant into the cavity of whichever starlet it was, his eyes above the bright green mask were dark with anger.

Forced to watch the rest of the boob job, I rethought the procedure. If I got out of here alive, a push-up bra would suffice.

However, making it out of here in one piece was looking less likely all the time, with big tits losing their appeal when I wouldn't be around to flaunt them.

The surgery seemed to take forever. To the point the scrabbling of my friends on the other side of the wall stopped. Chalky even abandoned jamming the gun into my back. In the end, the medics left through the double doors opposite where we waited, pushing the patient before them, and casting filthy looks in our direction.

The swinging doors hadn't had time to settle when Chalky

shoved me toward the operating table, blathering about what she planned on doing to me. If she was doing all that, she'd need to have her hands free. After faking a stumble into the trolley of discarded surgical items, I grabbed hold of a scalpel.

Meanwhile, Chalky flipped aside the sheet covering the operating table to reveal shackles welded to each corner. I was in deep do-do if she got them in place. Resistance I hadn't experienced in a long time reared its head. This time my throat didn't close on me, and I yelled my lungs out, hoping my friends were still nearby.

Pistol-whipped for my efforts, I dropped the scalpel, resulting in a reaction I'd rather have avoided.

"You fat bitch!" She raised her arm to whack me with the gun again.

Still woozy from the first hit, I grabbed at whatever came to hand on the trolley and fired it at her. If she was too busy fending off flying surgical equipment, she was too busy to clobber me.

It was obvious she didn't plan on shooting me. If what I had seen on that auction listing was to be believed, there was no demand for that.

It was a lame plan, but it was all I had. My hand rested on a stainless-steel kidney dish. I grabbed it, reared up, and smashed it into her face. Bloodied swabs fired all over the place, followed by her gun.

Dammit, I hadn't knocked her out, just slowed her down. But it gave me time to grab yet more items and fire them at her.

A glance toward the bolts holding the panel in place

suggested I didn't need to hold out much longer. It would be close, especially with Chalky on her hands and knees, desperate to get hold of the gun.

Oh, no, you don't.

Falling to the ground next to her, I grabbed the scalpel I'd dropped earlier and buried it in the back of her hand. It stopped her manicured fingers from closing around the handle of the gun, although not for long.

Rather than screaming as I had expected—hell, I had even relaxed a little—she slammed me with a deadly glare. She then pulled the scalpel free and flung it across the room.

Oh, hell.

The only weapon at hand now was the trolley itself, which had me summoning strength I didn't know I had. After grabbing it by two legs, I flailed it and flattened Chalky. This time, she yelled a string of obscenities, her carefully cultivated persona out the window.

Unable to keep bashing her with the trolley in such close quarters, I struggled with her. I was even winning when she pulled some sort of wrestling move. This had one of the skinny bitch's arms wrapped tight around my throat. That her insubstantial limb had the properties of a boa constrictor shocked me.

This was especially so when I tried breathing. Unable to fill my lungs, I panicked, clawing at her arm to loosen her hold. And the less air I had to play with, the more pathetic my attempts became. Damn it, they were now so lame that I was as good as massaging the evil cow.

While the black started out as spots, these soon coalesced into a solid wall of inky darkness. It was one that invaded my brain and chilled my thoughts. I was at the point of welcoming the void when the wall splintered and Hemi stormed through.

"Get your fucking hands off her!"

Need ... more ... air ...

31

When my eyes snapped wide, the now-dead theater light glared at me. For a horrifying second, I expected to find myself chained down. But moving my arms and legs proved this to be the remnants of yet another nightmare.

I swiveled my head first one way and then the other, seeing that only Ange and Bev were there with me. There was no sign of my nemesis.

"Where's Chalky? And the others? Did they get her?"

Bev struggled to find the right words, her face a mask of concentration, as if deciding what to tell me.

"No sugar coating, please," I said, taking stock of my wellbeing. I was feeling upbeat, despite Chalky having choked me to the point of passing out. My still being alive definitely helped. "Give it to me straight. I can take it." At least I thought I could.

It was all the encouragement Ange needed to share everything in excruciating detail, her verbal shorthand making it faster than if Bev had answered.

My gaze swung back and forth between the two women. "She got away!?" How was that even possible? I had clobbered her good with that trolley, and she still had her arm wrapped around my throat when Hemi busted through the wall.

Could it be that she'd gotten her hands on the gun after all? It was the only logical solution. After Ange helped me into a sitting position, I threw my legs over the side of the operating table, all the while looking around. The gun was no longer where it had been when Chalky and I were fighting.

"Here's hoping they catch her and soon." This last sentiment was as much for my benefit as the others.

Ange took my pulse again with a worried expression on her face. "You should be okay to move? You'll just need to take it easy."

"I promise I will, because I'm not staying here with that crazy tube of toothpaste on the loose. Let's get out of here and find my phone."

There was also the small matter of the king-size bars of 70% dark chocolate hidden next to it. If ever there was a time I needed chocolate, it was now.

Bev and Ange were already at the double doors the surgical team had left through earlier when I came to my senses. "Ah, I don't think it's a good idea going that way. You never know who we'll run into."

The women stopped, unspoken questions in each of their expressions.

"If we go back the way we've come, we know where we're going."

Also, if we retraced our steps, anyone we met would either be comatose, or as with the guards whose guns had exploded, plain old dead.

Convinced of my strategy, they nodded. When they moved in my direction, I received the ultimate confirmation that my plan was sound.

Walking through the hole Hemi had smashed in the wall, I found my cricket bat lying where I'd left it, a marker to my location as intended. There was a comfort in having it back in my hands. So comfortable that without my late husband to hold me back, I was going to resume play. There must be a Master's League I could join.

Before retracing our steps, I looked down the hallway as it disappeared off to the right. I knew the trolley with its pile of bodies had gone that way because of the drying trail of blood. A shudder racked my frame at thoughts of those poor women being butchered, with memories of that stark concrete room set to haunt me for the rest of my days.

"Did you find anything before you realized I was missing?"

Bev shook her head before putting her answer into words. "No, blast it! They disappeared through another one of those panels and the guys couldn't get it open no matter how hard they tried."

Logic said if we followed the trail of blood to its conclusion, we would find what we were looking for. Common sense said we shouldn't do that without the guys being with us. Waiting was fine by me, with all those unfortunate women long since past help.

We reached the fake linen closet without encountering a soul. Even the guards whose guns blew up were missing, although matching red streaks along the hallway said this hadn't been under their own steam.

In the lead, I had already grabbed hold of the decorative molding on the back of the shelving unit when the whole thing moved of its own volition.

This meant one thing. Swinging back to the others, I put my finger to my lips before double-handing the cricket bat high above my head.

I didn't have the luxury of knowing who it was before I acted. All I knew was that it wasn't one of our saviors and whoever it was, he was wearing camo. That was fine by me. The cricket bat stove in his cranium with a sickening crunch and he dropped to the ground, not knowing what hit him.

Rolling him over with my foot, I saw it was Piers, and thought about rearranging his prefrontal cortex to improve his personality. However, I couldn't quite bring myself to hammer him. "Here, take this." I held my bat out and Bev grabbed it, an inquisitive look in her eye.

After grabbing hold of one of Pier's feet, I waited for Ange to take hold of the other. Between us, we dragged him toward the mixing room, not stopping until we were next to the vat full of chocolate drink and vomit. I dropped his leg and grabbed an arm. Ange also dropped the leg she was holding, although she wasn't as quick to grab Pier's other arm.

I was about to speak when a moan came from a vat at the back of the room.

Damn, I'd hoped the workers would still be down for the count after being dealt with by Horse and Hemi earlier. I pointed at the vat before laying my finger across my lips. It was better all round if we kept our voices low. Even if the guards made it out of there in one piece, the less they knew about who was behind what was about to happen, the better.

While looking at the unconscious man, Ange wiped her hands down the side of her pants before moving closer to me so she could keep her voice low. "What do you have planned?"

"I was thinking about drowning. Apparently, it's a relaxing way to go."

"I don't think. Um, no. I can't do that," she stuttered out, not bothering to keep her voice low. She stumbled back, looking at me like I had two heads.

"Ange, they skinned women back there," I hissed at her. "They chopped them up with chainsaws. They drilled holes in them. I don't think they did it to them after they'd died of natural causes. This prick," I took time to kick him in the stomach, "raped me with a loaded gun without being asked by Chalky." I kicked him in the balls even harder. "And he made damned sure it hurt."

Despite this, Ange was still reticent about taking someone out. Fortunately, Bev had no qualms. After a muted, "Here, hold these." She handed Ange my cricket bat, along with her frying pan.

She didn't need any help to heft the now-moaning Piers up and over the top of the mixing bowl. A shove forward was enough to see him buried up to his shoulders in the gloop. However, it took our combined strength to keep him under until he stopped struggling.

While not a lot of fun, it was preferable to taking him and Lance to court for rape and us being on trial as much as they were.

Hell, if they got a good defense lawyer, they'd likely spin it that us not fighting back meant we were asking for it. Okay, that might be an exaggeration, but I'd heard enough horror stories to know there was no way I was putting myself through that.

Back in the hallway, I made sure I had their full attention before I spoke. "Remember, what happens at fat camp, stays at fat camp! Okay?"

Neither of them argued the point, nor was it discussed on our way back to the linen closet. Far better we concentrated on checking whether anyone else was around, than arguing the right or wrong of what had just happened.

Closing the door to the linen closet, I bemoaned the fact there was no key. There wasn't even anything we could use to jam it shut. Distance would be our friend in this case, and we wasted no time in taking off. The sooner I was away from there, the better.

We left the building using the same door we had entered through earlier. The difference was that rather than being the dead of night; the sun was peeking over the hills behind the spa. It was funny how things seemed less evil in daylight.

"Let's check on Tee." Ange didn't wait to see if Bev and I agreed. She was off through the flax bushes, leaving us to follow as best we could. It was as though she was trying to distance herself from us.

"I don't think she enjoyed seeing us take out camo boy," said Bev, as we scurried to catch up.

"If he had done to her what he did to me, she wouldn't be so squeamish. Anyway, it wasn't murder, it was an execution."

I thought we'd kept our voices down until Ange stopped in her tracks and spun to face us. "Okay, you two freaked me out. Cold-blooded murder freaks me out. I've spent the last twenty years of my life devoted to keeping people alive. I can't just flip a switch."

"Even when they're truly evil?" Bev looked intrigued.

"Yeah, when they've raped and murdered people in cold blood for money?" I added.

"I get it isn't straightforward. Just don't ask me to help. Okay?"

She got nods from both Bev and me. It was a good thing she couldn't see my fingers crossed behind my back because I thought there would be other executions before the day was out.

On entering Tee's room, we found her back in the middle of her bed and fast asleep, her loud snoring filling the room. It was as though the mayhem we had been through was a figment of our imagination.

We did our best to rouse her, but she was as dead to the world now as she'd been in the middle of the night. "I think we have to leave her here."

"You could be right," said Ange, even if she didn't look happy about it. "If we need to leg it, she'd never keep up."

Bev's face was a picture of concentration before she spoke. "I'd say if they haven't bothered her by now, perhaps she'll be okay."

This had me wondering if there weren't other reasons they'd left her alone. "Maybe she bought more than toast favors from the kitchen twins? Sheesh, for all we know, she could be one of their online stars."

"Now what do we do?" said Bev. "We can't get into town without a vehicle, and we've not seen that butt-ugly Hummer around."

Memories of when the beast had last fired up weren't happy ones, even if I'd escaped soon after. "I remember it roared out of the parking lot when Chalky was about to give me a hysterectomy with a power drill."

"She was going to do what?!!" Ange looked as horrified as Bev. Maybe it was because I had dropped it into our conversation without preamble.

Ange shivered. "She can't be that evil, can she?"

"Yes, yes, she can. Not once did she balk at doing what the pay-per-view crowd asked her to do to me. Not once."

We were each quiet with our thoughts when I caught movement through the large front window. It was Johnno, and he was striding across the open area toward the cliff. He had Chalky slung across his shoulders like a side of beef.

In unspoken agreement, we shot down the front steps and struck out to intercept him before he could reach the drop-off. However, he was wasting no time in wanting to be rid of her, his ground-devouring strides more than a match for our own.

"Wait!" I yelled at Johnno, but he didn't take a blind bit of notice.

"Stop! You stupid bastard!" boomed Bev from next to me.

Whether it was the volume or her calling him a stupid bastard, he stopped, allowing us to slow. Which was a relief, because so soon after coming close to being asphyxiated, I was in no fit state to be jogging.

"What?" barked Johnno, spearing us with a murderous gaze before continuing. "I don't need a fucking hunting license to get rid of this piece of crap."

No sooner had he said this than he swung back toward the cliff, and Chalky's gaze locked with mine. "You! This is all your fault. I told Scooter we should've put a bullet through your head."

The venom of her words had me reeling, and for a moment, I couldn't process them. "Scooter? You have a kid?" I wasn't sure what sickened me more. That she had given birth while I couldn't, or that her kid was part of the operation.

There was no amusement in her responding laughter, the high notes akin to nails on a blackboard. Her following words weren't any kinder. "You stupid ... fat ... slag. Of course, he's not my kid. He's only the best in the business, and if you think you're shutting him down, you're fooling yourself."

The business? What business? Was she talking about covert plastic surgery, or the whole deadly pay-per-view side of the operation?

Focused as I had been on her words, it was a nasty surprise to see that we had arrived at the cliff edge, my tummy flip-flopping as always. It seemed I wasn't alone in this reaction, with Chalky struggling harder than ever. Against Johnno's strength, she didn't stand a chance.

I was still working on another question about the mystery Scooter when, without warning, Johnno shoulder-pressed

Chalky up and over his head and propelled her out into the void. Contrary to her usual modus operandi, Chalky's descent was anything but quiet.

Her screams rent the air, only interrupted when she smashed into a few trees on the way down. However, after landing with a loud crash at the bottom of the ravine, she fell quiet.

But was she gone for good? It couldn't be that easy, could it? Next to me, Ange was a shaky mess. "But she was still alive," she stuttered.

"The fucking bitch is pig tucker now," said Johnno, before breaking into raucous laughter that only intensified when loud grunting came from far below.

This soon escalated to squealing, followed by the crashing of undergrowth. Personally, I didn't blame the pigs for wanting nothing to do with Chalky, dead or alive. Even if she was dead, as I suspected, with that much Botox on board, she'd be tougher than old boots.

We waited a couple more minutes, but all was quiet in the ravine, with Bev and me more than happy about this. Ange wasn't in agreement, even knowing how truly awful Chalky had been. "She should have faced justice. Gone to jail for what she did."

Johnno shook his head in disbelief before sending a large wad of spit over the cliff. "Lady, are you out of your effing mind? People like that don't end up inside. Never have. Never will. Who do you think pays for this shit?" He gestured toward the buildings that dotted the landscape, before including the three of us.

We were still contemplating this when Hemi and Horse joined us, with a quick summary on offer. According to the guys, the place was as good as dead. Any mercenaries not dispatched had long since left the property, with Horse even overhearing a couple talking about this shit being way above their pay-grade.

The only thing they weren't sure of was whether there were any from the medical side of things still around. But there had to be. There wasn't a chance the women so recently operated on would be in any fit shape to be moved.

Thoughts of running into any of them didn't worry me though, with that side of operations probably legitimate, if clandestine.

With concerns about running into mercenaries, Lance, Piers, or Chalky, off the menu, it released the pressure that had bound me for what felt like weeks, perhaps years. While I might not have lost weight during my time at The Vale, my sense of self was so much lighter.

Bev cleared her throat before looking at Ange and me. "We need to grab Tee and get the hell outta here."

She was right. It didn't matter that she was unaware of what had been going on. She knew our true identities. And for that reason alone, we couldn't leave her behind. The challenge we faced was how we were to get into town.

Tee wasn't up to walking through the bush to the guy's vehicles, which had been what we planned on.

Despite all this, we'd already talked about not hanging around waiting for the police to arrive. Especially not after what Hemi, Johnno, and Horse had gotten up to while saving us.

There was also the small matter of a chocolate-coated South African. I didn't think my ability to lie to the cops was up to a challenge like that.

Johnno, having overheard us, stepped up. "Yeah, you lot go wake your mate while we have a final gander around the place. See if we can't uncover anything else." The three men then split away, making for the dining hall and leaving us to carry on to Tee's room.

I was the first up the stairs when we got there. The three of us trooped in, lining up next to her bed, dismayed to find her sleeping as deeply as she'd been earlier. How she slept through the racket she was kicking up was anyone's guess.

Not one to muck about, Bev shook Tee until the poor woman's neck rolls were into tsunami territory, although even this didn't rouse the sleeping giant.

"They must have given her a massive dose." Ange reverted to her nursing status and grabbed Tee's wrist to take her pulse. "It's slower than it was last night, which is a good sign. Maybe she's just a deep sleeper."

"She'd bloody wake up if we told her we had access to enough of that chocolate shake to drown in."

No sooner had these words left Bev's mouth than Tee's eyes snapped open, from deepest slumber to alert in seconds. "What did you say?"

Not giving Bev a chance to answer, her gaze swung in my direction. "I thought you checked out?"

"Hah, I damn near did. Get dressed and we'll tell you all about it."

While sitting on the porch waiting for Tee, we admired the view. However, Johnno and Horse interrupted the serenity when they crossed the vista, a struggling guard slung between them. Even though I wasn't familiar with him, there was no remorse as I watched them pitch him over the cliff without a moment's hesitation. Ange, however, cried out in distress.

"Right," said Tee, walking out of her room, "you want to tell me what's going on?" We didn't have a chance, before she added, "We should have been called for breakfast by now."

"Trust me, when we tell you what's been going on, you won't be so keen on eating." Ange's tone said it would be a long time before she drank another smoothie, unless it was one she had prepared herself.

Tee looked at the dining room, while licking her bottom lip. "Don't bet on it. It takes a lot to put me off my chow."

Rather than wait, she took off, not bothering to keep to the raised boardwalk. As we followed in her wake, there was no missing her tummy rumbling, even from a good couple of feet back.

"We need to get there before her, otherwise she'll be headfirst into the fridge and hoovering whatever is on hand."

Bev raced after her, with Ange and me not far behind. Tee would never forgive us if we didn't tell her about the secret ingredient in those big-ass smoothies. Whether this would stop her from drinking one was anyone's bet.

The four of us were close to the doors to the dining room when Anton exploded through them, with Hemi in pursuit.

"Run, Anton, run!" said Ange, in a fair Forrest Gump parody.

I thought she was kidding until I saw she was wringing her hands.

Tee looked at Anton—who was close to being caught by Hemi—and back at Ange. There was bafflement written large on her face. "Why?"

Bev looked at the pursuit that, while doubtless deadly, had taken on a comedic air, with Hemi and Anton's physiques representing both extremes of the bell curve.

"Because if Hemi gets hold of him, he'll chuck him over the cliff, like all the others."

"You are joking." For once, Tee looked away from a source of food.

Ange continued to wring her hands. "No, she isn't."

"Like hell he will!" roared Tee.

She was fast for such a large woman, and Hemi was no match for her when she slammed sideways into him. She took him off his feet, landing on top of him. The oomph of air escaping his lungs confirmed she'd winded him.

"I'd better go see if he's okay," said Ange, already jogging in their direction.

Meanwhile, Anton, making the most of Tee's diversion, legged it toward the Sleeping Beauty Suites.

"Hell, I've just thought of something!" I didn't bother explaining, instead taking off after him.

I was gaining when he as good as disappeared into the row of flax that bordered the dense bush. If I hadn't been right behind him, I'd never have seen the gap, with no STAFF ONLY sign to denote this path. I shot through it without slowing down and soon enough, saw him not too far in front of me. Thinking he had escaped, he'd slowed.

Big mistake with me able to sneak up behind him and slam a hand on his shoulder before he knew I was there.

"Take me to your car!"

The words were menacing, even if inside my head I heard them in a "Take me to your leader" voice. Wrenching free of my grip, he spun to face me, his expression changing from terror to humor in a heartbeat. That was until I raised the cricket bat.

"Sheesh, okay, lady."

"You don't even know my name?"

He shrugged. "What's the point?"

Much as I would have liked to part his hair with my cricket bat in response to that attitude, I stopped myself. Was he saying this because he knew this was where fat women came to die, or that there were so many that remembering their names was impossible? For his sake, I hoped it was the latter.

"Your car?" I then prodded him hard enough that he staggered back a step or two.

In response, he turned and stormed off, leaving me standing there for a couple of seconds until my legs caught up with my brain and him. The parking lot was a decent slog, and doubtless why I had seen no cars other than the Hummer on the property.

Without warning, we cleared the bush into a large gravel parking lot. This was home to at least a dozen high-end vehicles and a large shed, the latter most likely a chop shop. Sure, a few of the cars likely belonged to the medical staff and Chalky, but the rest must belong to ex-residents or those getting under-the-counter surgery.

Anton took advantage of my being distracted to sprint to a hot pink Mazda convertible and jump in without bothering to open the doors. He started the car and left in a spray of gravel soon after. As I watched the stupid car fishtailing up the driveway, I wasn't that concerned. It would never have held the four of us, anyway.

There was a crunch of gravel behind me and I turned, expecting to see that the others had caught up with me.

Chalky's white smock was no longer pristine. Ripped, shredded, and smeared with dirt and leaf litter, it now suited her personality. The rest of her didn't look too hot, either. At the slightest movement, her right eyeball bounced against her cheek, courtesy of a tenacious optic nerve. And yet, despite being introduced to the bottom of a cliff the hard way, she looked in rude good health.

Held in place by the dead glare of the eye that remained in its socket, I did nothing, waiting to make my move. She persevered in her examination of me as she staggered around like a drunk, thanks to a broken tibia poking through the side of her calf muscle. "Well, well, well, Marilyn, I'm rarely surprised."

Why was that? That I was alive? That she was alive? Could I even tell with that botoxed deadpan expression of hers? However, there was nothing surprising about the manic look in her eyes—make that eye—with no missing the edge of madness. You'd have to be unhinged to be okay with the atrocities I'd seen. That she'd orchestrated.

"Did you think we'd let you and your little friends get away?"

On looking at the state of her, I wasn't sure how she thought she'd stop us. Unless she was talking about retribution for us having screwed up her little money-making pay-per-death initiative.

"I've worked too hard to let you get away with it. If I can recoup some of my costs, I will."

So conversational were her mutterings, that I didn't immediately notice the threat buried in their midst. All that changed when I caught sight of the gun she was holding. The gun aimed at my chest.

There was no time to think, just act.

33

I swung the bat hard, shattering Chalky's hand and disarming her. In my imagination, I followed this up with a full rotation that saw me smashing the bat into the side of her head. But I couldn't bring myself to do it.

If I did, then I'd be no better than her. I did, however, kick the gun under the nearest car where she couldn't get to it. Despite this, I kept alert, not trusting this crazy bitch to come at me despite her various injuries.

Hadn't she already proved herself to be indestructible by surviving that fall? While it would have been easier all around if she had died, a part of me wanted to see her locked away until she rotted. Somewhere with 24/7 CCTV, so she would know how it felt.

Chalky and I had been staring daggers at each other for a full two minutes before I realized the others wouldn't know where I was. They were too busy checking out the dining hall and taking care of the damage Tee had done to Hemi when I took off after Anton.

This had me pleased I hadn't thrown the cricket bat to the side in disgust, as had been my first impulse. Even as smashed up as she was, Chalky scared the crap out of me. Perhaps it was down to the evil that rolled off her in waves.

I hadn't been a fan of her since the start, and with her polished veneer now MIA, she was scary as hell. It was during our standoff that I noticed the watch on her undamaged wrist. "You skinny old cow, that's my dad's Rolex!""

I wasn't sure if it was that I'd screamed this, or my taking a step in her direction, but she hopped back, keeping the distance between us. I hadn't had time to get closer to her when I heard footsteps off to my left. Unsure who it was, I turned square on to the narrow track, my bat raised in readiness.

However, rather than a camo-wearing guard, as I'd feared, it was Johnno, his knife at the ready. He took one look at me before his gaze landed on Chalky. "This bitch? You fucking kidding me?"

A moment later, he stalked forward, although him sliding his knife back into the sheath on his leg still didn't bode well for my nemesis. As if sensing this, Chalky hopped off as fast as her good leg would allow.

Rather than chasing her down as I had thought he would, Johnno followed at his leisure, the dense undergrowth soon swallowing the pair.

After a while, the only indicator they had been there were

Chalky's crashing and banging, and Johnno's sing-song of, "I can still see you."

Then even that soundtrack fell silent, something that allowed me to hear the others making their way up the path from the main part of the complex. Tee was with them and holding half-a-dozen slices of toast.

As I had done earlier, they looked around the parking lot, taking in the late-model luxury cars. "There's mine!" This discovery by Bev was an immense relief, meaning we could get away without having to steal a car.

It was only then I discovered that Ange and Tee hadn't received instructions to park in the middle of nowhere, as I had.

"Kinda hard when you don't own a car," said Ange, before adding. "I got the bus."

"I caught the ferry from Auckland," chimed in Tee.

It was a moment before rational thinking kicked in. Was it that Ange and Tee were worth more alive than dead? That Bev, having put her husband as next of kin, would never disappear.

Once again, the emptiness of my life threatened to overwhelm me, and I restated the promise to myself that from there on in, I would make better choices.

My introspection took a back seat when Bev reported that the key to her Land Cruiser was still in the ignition. However, much to her chagrin, there was only a quarter of a tank of gas left, meaning someone had been using it. "Those cheeky bastards!"

Even with her having climbed in and started the engine, we couldn't leave just yet, not without our handbags and other belongings. The minutes stretched with no sign of Johnno or Chalky. Horse and Hemi were even talking about going off to help when we heard a blood-curdling scream.

As suddenly as it started, so did it stop.

Ange's gasp was loud enough to have me looking away from the bush and in her direction. Sure enough, she was covering her face as if this would somehow save Chalky from her fate. Personally, I was less inclined to worry about the spa manager's welfare. She sure as hell hadn't worried about mine.

On rejoining us in the parking lot, Johnno was grinning. "Nasty place, that Coogan's Bluff."

Next thing I knew, Ange was all up in his face. "You killed her? Again? How could you? It's not your place to hand out justice!"

Rather than ripping into her as I had expected, Johnno laid his hand flat on his chest, his expression one of manufactured outrage. "How can you say such a thing? She slipped is all."

Next to him, rather than smiling, Hemi looked grim. "Coogan's Bluff? That's fitting." Soon enough, Horse was nodding his agreement, although I didn't know why.

I didn't need to wonder for long, with Hemi's gaze soon catching mine. "That's the one where Bill died." He didn't need to say anything else. I knew while rough-and-ready, the guys had a soft spot for the old man.

After a moment's silence, it was Horse who outlined how we should proceed. While he was the quiet member of the group, his reasoning was sound. Our priority was to find anything that could identify us, including any items confiscated.

"Handbags, we'll need to get ours out of your room, Tee." I didn't want to go into details of how we'd found them and put them there without her knowledge. We could bring her up to speed after we got out of there.

With her last slice of toast taken care of, barring a few crumbs around her mouth, she was quick to bring up the subject of her own handbag. "Chalky took it off me when I checked in."

"What did it look like?" Ange asked.

No sooner had Tee said it was an orange tote than Bev, Ange, and I looked at each other. Unfortunately, we knew where her bag was, and I, for one, didn't want to go anywhere near it.

What if that guy was still alive under the trapdoor? With Tee's bag one of the first to be piled atop it, we would need to move everything else to get to it, including that guy's hand. It was enough to have me swallowing and looking at the men. "Can you guys come with us? We'll need your help with a couple of things."

With the plan of action agreed to, we walked single file back down the track to the main part of the complex. I was second to last, with Johnno bringing up the rear.

We'd not gone far when he tapped me on the shoulder. It was enough to have me slowing and looking back. When I saw what it was he was holding out to me, I knew Chalky didn't go over the cliff of her own volition. And as I fastened the Rolex onto my left wrist, I decided I was okay with that.

We cleared the bush and were walking abreast when Horse raised something I had been thinking about myself. "You know you lot can't go to the cops about this?"

Tee stopped dead in her tracks, with it working like a land anchor on the rest of us. "Why not! I'm ready to spill my guts on TV."

Not content, she carried on, determined to claim her fifteen-minutes-of-fame. "I've got no problems being plastered all over the news and in the women's magazines." It didn't matter to her that everything she had heard was second hand. She wouldn't let that fact stop her from giving a tell-all.

It was Hemi who pointed out that her wanting to go public wasn't the best idea. "We didn't get everyone. If they think you're helping the cops, they'll take you out." He put his hand on her shoulder and squeezed it as if to soften the blow, although there was nothing gentle with his next words. "Lady, the guys behind this wouldn't think twice about killing you to keep their nasty little secret safe."

Horse backed this up. "Yeah, if they'll kill an old guy by slitting his throat and leaving him for the pigs, what do you think they'll do to you?"

As harsh as his words had been, they cut through the potential B-List Celebrity that had been clouding Tee's judgment. Rather than being photo-ready, she was now pasty white, her eyes wide, jaw slack.

However, it was Johnno who said what the others hadn't.

"Yeah, and if they find you, they find us, and I don't fancy spending the rest of my life inside."

I only knew I was nodding my agreement to this when I saw Bev was doing the same. And while Ange also nodded, there was a proviso. "While I don't condone your actions, the cops won't hear about it from me."

Bev wasn't as squeamish. "I have no problems with what you guys did. When it came down to us or them, I was happy it was them."

In unspoken agreement, we then all turned and looked at Tee, with her holding her hands up in surrender. "Fine, fine, I won't say anything." I could tell her promise hadn't come easy. Minor celebrity within her grasp.

No one spoke for the rest of the walk to Tee's room, each of us alone with our thoughts. It was only when rummaging through my handbag on our way to find the three tofu eaters that I noticed I was missing something.

My bottle of beta-blockers. It didn't take me long to remember when I had last seen it. I was in Chalky's bathroom having downed two capsules when Ange found that control room. Damn it, I must have left the bottle on the bathroom vanity. The bottle with my real name on it. There was no point doing a runner before the cops arrived if I left that behind.

"Bev, Ange, do you want to search for the tofu eaters, while Tee and I go grab her handbag?" On their agreeing to this, I added, "It might be best if they stay put until the cops arrive."

There was also the fact that moving the woman with the flayed back wouldn't be possible without an ambulance in the mix. "Ange, can you check on the woman I told you about? She was in a hell of a mess."

Much to my surprise, when Ange and Bev veered away, Johnno accompanied them, which was a good thing, given there could still be others hanging about. He was a guy to have in your corner in cases like this. Meanwhile, Tee and I headed for the administration block, with Hemi and Horse in tow.

We were nearing it when I heard the distinctive sound of the Hummer roaring into life, there no mistaking its throaty roar. Hemi and Horse took off, with me right behind them. I shot around the corner of the building to find the men standing out front, clouded in dust.

The last I saw of the gold monstrosity was it shooting through the wide-open front gates. It was the first time I'd seen them like this since entering.

The one unknown in all of this was who was behind the wheel and what did they know about us? We needed to get out of here, and soon.

34

Not knowing the identity of who'd just left, we approached the admin building with care. Put it down to me having seen far too many action flicks, but if it was me, I'd have booby trapped the hell out of the place.

As always, Horse entered first, although he wasn't gone for long. "Coast is clear."

Despite knowing the small building was empty, I was slow up the front steps. I took a quick look at the storage room off Chalky's office and could see everything was as we had left it. Good, the guy who had lost his hand must have succumbed to his injuries or gone back up the tunnel.

"Hemi, are you able to help Tee grab her handbag? It's under that lot." I paused for a second before adding, "Whatever you do, don't lift the trapdoor."

I didn't bother going into details about what else they

would find in there. Hemi was stoic enough that I doubted finding the guy's hand would bother him. A muffled shriek soon let me know the same wasn't true of Tee. It was a good thing for Hemi that the large woman wasn't sick like Bev, Ange, and I had been earlier. And anyway, something as trifling as a severed limb would never dislodge that cardboard toast.

After Hemi put the amputated hand on Chalky's desk, he and Tee were soon rummaging through the pile of shelving and handbags.

Leaving them to it, I made my way through to Chalky's bathroom, spotting my bottle of pills tucked in behind the faucets. I was about to head back to reception when I decided I wanted to show someone else what we'd found.

"Hey, Horse, check this out." After he joined me, I slid the pocket door to the side and stepped back to give him free access.

After a cursory glance inside, he looked at me, one brow raised in query. "Yeah, what of it?"

"This is where they ran the auctions from."

On seeing him tip his head to the side, I knew something was up. While this guy might be quiet, he had never struck me as slow. On joining him, I couldn't believe my eyes. Gone were all the electronics, replaced with row upon row of those butt ugly white smocks.

"But, but, that's not right." I stepped inside and wrenched the hangers to the left and right. It was a pointless exercise with nothing but a few random cables still in evidence. "There were rows of monitors, a large computer, electronic stuff!"

I spun around to find Horse looking at the ceiling, which

had me doing the same. Sure enough, there, disappearing through a hole in the corner, was a thick cord of cable that was way beyond anything you'd see behind most home theater setups. Doubtless, these had once connected the control desk to the satellite dishes on the roof.

Horse soon put into words what I was already thinking.

"There's no way that crazy ghost of a woman survived going over Coogan's Bluff."

He was right. Nor would she have had time to get from the top of the property down here and load everything up. No, that was down to whoever had just left in the Hummer. It also said that whoever it was, they weren't a grunt, because I doubted any of those guys knew about the control room.

It'd have to be someone further up the pecking order than that. Could it be the mysterious Scooter that Chalky had raved about?

I was still working through the ramifications of what this meant for us when Horse stiffened. Soon enough, he bent down and grabbed something off the floor. However, rather than showing it to me, he pocketed it, proving that whatever it was, it was small. I opened my mouth to ask what it was when he spoke.

"Memory stick." After retrieving it, he tossed it up in the air, caught it, and slid it back into his pocket in one smooth move. "I've got a mate who can check it out."

In the past, I'd have suggested we hand this over to the police. However, if there were people I should be worried about, I'd rather hear about it sooner than later. The authorities would always be slower to react thanks to all that red tape, something I doubted would bother Horse's mate.

"You'll pass it onto the police, right? When your friend's done with it?"

In return, I got a bright grin and a jaunty salute, which amounted to a yes in my books. Unfortunately, his smile soon faded.

"In the meantime, you need to lie low, because the filth behind this place has to know who you are. Even if they don't know what you got up to."

Damn it, he was right. Chalky, having helped herself to my identity, said that. All I could hope was that she hadn't gotten her hands on my settlement money. Kinda hard to hide if you're penniless.

As to the Megans—the tofu eaters—while caught up in everything, they didn't know as much about the operation as Bev, Ange, and I did. As it stood, they were our only hope that justice would be served.

But without the electronics to point the cops in the right direction, the chances of those ultimately responsible being caught were slim. And that didn't sit well with me. Not at all.

"Horse, whatever you find on that memory stick, promise me you'll share it far and wide." I thought about it for a second. "But just be careful."

Johnno was right. It was all too easy for the rich and famous, and those with connections, to get away with blue murder, or in this case, just murder. To flash the cash and have their problems disappear.

Hadn't I seen that firsthand with my late husband and his associates? Well, not this time, and especially not for someone with as idiotic a name as Scooter.

With that moniker, and enough hints made public, it shouldn't be too hard to identify him.

All too soon, we were back in the top parking lot, stowing our things in the back of Bev's Land Cruiser. A last sweep of the property had me finding my suitcase in the dumpster behind the Sleeping Beauty Suites.

Likewise, everyone else had found anything that could identify them. So far as we knew, there was nothing left on site to show we'd ever been there.

It wasn't until Bev had driven out onto the road into town that the men melted into the bush. Johnno was off to a forestry contract down south, while Horse was returning to his city lifestyle. Meanwhile, Hemi planned on hiding out at a mate's place up the coast until things cooled down.

And just like that, they were gone.

The only evidence they hadn't been a figment of our imagination was Horse's number programmed into my iPhone. I couldn't blame them for taking off, with an absence of hunting licenses reason enough not to hang around. Add to this the sheer number of corpses left on the property, and they were better off disappearing like us.

We were trundling slowly down the road into town when we called the local police station using a burner phone we'd found in our last sweep of the property. As preposterous as our story was, they believed us, thanks to what little the tofu eater who had run into town told them before collapsing.

Despite promises we would be in to fill out a proper report, we had no such intention. We gave them as much information as we dared, and definitely enough to know where to look when they got around to searching the property.

After ending the call, I'd turned the phone off and biffed it into the bush. And while this wasn't as far as I would have liked, the drop off and density of the bush meant the chances of it being recovered were slim.

After dropping Tee and Ange at the ferry, Bev took me to collect my Lexus, with Gary eager to hear all about my time away with friends. It had been an interrogation that had left me both scrambling for words and relieved it wasn't the cops questioning me. Never great at telling lies, I had resorted to a word salad that appeared to satisfy his curiosity.

With my car collected, there was only one other thing I needed to take care of before leaving town. And that was emailing Lorraine to apologize for not following through on checking into The Vale. It was easier to tell her I had chickened out and booked a holiday cottage instead than have that blabbermouth outing me to the cops.

That done, I was soon following Bev down the main road on my way to spend a month in the country, working on my recovery and reclaiming my identity.

EPILOGUE

Unable to stay with Bev and husband, Stan, any longer, I was back in the city. I hadn't committed to a house or even an apartment, and was staying in an upmarket B&B close to my old haunts. The decision about what I wanted to do with my life going forward had taken more energy than I would have thought possible.

Online counseling with an overseas' shrink had helped with me being able to unburden myself without risk of exposure. And after reading what the authorities had put the tofu eaters through, I was glad of our decision not to go public.

Thank goodness those women didn't know who we were, and especially not our real names. Despite the cops searching for us using our alias, they'd had no success. And with The Vale having covered our tracks as effectively as their own, our secret was safe.

One thing that was missing was any news about what Horse's mate found on that memory stick, with no mention on the news. I knew the guy was still working on it thanks to a text from Horse, but that was weeks ago.

While vigilante justice had taken care of most of the guilty, those behind the endeavor were still at large, and that didn't sit well with me. The one surprise in all of this was that despite several attempts, Chalky hadn't been able to access my bank account, thanks to my new accountants. I hadn't been keen on starting over, and if my plans went ahead, I'd need every cent.

On looking around my chintzy room at the B&B, I marveled at how different my life was these days, and how very different it was about to become. Being close to death caused a shift in my priorities, with lunching and constant clothes shopping no longer appealing.

Today, though, I had lunch with Lorraine and the others, although I'd be a self-confessed idiot to think this was so we could have a lovely catch up. No, this was all about Lorraine giving me grief for not acting on her recommendation. For her to gloat at what she was sure would be my lack of weight loss.

After stepping out of the shower, I made quick work of drying myself. I didn't bother blow-waving my hair, instead finger-combing some mousse through its much shorter—and blonder—length. In an ultimate show of defiance, I messed it until it was a riot of curls. So many hours wasted over the years, maintaining the smooth, helmet-like bob David had preferred.

My clothes laid out before my shower, saw me dressed in minutes. Thanks to the tan I'd gained on my daily walks at Bev's place, I left my make-up at mascara and lipstick.

I was so much lower maintenance than I used to be, and I loved it. I was nothing like the corporate wife who'd left town. I was thinner, healthier, and happier in my skin. The only dark clouds that remained were those clogging the part of my brain devoted to memories.

The restaurant wasn't far, so rather than drive and waste ten minutes looking for a parking space, I walked. Winter hadn't quite got us in her icy grip, and the sunshine was still warm. I'd also eschewed heels for sneakers bought from a surf shop that'd allow me to walk at a good clip. It was the sort of place I'd never have visited in my old life.

Lorraine's strident tones greeted me before I even saw her, flying like birds of prey over the high wall that surrounded the alfresco part of the restaurant. "Has anyone seen her since she got back to town?"

It wouldn't take Einstein to know she was talking about me, and my steps slowed of their own accord when she got a volley of "No" in response. Rooted to the spot, I waited to listen to what else the nasty piece of work would say.

"Twenty says she hasn't lost an ounce." I didn't need to see Lorraine's expression to know malice was now fighting her facelift for supremacy. "Serves her right for ignoring my recommendation."

She'd have heard by now what was going on at The Vale, making it even more awful that all she could focus on was me not following her advice. Why did I ever bother with this spiteful woman before? That's right, our husbands did business together.

I walked in with back straight and head held high. A dozen steps, and I was next to their table, although it took a few seconds for my presence to be registered.

"Yes?" Lorraine looked both up at me and down her nose at the same time. Just this one word, and I had to fight my response to cower. I wanted to make myself smaller, to apologize, even though I'd done nothing wrong.

It was then I remembered how strong I could be when push came to shove. I was strong enough to take on Chalky, meaning Lorraine was a doddle by comparison.

The old me would have ignored the bitchy comments I'd overheard on arrival. The new me had no compunction about prodding the elephant sitting in the middle of the large round table.

"As you can see, Lorraine, I've lost more than an ounce."

"Marilyn, is that you?" Deidre, albeit as shocked as Lorraine, hadn't been bad-mouthing me. She therefore had no trouble asking me if I was indeed me.

Meanwhile, the skinny orange cow sporting the fake boobs was still mute. The thought alone was enough to have me breaking out in a wide smile.

Imagine if I said it?

Rather than answer Deidre, I held my arms wide and turned, giving them plenty of time to stare. My body had changed beyond recognition and so had my clothes. Gone were the designer outfits David insisted I wear and that these women still favored. Instead, I was wearing jeans and a long-sleeved T-shirt, along with a weathered leather jacket bought at a charity shop.

I knew damned well I looked good, with more than one guy trying to catch my eye on the walk here. Backing this up, the pure hatred in Lorraine's eyes said it all.

"I'd love to join you for lunch, but I've got packing to take care of."

"Packing?" said Claire. "Are you off on vacation?"

"Nope. I'm moving out of the city. Away from here. Away from all the terrible memories." I paused, making sure I had Lorraine's attention. "Away from skinny orange cows with poached-egg tits."

Oooh, now that felt good.

I didn't wait for a response. Instead, I swung around and left the way I'd come in. I was on the other side of the high wall before Lorraine put a voice to her anger.

"Well, I've never been so insulted in all my life!"

"She looked good though, didn't she?" said another.

"Yes, thank you, Audrey. If I wanted your opinion, I'd have asked for it."

A magnificent grin made itself at home as I strode off along the sidewalk. Back to finish packing for my new life at the beach.

It had taken me a long time to decide what to do with my future, to see that in healing myself, I could help others. It was this that had seen me purchase a large home high above Muriwai Beach.

I hoped that come next summer the place would be ready for guests, with Sue-Ng already hinting at a couple of potentials. I wanted to provide a sanctuary to those who wanted to move on with their lives, to leave the past behind. Perhaps if there'd been something like that when my marriage ended, I wouldn't have booked into The Vale.

A quick look at what time it was, and I slipped my ear buds in, eager to hear the news. Maybe today would be the day. Soon enough, the newsreader had been through all the death and mayhem, both from here and abroad. I was about to pull my buds free when they announced they had exciting entertainment news.

The DJ positively gushed when she announced that Scooter Bradshaw, the self-proclaimed godfather of reality TV, was in town. The mastermind behind the award-winning series Weight Loss Warriors was working on pre-production for Natural Selection, a new island-based reality show.

I was pleased I hadn't stopped for lunch with the others, because now all I wanted to do was throw up. Instead, I placed a call to Horse, not trusting my fingers to text.

"I've got a lead on Scooter." Without waiting for him to respond, I rattled through what I'd heard on the radio, worried I'd forget something in my haste.

After a brief silence, Horse's smooth voice came back. "I'll look into it. Just be careful, okay?"

I nodded to myself, even though he couldn't see me. "Always am."

On ending the call, resolve washed over me. Scooter Bradshaw may have thought he'd escaped the consequences of what happened at that bloody spa, but he was wrong, perhaps dead wrong.

As I made my way back to the B&B, I decided that if Scooter ended up paying the ultimate price as the other lowlifes had, I could live with that.

Could you take a life to save your own?

Talented artist Paige Masters is trapped in a prison of her own choosing. It doesn't matter that it's architecturally-designed with stunning views, it's still a prison.

With de facto partner, Greg Walker, chipping away at her self-worth, she needs to get out while she still can. Away from the sniping, the comments on her appearance, her mental health and, most damaging of all, her art.

If he takes that, she's got nothing.

Without the support of friends or family thanks to a flurry of no-shows or Greg insulting them, Paige is on her own. So, when in a bizarre twist of fate, she's gifted someone else's life, she doesn't think twice.

Dumped on an island with eleven strangers, she finds herself in the middle of the top-rated reality TV show, *Natural Selection*.

Week one and thanks to the show's much-touted THERE'S NOWHERE TO HIDE slogan, Paige is close to losing her mind.

Week two and the biggest challenge isn't losing her mind, it's losing her life.

Scheduled for release early 2025 when it will be available from all good online retailers. It can also be ordered in by your local independent bookstore or library.

BOOK CLUB QUESTIONS

- What was your favorite scene?
- What was your least favorite?
- Did you race to the end, or was it more of a slow burn?
- Which scene has stuck with you?
- What did you think of the writing? Are there any standout sentences?
- Did you reread any passages?
- Would you want to read another book by this author?
- Did reading the book impact your mood? If yes, how so?
- What was it that surprised you most about the book?
- What is the craziest diet you've ever been on?
- If you could ask the author anything, what would it be?
- Did this book remind you of any other books?
- How did it impact you? Do you think you'll remember it in months or years to come?
- Would you ever consider re-reading it? Why or why not?
- Who would you like to read this book and why?
- Are there lingering questions from the book?
- Did the book strike you as original?

BOOK CLUB EXTRAS

Just as you can pair a fine wine with fabulous cuisine, we believe in the perfect drink to accompany a spirited book club discussion. Read on for a few recipes to get you started.

SIMPLE CHOCOLATE MARTINI

- Cocoa powder (for rim), garnish
- 1 1/2 ounces chocolate liqueur, plus extra for rim
- 2 ounces vodka
- 1 piece chocolate candy, garnish

DIRECTIONS

- Step 1: Rim a cocktail glass with cocoa: Wet the rim by dipping it in a small dish of the chocolate liqueur, then dip or roll it in a dish of cocoa powder.
- Step 2: Pour the vodka and chocolate liqueur into a cocktail shaker filled with ice cubes
- Step 3: Shake vigorously
- Step 4: Strain into the prepared glass.
- Step 5: Garnish with chocolate candy
- Step 6: Serve and enjoy

OBITUARY COCKTAIL

- 2 ounces gin
- 1/4 ounce dry vermouth
- 1/4 ounce absinthe

DIRECTIONS

- Pour the ingredients into a mixing glass filled with cracked ice
- Stir well
- Strain into a chilled cocktail glass.
- Serve and enjoy, but be careful – as the name implies, this cocktail isn't for the faint hearted

CORPSE REVIVER #2

- 1 ounce gin
- 1 ounce orange triple sec
- 1 ounce white vermouth
- 1 ounce fresh lemon juice
- 1 dash absinthe

DIRECTIONS

- Step 1: Put ice and water into a cocktail glass to chill
- Step 2: Put all ingredients into a cocktail shaker
  with ice and shake like you mean it
- Step 3: Empty the glass ready to take your cocktail
- Step 4: Strain into the cocktail glass and garnish
  with some orange peel

Lastly, remember to drink responsibly even if the first rule of your book club is 'What happens at Book Club, stays at Book Club'. Have fun.

THANK YOU

First off, thank you to my critique partner and fellow author Kirsten Mackenzie for her unwavering support and input.

I'd also like to thank Lee Murray for her invaluable help on the first edition all those years back. The tweaks you suggested made all the difference and have stood the test of time.

Next a shout-out to Catherine Robertson for her input and feedback on this edition and to Helen for spotting all those little things that I'd missed.

Finally, I'd like to thank family and friends for all the times I've canceled on you, because I just had to keep going when I was mid-flow. I promise I'll make it up to you, although there is this one other project...

ALL ABOUT SYDNEY

Sydney has a love of writing passed down to her by her mother. Although, if her mom was still alive, she'd be smacking Syd across the back of the head given the direction her writing has taken. Irreverent, cutting and with humor that is very dark in places, it's not for the faint-hearted.

After twenty years in advertising, Sydney decided it was time to put all those stress-induced nightmares to better use by including them in her writing. She might also take perverse delight in eviscerating a few old bosses along the way.

Pet hates include reality television and dieting.